Berkley Prime Crime titles by Maggie Sefton

KNIT ONE, KILL TWO
NEEDLED TO DEATH
A DEADLY YARN
A KILLER STITCH
DYER CONSEQUENCES
FLEECE NAVIDAD
DROPPED DEAD STITCH
SKEIN OF THE CRIME
UNRAVELED
CAST ON, KILL OFF
CLOSE KNIT KILLER
YARN OVER MURDER
PURL UP AND DIE
KNIT TO BE TIED
ONLY SKEIN DEEP

Anthologies

DOUBLE KNIT MURDERS

Only Skein Deep

Only Skein Deep

Maggie Sefton

BERKLEY PRIME CRIME
New York

BERKLEY PRIME CRIME
Published by Berkley
An imprint of Penguin Random House LLC
375 Hudson Street, New York, New York 10014

ISBN: 9780425282526

Library of Congress Cataloging-in-Publication Data

Names: Sefton, Maggie, author.
Title: Only skein deep / Maggie Sefton.
Description: First edition. | New York : Berkley Prime Crime, 2017. | Series: A knitting mystery ; 15
Identifiers: LCCN 2017000409 (print) | LCCN 2017005626 (ebook) | ISBN 9780425282526 (hardback) | ISBN 9780698405929 (ebook)
Subjects: LCSH: Flynn, Kelly (Fictitious character)—Fiction. | Knitters (Persons)—Fiction. | Murder—Investigation—Fiction. | BISAC: FICTION / Mystery & Detective / Women Sleuths. | GSAFD: Mystery fiction.
Classification: LCC PS3619.E37 O55 2017 (print) | LCC PS3619.E37 (ebook) | DDC 813/.6—dc23
LC record available at https://lccn.loc.gov/2017000409

First Edition: June 2017

Printed in the United States of America
1 3 5 7 9 10 8 6 4 2

Cover art by Chris O'Leary
Cover design by Rita Frangie

Cast of Characters

Kelly Flynn—financial accountant and part-time sleuth, refugee from East Coast corporate CPA firm

Steve Townsend—architect and builder in Fort Connor, Colorado, and Kelly's husband

KELLY'S FRIENDS:

Jennifer Stroud—real estate agent, part-time waitress

Lisa Gerrard—physical therapist

Megan Harrington—IT consultant, another corporate refugee

Marty Harrington—lawyer, Megan's husband

Greg Carruthers—university instructor, Lisa's boyfriend

Pete Wainwright—owner of Pete's Porch Café in the back of Kelly's favorite knitting shop, House of Lambspun

LAMBSPUN FAMILY AND REGULARS:

Mimi Parker—House of Lambspun shop owner and knitting expert, known to Kelly and her friends as "Mother Mimi"

Burt Parker—retired Fort Connor police detective, House of Lambspun spinner-in-residence

Hilda and Lizzie von Steuben—spinster sisters, retired schoolteachers, and exquisite knitters

CAST OF CHARACTERS

Curt Stackhouse—Colorado rancher, Kelly's mentor and adviser

Jayleen Swinson—Alpaca rancher and Colorado cowgirl

Connie and Rosa—House of Lambspun shop personnel

Cassie Wainwright—Pete's young teenage niece, who has come to live with him after her grandfather, Pete's father, died

Eric Thompson—Curt Stackhouse's teenage grandson and a friend of Cassie

Only Skein Deep

One

"Does that feel good?" Kelly Flynn asked her Rottweiler as she rubbed behind one of his silky black ears. "Does it, Carl?"

Carl, for his part, had already given Kelly an answer with his doggie sounds of pleasure. He bent his head slightly, the better for Kelly to rub behind the "special spot."

"Is that your favorite spot?" Kelly said to her dog as she stood beside him on her cottage's outside patio. Carl replied with a little crooning sound. *Yes! Yes! That's it!*

Kelly rubbed for a few more seconds. "Okay, that will have to be it for now, Carl. I have to leave."

Carl looked momentarily surprised when she stopped rubbing. Then he held his head in the way only dogs can do and trotted over to his water dish.

As Carl slurped several large gulps of water, Kelly caught sight of a pair of golfers strolling toward the green that was closest to the edge of the golf course. And the closest to Kelly's backyard.

"Looks like you'll have some golfers nearby, Carl," Kelly advised her dog as she slid open the glass patio door. "Try not to scare them to death."

Either Carl understood exactly what Kelly had said, or the golfers happened to edge into his peripheral vision at precisely that moment. Carl's head jerked up, and he let out a loud, "Woof!" He followed up with a string of sharp barks as he charged for the back fence. There, he stood up on his back legs, front paws on the chain link, and barked more threats to the unlucky twosome who dared to visit "his" course. The two golfers turned around at the sound of an authoritative Rottweiler bark. Then one waved toward Kelly before they both returned their concentration to their next golf shot.

Kelly waved back then glanced at the sunny Colorado sky above. It looked like they were really moving full steam into early summer. Springtime temps of the high seventies and now the low eighties were teasing everyone. April and May flowers were sprouting everywhere. She loved it.

Kelly walked over to the cottage kitchen counter and retrieved her medium-sized plastic mug. Ever since she'd reached the start of her ninth month of pregnancy, Kelly noticed that fast movements and turns had become harder to manage. Her round, bigger-than-a-basketball belly led the way.

At that moment, the baby inside gave a sturdy kick, and Kelly placed her hand over the spot. "Starting soccer practice already?" she teased the baby. "Okay, I'm going to settle into the armchair and attempt to get some work done, so try to keep the goals to a minimum."

Mug in one hand, Kelly retrieved her laptop and sat in the comfy old armchair that Jayleen had given her. "Every mom needs a comfy chair before the baby's born and a sturdy rocking chair after the baby's born," Jayleen had told her with a tone of authority.

Letting the armchair's comfortable embrace surround her, Kelly popped open her laptop. She wanted to add the last of this week's condo expenses she'd calculated for her real estate investor client Arthur Housemann. She'd entered two rows of expenditures onto the spreadsheet when several sturdy kicks from the baby made Kelly's belly bulge in one spot then another.

"Are you running down the field, Jack?" Kelly said as she watched what she'd come to recognize as a baby foot create another bulge. Kelly placed her hand over the spot. "Or was that a goal? If it was winter, I'd swear you were playing ice hockey," she laughed softly. Suddenly, that bulge disappeared and she felt more movement inside, then another bulge appeared on her left side. "Goal!" Kelly cheered then laughed.

Just then, her cell phone rang beside her elbow. Steve's name flashed on the phone screen.

"Hey there," Kelly said on answering. "He just scored a soccer goal."

Steve's laughter came over the phone. "Atta boy. Lots of kicks, huh?"

"Oooooooh yeah," Kelly said, settling deeper into the armchair's embrace.

"How're you doing?" Steve asked.

"I'm doing fine, just trying to get some work done on Housemann's accounts, but Jack's running up and down the field and the laptop keeps jumping."

"You're exaggerating," Steve said after another short burst of laughter.

"No, I'm not," Kelly said, watching her belly move again. "This kid keeps kicking goals."

"Did you have a second cup of coffee or something?" Steve asked, in a slight tone of concern.

"No!" Kelly protested. "I'm being so good, I don't even recognize myself." She had to laugh. "One cup of half-strength black coffee a day, as Sheriff Megan decreed."

"Atta girl," Steve cheered. "Megan will be proud. We're all proud of you."

"Yeah, yeah, yeah, you guys aren't having to try to stay awake in the afternoons, either. I swear, I'm gonna drink two huge mugs of black coffee after Jack's born."

Steve laughed softly. "It won't be long now. At least I hope. I keep talking to guys who say their wives went past the ninth month."

"Bite your tongue," Kelly teased. "I swear, I think I'm big as a house, but all the moms at Lambspun keep telling me I'm not that huge. You wouldn't believe all the stories I hear."

"Yeah, I would. Guys are always telling me stories. I swear, Dutch has a huge family, and everything that happens to them is drama and trauma." Steve chuckled.

At the mention of Steve's longtime construction foreman, Kelly asked, "Is Dutch doing okay? He's still only working half days, I hope."

"Oh yeah. He keeps wanting to work longer, but I've laid

down the law to him. It's only six months after his heart surgery, so he's still in the rehab period as far as I'm concerned. He hates it when I say that, but I've told the guys to grab his tools if necessary. Whatever it takes to get him to stop working."

"You know, some guys have to work. It's part of who they are," Kelly observed as she felt Baby Jack move about. "You and I have both heard stories about men who didn't live very long once they retired from their jobs. Their work is part of their identity, and it's like they don't know how to live without it. I really believe the reason that Burt has never had another heart attack is because he's had the chance to involve himself with the programs that help men who are recovering alcoholics."

Some stray memories suddenly popped into Kelly's head. "Oh, and don't forget, Burt regularly helped me whenever I was sleuthing around."

Steve gave a short laugh. "How can I forget that? Listen, I see Dutch signaling me. The guys just finished digging out that basement space. Gotta check it out."

"Sounds good. That must be the third or fourth basement they've dug on your new building site. How many town houses will be there?"

"No more than twelve. It's a small site, but it's an infill lot. The city doesn't have many of those, and they're prime spots. I'll talk to you later. Take it easy."

"Will do," Kelly said, then heard his phone click off. She returned to her accounting activities, methodically entering expenses and revenues. Baby Jack had quieted down, so this was a perfect time to get some work done. She drained her mug of unsweetened grapefruit juice, hoping that Afternoon Sleepiness wouldn't attack. But she could feel the combination of the comfy armchair and a warming spring afternoon was about to take its toll. What she wouldn't give for a cup of Eduardo's full-strength Black Gold right now.

House of Lambspun shop owner Mimi Parker looked up from stacking bundles of bubblegum pink yarn on the antique dry sink in the shop foyer. "Kelly! I was hoping you'd come in this afternoon," she declared with a big smile as Kelly stepped inside the knitting shop. "I wanted to show you some of the adorable baby outfits two of the knitters in this morning's group created."

"Oh wow. Did they really make them for me?" Kelly said as she paused by one of the tables in the entryway. Several fat skeins of lime green fiber were stacked in a neat pile. She stroked one of the skeins. Soft. Cotton, maybe? Examining the label she read that it was one hundred percent cotton from India. Kelly was always surprised how good her fingers were at detecting different fibers just by stroking them. In the nearly ten years she'd been coming to Lambspun, Kelly had gone from someone who had never knitted anything in her life to what she referred to as an Intermediate Advanced knitter. The word "Expert" never felt comfortable to her mind.

"They're not for you," Mimi said with a grin as she walked over to Kelly. "They're for Baby Jack." She reached out and gave Kelly's tummy a soft pat. "How're you doing, Jack?"

"Oh, he was playing soccer earlier when I was trying to

get some work done. Since it's springtime, I figured it was soccer."

"Were you racing around, Jack?" Mimi said with a little laugh. "You can't wait to get out, can you?"

"Well, since Jack's six pounds, the doctor says he could come in a couple of weeks or maybe he'll hang around longer. Who knows?" Kelly said as she walked toward the main knitting room.

Mimi followed after her. "Well, you're still carrying Jack a little high, so the baby hasn't dropped yet. You probably have a couple or more weeks to go."

Kelly smiled. "That term always makes me laugh. Dropped. It sounds so funny." She placed her fabric knitting bag on the long dark wood library table that dominated the main knitting room of the Lambspun shop. Kelly settled into one of the wooden chairs that bordered the table and glanced around the room.

Three sides of the room were lined with shelves. One entire wall contained open bins where yarns of every description spilled out. Since it was springtime, Mimi and the shop staff—the Lambspun elves, as Kelly called them—had filled the shelves with bright spring colors. Pink lemonade, lime green, lemon yellow, tangerine, blueberry. Cotton yarns, merino wool, alpaca, even bamboo. The yarn bins were stuffed to overflowing. Just like the central yarn room located between the foyer and the main room. Every wall there was stacked high with bulging shelves.

And both in the foyer and in the central yarn room hung beautiful handmade creations. Knitted, crocheted, and woven.

Scarves, baby sweaters, cloche hats and berets, and socks both multicolored and patterned.

Mimi laughed lightly. "Yes, I always thought it was funny, too. But it's very apt. Suddenly, one morning you notice something is different. And when you look in the mirror, you see that your tummy is definitely lower." She pulled out a chair next to Kelly. "I'd be glad to get you a cup of strong black tea. Extra strong and black. Even strong tea still has less caffeine. You were able to enjoy that, I remember."

"Enjoy is an exaggeration," Kelly said, eyeing Mimi. "I choked it down."

"Okaaaaaay," Mimi said. "How about some milk?"

Kelly shook her head. "Not now. It'll make me sleepy. I usually have some in the evening."

"How about some almond milk or coconut milk instead?"

"Actually, those taste good, but they'll make me sleepy, too. Everything seems to make me sleepy nowadays." Kelly reached inside her fabric knitting bag and pulled out the fiber project she'd just started. A small baby hat made of azure blue and smoke gray yarns.

"Well, let me go get some of that new Yorkshire tea I bought yesterday. That's definitely stronger than most teas you find in the grocery stores, so maybe that will taste better." Mimi pushed back her chair.

"It doesn't have any strange ingredients, does it?" Kelly asked.

"No, no. Simply strong black tea. I'll make a half cup. That way you can give it a try," Mimi said as she walked away toward the café that adjoined Lambspun knitting shop.

Kelly had long ago learned to give in to any of Mimi's

suggestions. "Mother Mimi," as Kelly and her friends called the sixtyish shop owner, had become a second mother to Kelly and her closest friends, Jennifer, Megan, and Lisa. Mimi's only child had died in an awful accident many years ago. He was a freshman at the local Colorado State University and had gone up into the neighboring Poudre Canyon to a friend's house for a weekend party. Unfortunately, several of the other college students were taking drugs, and Mimi's son joined in. He had a very bad experience and wandered away from the house into the surrounding mountainous terrain. He fell to his death on a rocky ledge below.

Alone in the main knitting room, Kelly wasted no time in returning to her knitting project. She picked up her stitches where she left off with the baby hat. She wanted to have the hat finished before the baby came, and according to everyone, that could be anytime this month. *A May baby*, she thought, as her fingers went through the familiar knitting movements. A spring baby. With luck, maybe she could play a few softball games before their softball season ended in the fall.

That cheerful thought brought a smile as Kelly pictured herself slender again and running the bases under a sunny sky. The shop's entry doorbell tinkled while summer scenes filled her mind. Taking the baby out to the games like Megan and Marty did with their baby, Molly. Perfect.

"Hello, Kelly. How're you doing?" a familiar voice said behind her.

Kelly turned to see retired Fort Connor police detective Burt Parker walk into the room. "Hey, Burt. I'm doing fine. What have you been up to?"

Burt pulled out the chair beside Kelly. "Errands, as usual. Mimi had a list as long as my arm today, I swear." Burt chuckled.

Kelly smiled at her longtime mentor. Once he and shop owner Mimi had married a few years ago, Burt was at the shop every day. Kelly really enjoyed that, since she'd lost her own father to lung cancer many years earlier. "Face it, Burt. You love staying busy and doing those errands. Otherwise, I bet we'd see you here in the shop looking for stuff to do."

"You're right, Kelly. There're always things to do here." He leaned closer to Kelly's belly. "And how are you this afternoon, Baby Jack?"

"Oh, he's been having a great time playing soccer. I swear he scored several goals while I was trying to do my accounting earlier."

Burt chuckled. "Well, he's probably anxious to come on out and meet us all."

"Not until I finish his hat," Kelly teased, holding up the baby hat. There were only a few rows of blue and gray cotton yarn on the knitting needles.

"You've got another couple weeks or so, don't you?" Burt asked, with a concerned look.

"Yeah, but the doctor said since the baby is a little over six pounds now, and I'm just about full-term, then Baby Jack could come anytime."

Burt nodded in his usual way, his lined face wrinkling in a worried expression that Kelly recognized. "Well, I'm making sure that the car is filled with gas and ready to go, just in case Baby Jack decides to come earlier rather than later."

Mimi walked into the main room then, a small mug in

her hand. "Here you go, Kelly. Half a cup of Yorkshire black tea. Give it a try and see what you think." She set the mug on the table in front of Kelly. Then Mimi leaned over and gave her husband a quick kiss. "Hello, dear. Were the shops really crowded?"

Burt shook his head. "Nope. I actually finished in good time. Then I stopped at the Starry Night coffee shop for a cup of coffee and to chat with that shopkeeper you mentioned." He eyed Kelly with a raised brow. "Kelly's trying some hot tea. This is a momentous occasion."

Kelly gave them both a sardonic smile. "Don't either of you get your hopes up. I haven't liked any hot tea yet." She picked up the mug, blew on it, then took a small sip. Kelly closed her eyes so she wouldn't grimace. Nothing tasted as good as her beloved extra strong black coffee, but she had promised herself she'd give other things a try. She tasted the hot tea then swallowed.

"Well, it's not as awful as some of the other ones I've tried," she said, screwing up her face.

Burt chuckled. "Damning with faint praise."

"So it's not totally awful?" Mimi asked.

"But it's still not what I'd call good."

"We'll take that, won't we, Burt?" Mimi said with a smile.

"We will indeed," Burt said as Kelly took another small sip to please her dear friends.

Two

Kelly closed the front door to the cottage she'd inherited after her aunt Helen's death nearly ten years ago. Kelly had returned to the city where she grew up in Northern Colorado to settle her beloved aunt's financial affairs. And she was shocked to learn that her aunt Helen had left Kelly the cottage and separate garage in her will. Kelly's father had moved around frequently when she was growing up, so the closest thing to a childhood home for Kelly was Uncle Jim's and Aunt Helen's farmhouse. They had raised sheep for a lifetime. Kelly still remembered how her uncle would sit in a small patio close by the front entry door to the farmhouse and watch over his large flocks.

Unable to run the sheep farm alone, Helen had sold off the acreage that once held sheep pasture when Uncle Jim died. But she moved from the large farmhouse right across the driveway to a small, cozy cottage that sat on the edge of the pasture. The large farmhouse was sold to a real estate investor who rented the property to Helen's favorite yarn and fiber shop, Lambspun. Lambspun's owner, Mimi, needed room to grow her successful fiber shop, and the farmhouse was the perfect spot. Located on the corner of two streets on the east side of Fort Connor's Old Town, the 1930s beige stucco, red-tile-roofed shop soon became the favorite of many of the area's fiber workers. Knitters, crocheters, spinners, and weavers were all welcomed. Shop owner Mimi was accomplished in all four of the popular fiber pursuits, so her regularly scheduled classes attracted a growing following.

Kelly walked across the driveway separating the cottage from the knitting shop. But instead of heading toward the shop's front door, Kelly aimed for the patio that sat directly behind the Lambspun shop. Filled with spring and summer flowers, Kelly eyed the planters and gardens that Mimi and her Lambspun elves had planted all around the back patio. The outside patio tables were still populated with lunchtime customers of the popular Pete's Porch Café.

She scanned the farthest tables and found one of her favorites was empty. Smaller than the rest, Kelly didn't feel bad occupying that back table and working outside in the beautiful spring weather. Café owner Pete had run the successful eatery ever since Kelly first stepped inside Lambspun. Waitress Jennifer was the first friend Kelly made when she first came to Fort Connor. She had walked across the driveway to her aunt's favorite yarn and fiber shop and stepped inside to an entirely new world. Kelly referred to the experience as "falling down the rabbit hole." Once she stepped inside Lambspun, she found herself in a magical place of color and texture. An absolute treat for the senses.

Kelly set her fiber briefcase bag onto the wrought iron patio table and settled into a matching outside chair. Shaded from the sun by the leaves of a large cottonwood tree in that corner of the outside patio, Kelly retrieved her laptop from the briefcase bag. Baby Jack was not playing soccer at the moment, so this was a good time to get a little accounting work done.

She wanted to make sure all the client accounts were up-to-date once the baby was ready to come out and meet everyone. After working for several years in a big Washington, DC, corporate accounting firm, Kelly moved back to Fort Connor after her aunt's death. Thanks to recommendations from friend, mentor, and adviser on all things ranching related, Curt Stackhouse, Kelly's practice now consisted of two very successful clients only. Arthur Housemann was a savvy real estate investor in Fort Connor and Northern Colorado, and Don Warner was an equally successful and savvy real estate developer. Both men were delighted with having the experience and expertise of a corporate-level CPA at their service.

Kelly popped open her laptop and was about to click on the accounting software when her best friend and café waitress Jennifer approached the table.

"Hey there, girlfriend. What can I get you? And please don't say, 'Black coffee, extra strong.' Megan would smell it on your breath. And you don't want to anger Mighty Mouse."

Kelly joined her friend's laughter. "Oh, if Megan ever heard us say that nickname, she'd fuss at us for a week."

"At least," Jennifer agreed. "Why don't you let me bring you a nice cup of black tea?"

"Actually, why don't you bring me some of that Yorkshire tea that Mimi made for me yesterday? It's a poor substitute for coffee, but not as bad as all the others I've tried. It's actually drinkable."

"Good heavens!" Jennifer exclaimed wide-eyed. "Did you feel the earth move just now? I swear it shifted a little."

"Yeah, yeah, yeah. Don't tell anyone. I want to keep my wayward pregnancy habits to myself. You and Mimi can be trusted not to tell."

"You are so funny," Jennifer said, pulling out a chair across the table from Kelly. "Your tea indulgences are safe with me."

"Blame it on Pregnancy Brain," Kelly said, relaxing back into the wrought iron chair. "That's what one of the moms-to-be at my exercise class calls it."

"Love it."

"She says she's constantly forgetting where she put her car keys. And when she finally finds them, she can't remember what errands she has to run." Kelly chuckled. "I have to confess I spent ten minutes yesterday morning looking for my key chain."

"Put a hook on the wall near the garage back door," Jennifer suggested.

"Actually, that's exactly what Steve did last night." She laughed again. "Thank goodness."

"How're you feeling?"

"Really good," Kelly said with a nod. "No Braxton Hicks contractions down low, so I guess Baby Jack will stay in full-term. Plus, every other mom has said he 'hasn't dropped yet.'" Kelly wagged her head. "That's such a funny term."

"Well, you'll be able to tell when he does," Jennifer added. "I've known many girls over the years who've been pregnant, and it's very obvious that one day, the baby is lower than before. It sounds funny, but it's pretty descriptive."

"I've never paid that much attention over the years, so it's just these last few months when I've been scrutinizing other pregnant moms. Say, are you two coming to the softball games this weekend? We'll be there to cheer on Megan and the rest of the team. City Park fields."

"Pete and I will try to catch their game, but Cassie's team is playing on the Rolland Moore fields. Eric's team will be at City Park, so we'll swing by there after Cassie's game is over. It's at nine o'clock in the morning."

"Okay, we'll cheer on Cassie and Eric, then go cheer for Megan and the team. Tell Cassie I'll look forward to seeing her this weekend."

"Will do. But you should think about staying at home with your feet up this weekend. You need your rest."

A small truck traveling down the driveway slowly caught Kelly's attention. She watched it pull into a parking space. She'd only glimpsed the writing on the truck's side panel. A middle-aged woman stepped out of the truck and headed toward the back of the vehicle.

"Is that a new shop making a delivery?" Kelly asked. "I don't recognize the logo."

"I don't know. It may be the new vendor that Mimi mentioned the other day. Someone selling candies and other packaged goodies."

"Oh great. Just what I need," Kelly said with a sigh. "More temptation."

Jennifer started to laugh and Kelly joined in. Sweet treats tempt everyone.

"Here, take my hand," Steve said as he helped Kelly step up to the second row of the outside bleachers at Rolland Moore Park ball fields. "I figured this row was good because you can easily get out for bathroom breaks." He gave her a wink.

"Good thinking," Kelly said as she settled on the wooden bleacher. She was beginning to notice for the first time how hard those bleachers were. Kelly figured she'd probably never noticed before because she was observing a lot of different things now that she was pregnant.

"I was going to get something to drink from the concession stand. What would you like? Rather, what's allowed by the powers that be?" He grinned.

"You mean the Nutrition Guru, Megan?" Kelly joked. "I'll have an iced tea. If I had a cola, Megan would fuss about how bad colas are." She stretched out both her legs on the lower bleacher. "Once Jack comes, Megan can shift her focus totally to Lisa. You and I will be up to our butts in diapers and such."

"And middle-of-the-night feedings, from everything I've heard. The guys at the work site are trying to scare me. It hasn't worked."

"Hopefully, we'll be one of the lucky ones and Jack will start sleeping through the night early on," Kelly observed as she looked over the ball field and the teenagers practicing there. "I swear, Megan and Marty were getting up in the wee hours for months with Molly. She never slept more than three hours, Megan said." Kelly looked up at Steve.

"Let's keep our fingers crossed. Molly is high maintenance, for sure."

Kelly laughed. "Kind of like Megan. So, no surprise." She glanced across the field again and glimpsed a familiar figure walking toward the bleachers. "Here comes Cassie."

"Hey there, girl," Steve said, giving Cassie a hug. "Who're you guys playing today?"

"West Longmont. It should be a good game. We're pretty evenly matched," Cassie said with a smile and the tone of teenage confidence.

Kelly observed the fifteen-year-old girl who was swiftly changing into a young woman. Taller, with all feminine curves filled out completely now. Plus, Kelly detected a new air or attitude was coming into being. A new confidence.

"You guys will do great," Kelly predicted with a big smile. She leaned back onto the bleacher row behind her.

"And how's Baby Jack doing?" Cassie asked, then reached out and gave Kelly's tummy a rub. "Bring me luck, Jack," she said with a grin.

Kelly laughed. "Nobody talks to me anymore. Have you noticed? Everyone talks to my belly."

Cassie grinned. "Are Lisa and Greg coming? Or is she still feeling yucky?"

"Yeah, pretty much, Greg says," Steve commented as he settled on the bleachers beside Kelly.

"She's able to teach her class at the university once a

week," Kelly added. "But she's staying at home most of the time. She's having a hard time with that early morning nausea. Morning sickness."

Cassie's expression changed to concern. "Wow. I hope she starts to feel better. Neither you nor Megan had those problems, Kelly. At least I don't remember your throwing up at all."

"I was lucky, I guess. I'd feel upset to my stomach a few times. But I'd go sit down with my head between my knees, and it would go away. Poor Lisa has definitely had a harder time. I went over to see her at their house the other day, and she was feeling fine. So I guess it comes and goes."

"How far along is Lisa, again?" Steve asked.

"She's just about three months. That's kind of the prime time when women feel queasy. A couple of weeks from now, Lisa should be fine. I hope." Kelly gave a crooked smile.

"Poor Lisa. Maybe Eric and I can go over after homework some night and take her a carton of cola drinks or ginger ale. Jennifer says that settles the stomach, but I'll check with Megan if they're okay during these early days of pregnancy."

"That sounds like a great idea," Steve said with a grin. "Why don't you drop by and see all of us at the same time. Friday night the gang is gathering at our house for movies and popcorn. You and Eric can say hi and grab a bag of popcorn before you go out with your friends."

"Hey, that sounds good to me. I'll tell him. His game has been moved over to these fields today." Cassie smiled, then glanced toward the parking lot. "Here come Pete and Jennifer." She waved her arm above her head. "Kelly and Steve are already here," she called out.

"I think I see Eric's team warming up. Can I get you anything from the concession stand, Cassie?"

Cassie wrinkled her nose. "Naw. Well, maybe one of those ice cream pop-ups. Thanks a lot."

"How're your classes going? You guys will be getting ready for final exams pretty soon, won't you?" Kelly asked.

"Oh yeah. We'll start reviewing next week. May is exam month, so they're coming up." She pointed down the sidelines. "Excuse me, guys. I see one of my friends I have to talk to. Be back in a few minutes." Cassie hurried away.

"Hey there, you two. Glad you're here," Jennifer called as she and Pete walked up to the bleachers.

"How're you feeling, Kelly?" Pete asked, his kind face concerned.

"I'm fine, Pete. I'm doing my exercises every morning, either at the fitness club or at home. So I'm feeling good."

Pete smiled as he and Jennifer settled on the bleachers down from Kelly and Steve. "Good to hear that. Don't forget to let me know if you have to get to the hospital fast. I'm right there next to the shop so I can get you there quickly and call Steve on the way."

Jennifer laughed lightly and patted Pete's back. "He's been working out various scenarios. And he's found the fastest way to the hospital, too."

"Well, I'm hoping Kelly will be home relaxing with me, so I can take her to the hospital," Steve said with a grin. "I've even stopped going to the Denver work site, and I'm just checking the new site in Wellesley."

"Remember, guys, about best-laid plans," Jennifer said. "Marty had everything all planned out, too. Then Megan got her first contractions in the middle of the night. And they started coming so fast, they were racing to the hospital, Marty said."

"I remember Megan telling me that," Kelly said. "Well, Steve and I will make sure we have our sneakers beside the bed so we can race if we have to."

"Uhhhhhh, I don't think you'll be racing anywhere, Kelly," Jennifer said, patting Kelly's tummy. "How's Baby Jack doing?"

"Playing soccer. And scoring goals, I figure from all that activity. I swear, he moves from one side of my belly to the next. So I guess he's running down the field."

"Hey, isn't that Marty walking over with Molly on his shoulders?" Pete said, pointing toward the parking lot.

"You're right. Let me head over to the concession stand now," Steve said.

"Don't forget to get something for Molly or there'll be heck to pay," Jennifer joked.

"Got it," Steve said as he walked away.

"Where's Megan?" Kelly wondered out loud as she peered toward the parking lot. "I see her now. She's getting something from the car. Oh, it's the stroller."

"Good luck with that," Jennifer said in a wry voice.

"Oh yeah. I've watched Molly climb out of everything Megan's ever put her in," Kelly added. "Child carrier, car seat even when she's strapped in. Don't know how she manages that. Even the high chair. She nearly gave Megan heart failure when I stopped over there a couple of months ago. She waited until Megan was showing me something on the dining room table, then we turned around and saw Molly balancing on the edges of the high chair." Kelly laughed softly. "Brother, if Baby Jack starts doing that, I'll start feeding him from the car seat on the floor."

"On the floor?" Pete said with a laugh.

"Yeah. The floor is a lot closer," Kelly replied. "Believe me, I've learned a lot just by watching all the crazy things Molly has done."

"And speaking of my favorite redhead, here's Molly!" Pete said, smiling as Marty walked up to the bleachers, Baby Molly riding high on her daddy's shoulders.

"Hey there, guys!" Marty said with his trademark big grin and red hair framing his face. "How're you doing, Kelly?"

"Doing good. Feeling good, too. Baby Jack is still comfy where he is. I don't think he wants to move out anytime soon."

"Hi, folks," Megan said as she approached, overstuffed diaper bag over her shoulder. "How're you feeling, Kelly?"

"Feeling good. Doing fine," Kelly repeated with a smile for what felt like the millionth time.

It felt good to have so many people care about her. It had just been her dad and her during Kelly's childhood and young adulthood. Up until her dad died too early from lung cancer. A lifetime of smoking cigarettes. Those early years of her career in a corporate CPA firm didn't allow for much of a social life. But her life changed once she returned to Fort Connor and walked across the driveway from her aunt's cottage and into the warm, welcoming atmosphere of the Lambspun shop. There, Kelly found more friends than she'd ever had in her entire life. She'd actually found more than friends. She'd found a family.

"Hey, Molly," Pete said with a bright smile. "Wanta come to your uncle Pete?" He clapped his hands then spread his arms wide. A mop of bright red curls surrounded toddler Molly's face, which spread now with a wide smile.

"Peeta, Peeta," she cried, reaching for him.

"Wait a minute, honey, let me lift you . . ."

"Molly, wait . . ." Megan urged her daughter.

But Baby Molly ignored both parents and halfway dove from her daddy's shoulders toward Pete's arms.

"Whoa!" Pete leaned forward quickly and scooped up Molly as she leaped from Marty's shoulders.

"Oh no!" Jennifer exclaimed, reaching forward just like horrified Megan beside her.

Completely oblivious to all the adult concern, Molly chattered away to Pete as he held her safely in his arms. Megan and Marty exchanged grateful yet concerned parental glances.

Jennifer sat on the bleachers, hand to her breast. "My heart is beating a mile a minute."

"Mine stopped," Pete said. "You've gotta stop scaring us, Molly girl," he said with a grin. "You're gonna give us all heart attacks with your gymnastics."

"Tell us about it," Megan said, rolling her eyes, and she and Marty collapsed on the bleacher below.

Kelly's heart was still pounding, too. *Good Lord*, she thought to herself, observing Megan's and Marty's shell-shocked expressions. Then she wondered if she and Steve would be playing circus catcher in a few months.

Steve walked up to them with a box filled with cups of soft drinks. "Hey there. Who wanted the cola, who wanted the orange drink—?" He interrupted himself because Jennifer reached forward and grabbed one of the tall cups, gulping it down.

Steve started to laugh as he set the box on the bleachers. "Looks like I got here at the right time."

"Oh yeah," Kelly said to him as he sat beside her.

Picking up on her tone of voice, Steve asked, "What'd I miss?"

"Just heart-stopping acrobatics, that's all. I think we'd better brace ourselves," Kelly said with a rueful smile.

Three

"Well, hello, Kelly," an older woman said as she entered Lambspun's main knitting room. "How're you doing?"

Kelly looked up from her needles and recognized one of Lambspun's regular knitters, a familiar face around the shop's welcoming table. "Hi there, Geraldine. I'm doing fine. I feel great, and the baby must, too, because he's jumping around a lot."

Geraldine's lined face creased into a wide smile. She pulled out a chair on the other side of the table and settled into it. "That is so good to hear. My own daughter had all sorts of troubles with that morning sickness every time she was pregnant. But the babies were all healthy, thank goodness." She opened her bright red fabric knitting bag and removed a lemon yellow bundle of yarn with needles dangling.

"That's the important thing," Kelly said, her fingers working the soft blue and gray yarn onto the circular needles. Her hat was progressing slower than Kelly had hoped, because she simply no longer had the time to knit. Before she'd reached her ninth month, Kelly had been able to take some time to relax in the afternoons before she had to start the next round of activities. But now Kelly found herself falling asleep in the afternoons. She would nap close to an hour, which shocked her. Kelly had never napped before in her life. Not in college, not even when she was sitting next to her father all those nights in the hospital as lung cancer took his life. She had tried napping at times like that, but her busy mind simply wouldn't stop. It wouldn't even slow down long enough for her to drift off. Kelly was amazed. Pregnancy had turned her into a napper. How strange.

"Are all your grandchildren in school yet?" she asked once Geraldine had settled into knitting the yellow yarn.

Geraldine chuckled. "Oh yes. They've all gone to school and gotten multiple degrees and started their careers. All of them are successfully employed and working, thank goodness. Not everyone nowadays can say that."

"Wow, I'm impressed, Geraldine," Kelly said with a smile as her fingers continued with the blue and gray yarn.

The shop doorbell jingled then, and another woman Kelly recognized walked into the main room. "Oh good. You two are here. I like it better when there are other folks around the table." The middle-aged brunette pulled out a chair farther down from Kelly and plopped her navy blue fiber knitting bag on the table in front of her.

"Hey there, Marie," Kelly greeted her. "Sit down and join us."

"Thanks, Kelly," Marie said as she settled into a chair and removed a pastel blue baby blanket from her knitting bag.

Kelly wondered if she needed to buy another baby blanket. She had a blue one and had made a super soft light yellow one with a pattern of farm animals on it. Then she remembered that several friends had already given her packages with extra baby blankets layered in between other gifts.

"That's a very pretty shade of blue," Kelly observed, looking at Marie's knitting project.

"Thanks, Kelly. I'd give it to you, but it's already claimed by a friend of mine," Marie said with a smile. "You're looking great, by the way. Are you feeling as good as you look?"

Kelly had to laugh. Ever since she'd become pregnant, people started watching her and commenting on how she looked or how she was doing. "Yes, I am. And thanks for saying that. I feel like I'm carrying a big bundle in front of me, but I actually feel fine."

"I'm glad to hear it," Marie said as her fingers worked the yarn. "I sailed through pregnancy, too. So, you and I are lucky, I guess. Some women seem to have a lot of problems. Or, in some cases, they like to complain about the problems they have. Different types."

The doorbell jingled again, and the middle-aged woman Kelly had noticed the other day appeared in the central yarn room, walking their way. "Well, hello, ladies," the woman said with a smile. "I'm Beverly, and I've taken over the snack and sweets business that your elderly vendor Gordon ran for years. I've been dropping by to introduce myself and some of the newer line of healthy and organic snacks we're selling."

"Nice to meet you, Beverly." Kelly spoke up first since Beverly was looking her way. "And yes, I noticed you came to the shop the other day when I was working on my laptop out there in the café garden."

"Yes, now that you mention it, I saw you, too. And if I'm not mistaken, it looked as if you might be expecting a baby." Beverly gave Kelly a warm smile.

"You're definitely not mistaken, Beverly," Kelly said with a grin. "I'm in my ninth month now. And we already know it's a little boy."

"Well, congratulations," Beverly said with a maternal grin.

"And they've already named him Jack for Kelly's father, right?" Marie added.

"Yes, we have," Kelly said, giving her belly a pat.

"Well, you deserve a nice organic snack. Take your pick, Kelly. It's on the house. Expectant mother special."

Kelly laughed lightly. "That's sweet of you, Beverly, but you don't have to—"

"It's my treat. I insist," Beverly said.

"Go ahead, Kelly. I've already had some of Beverly's items, and they're yummy," Marie said, turning in her chair, knitting dropped to her lap. "You can give me those chocolate-covered cherries, please. Two packages this time."

"You got it, Marie," Beverly said with an accommodating smile. "And what about you, Kelly? We have some organic nuts and dried fruits, if you'd like."

"Hmmmmm, that does sound nice. What kinds of nuts do you have?"

"I've got organically grown peanuts as well as cashews. Which do you prefer?"

"Oooo, I like both, but I'll take the cashews, please."

"You got it. What about you, ma'am?" she asked Geraldine, who had been sitting quietly, knitting and watching the other women.

"Oh, I'm fine for now," Geraldine said. "I'll give those treats a try another time."

"Certainly, ma'am. I'll be dropping by every week. Now, excuse me for a moment, ladies. I'll be right back." And Beverly swiftly walked out of the main room.

"I really don't need anything," Kelly said to Marie, "but it's pretty tempting when the treats come to you, isn't it?"

"Way too tempting," Marie replied with a sigh. "I need chocolate-covered cherries like I need a hole in the head."

Beverly returned in less than a minute, small packets in both hands. "Here we go, ladies," she said, handing both of them their treats with a flourish. "Cashews for Kelly and chocolate-covered cherries for Marie."

Kelly noticed the colorful packaging and flipped it over, reading the information printed there. Beverly was right. The package stated that the nuts had been organically grown.

Mimi walked into the main room then and burst into one of her tinkling little laughs. "Well, I see you folks have met our new Lambspun vendor. Beverly may not have yarns, but she definitely has other treats."

"Hello there, Mimi. Can I interest you in anything? I believe you tried the pecan candies last week, correct?" Beverly said with an engaging smile.

"Oh, you are a temptress, Beverly," Mimi said. "Why not give me those pecan candies again. I just love pecans!"

"Absolutely, Mimi," Beverly said, then retreated once again into the foyer where Kelly thought she glimpsed the top of a metal shelving unit. She returned quickly with Mimi's package of pecan candies. "Direct from Florida," she said with a grin. "I brought some plantain chips for you folks to try. When I visited Miami years ago, I think I visited every Cuban restaurant I saw. I just love their cooking. Fried plantains, yummy sauces, and deadly desserts. And black beans to die for." Beverly closed her eyes. "Delicious."

"Now you're starting to make me hungry," Geraldine said with a laugh as she glanced up from her knitting.

"I had some of those Cuban dishes when I vacationed there years ago," Marie said. "And I agree with you. I enjoyed some of the most delicious meals at the cafés there. In fact, the whole vacation week we ate out every night. I swear, my husband and I must have gained five pounds each."

Mimi and the others all laughed. "I declare, you've made me curious, Marie. And you, too, Beverly. I'm tempted to go to the bookstore and find a Cuban cookbook and make some of those dishes myself."

"Well, if you do, Mimi, please make sure you save some for us. We can have one of our potlucks one day for lunch," Geraldine suggested.

"I just might do that, ladies," Mimi said with a nod.

Kelly raised her hand. "If you do, please make sure to invite me, Mimi. I can't cook worth a darn, but I really enjoy good food. And those Cuban recipes sound delicious."

"You can bring the napkins and paper plates, Kelly. That's safer. Just in case Baby Jack decides to come." All the women started to laugh, and Kelly joined in.

"Frankly, I'm amazed you haven't had that baby yet," Arthur Housemann said to Kelly as she settled into one of his office chairs.

Kelly smiled at her fatherly client who had been more solicitous than usual since she'd announced her pregnancy. "It's not time yet, Arthur," Kelly reminded him. "I've only begun my ninth month. Baby Jack needs more time in the oven."

Housemann wagged his silvered head. "Well, Baby Jack is going to be a very big boy, then," he teased. "You look like you're ready to drop him."

Kelly laughed out loud at that. "Oh, Arthur. You simply have not been around many pregnant women for a long time. Half the women in my exercise class are due around the same time, and most of them are bigger than I am. I've actually kept doing exercise, so I think that's helped."

Arthur laughed softly. "You amaze me, Kelly. Why am I not surprised? Of course you're doing exercises. How's Steve holding up? Getting excited, I imagine."

"Oh yes. He's starting on a new development just east of the interstate. Not far from the new big-box shopping center."

"I heard about that. I'll have to drop by and see what he's up to over there."

"Steve loves it whenever you just 'drop' in. He tells me you're always full of ideas."

"I love seeing what Steve and his crew are up to," Arthur said. "By the way, how's your friend the physical therapist who works at the orthopedic clinic? I think you mentioned that she's expecting, too."

"Lisa? Yes, she's early in her pregnancy, so she's not due for a while. And I'm afraid she's having a lot of episodes of morning sickness, so it's a little rough right now. She's had a hard time taking care of her physical therapy clients as well as handling her psychology grad classes at the university."

"Goodness, she does have a heavy schedule," Arthur observed.

"Yes, she does. So I hope she passes through this rough patch pretty soon." Kelly held up two crossed fingers.

"Oh Lord, I remember my wife going through morning sickness. Quite a few years ago," Arthur said, gazing out his office window, which looked out on the east side of Fort Connor. Kelly remembered when she first came to Fort Connor, that view to the east of the city was mostly farmland or cattle ranches. Now all that property was divided up into subdivisions and filled with houses. Sometimes Kelly wished there were some farmlands left in between the subdivisions like some of the developments on the other sides of town had done. It was more pleasing to see houses separated by stretches of land. Greenery between the buildings. You could also see the mountains better.

"I must be getting older, Arthur, because I was just remembering what that land east of here used to look like when I first came to Fort Connor nearly ten years ago." She pointed out the window.

Arthur chuckled. "Nostalgia is a funny thing, Kelly. It creeps up on us out of nowhere," he said as he leaned back into his chair and gave her another fatherly smile.

Kelly shifted in the patio chair outside Pete's Porch Café. The May weather was beautiful, temps were actually mild in the mideighties, and the Colorado springtime morning sun was playing hide-and-seek in the cottonwood tree branches above. A perfect day to work outside, to Kelly's way of thinking. She'd been working on the accounting for an hour or so and had already entered all of Arthur Housemann's real estate investor monthly revenues for this month. Now for the expenses. Kelly had barely clicked on the expense spreadsheet when she heard it. *Thunder.* One rumble.

Kelly looked up to notice that the sky was no longer sunny. It was cloudy now, and some of those clouds coming across the Front Range of the Rockies along the western edge of town—the Foothills, as longtime residents called them—weren't white and puffy anymore. They were now gray and looked stormy to Kelly.

When did that happen? Last time she'd glanced up from the spreadsheets, the skies were sunny. Of course, she'd been working on her spreadsheets for quite a while now. Long enough for an early summer storm to blow in over the Foothills.

Another low rumble of thunder, then another. Longer this time. *That was it*, Kelly thought to herself, and clicked her laptop into Sleep mode then gathered up her client files. She'd lived in Colorado long enough to learn the signs of a summer storm. Thunder meant lightning was striking somewhere already. And she'd learned to never mess with lightning, especially in a mountain state like Colorado.

Kelly shoved everything into her fiber briefcase bag and headed out of the patio and around to Lambspun's front entry. She walked slower up the steps than she used to and heaved open the heavy wooden entry door. One of Lambspun's longtime knitting staff, Rosa, looked up from a pile of electric blue yarns she was stacking on the dry sink in the foyer.

"Goodness, Kelly. You got here just in time. Those clouds are going to open up any minute," she said.

Another rumble of thunder echoed then. Much louder than before. Followed by a loud crack! Both Kelly and Rosa jumped at the sudden sound.

"Whoa, I did escape just in time," Kelly said, patting her belly.

"Good thinking. You and Baby Jack don't want to be around that summer lightning. You never know where it will strike." Rosa's dark eyes were wide with warning. "I had a friend who always wanted to stay out in the rain, and one day she was actually struck by lightning." Rosa's eyes widened even more.

"Oh no!" Kelly said, horrified. "Did it kill her?"

"No, but it seriously injured her. Her brother said she dropped to the ground and lost consciousness for a moment. And some of her movements weren't the same afterwards. Like her walking. She still has a little limp."

"Wow, that is a scary story. I think I'll go inside faster from now on."

"Smart. There's two of you nowadays, so you have to be more careful than usual," Rosa said.

Kelly walked through the central yarn room and headed for the main knitting room. She noticed Marie and Geraldine were already there. "Hey there, you two, did the thunder scare you inside as well?" Kelly plopped her briefcase bag onto the library table and settled into one of the chairs across the table from the two women.

"Oh yes. I saw those clouds forming as I was parking my car." Marie was working on a pink and white knit piece.

"I got here before Marie," Geraldine said. "I noticed you

working outside in the garden, Kelly, but I didn't want to disturb you. You were obviously lost in accounting thoughts." She chuckled.

"Oh yes. Deep thoughts," Kelly said as she reached inside her knitting bag for the baby hat.

"How's Jack's baby hat coming along?" Geraldine asked. Her own needles were filling with rows of butter yellow yarn.

"Slowly, I'm afraid," Kelly said as she picked up her stitches where she'd left off. "I hope I finish it before Jack arrives to use it." She glanced toward Marie and pointed at the yarn on her needles. "Is that a sweater?" she asked.

"Well, it's supposed to be. But these sides are slightly uneven. I'm hoping they can be straightened out when I block the piece." She yanked one corner of the rectangle.

The doorbell jangled loudly, and laughing women's voices could be heard in the foyer. "Just in time," one said.

"You're right. Now where's that café you talked about?" the other woman asked.

Kelly, Marie, and Geraldine all looked up as two women walked through the central yarn room, clearly heading toward the hallway that led to the café at the back of the knitting shop.

Café owner Pete had started the café a few years before Kelly walked into Lambspun. Pete noticed that the farmhouse turned knitting shop had been used as a restaurant many years earlier. And it still had a restaurant set up in the kitchen area at the back of the farmhouse. He offered to rent that restaurant space from the investor who owned the entire property, and the successful combination of welcoming knitting shop and popular café was started.

Lambspun owner Mimi had truly transformed the older building into a warm and welcoming fiber retreat that beckoned everyone to come inside and explore. For knitters, crochet lovers, spinners, and weavers, Lambspun offered nooks and crannies and tactile delights around every corner. Visitors who walked inside out of curiosity often became regulars. Yarns and fibers of every description filled each room.

Marie checked her watch. "Those golfers are lucky that Pete's Café is still open."

Kelly looked over at Marie. "How did you know those two women were golfers, Marie?"

"Well, I know one of the women, and I've heard about the other one. They're both golfers. The brunette is a really, really good golfer and has won several local tournaments."

Kelly looked back at the blue and gray yarn. "There's no way I could hit one of those little balls on a golf course. It's hard enough chasing down and hitting tennis balls."

"You've got that right. Tennis is way more strenuous than golf, too. You have to race around the court chasing a tennis ball and hitting it back over the net fast. And then, the ball keeps coming back." Marie laughed. "I was never any good at tennis. And I'm not very good at golfing, either, but at least the balls land on the green. Then they lie still and wait for you to hit them!"

Kelly pictured the golf ball lying docilely in place compared to the restless tennis ball that kept coming back over the net, and she had to laugh, too. "That is so funny. Now I'm picturing passive golf balls lining up on the green."

Marie's laughter and smile vanished. "That younger blond woman is a newcomer and another golfer who's starting to win some tournaments. She's also the new wife of William Callahan, the president and founder of that successful local equipment company. Unfortunately."

Four

Kelly was surprised by the addition of that word. "Unfortunately." There was definitely a story there.

"Yes, I recognize the name Callahan," she said. "He started that company locally several years ago and built it into a national success, right?"

"He and his wife both made that company successful," Marie said emphatically.

Kelly couldn't miss the emphasis put on the word "wife." "It sounds like his wife was very much involved in the company, too."

"She certainly was," Marie replied. "Meredith helped test and modify some of the sports gloves they sold. Baseball gloves, softball, too. Meredith used to play a lot of softball in her younger days."

Kelly considered the way Marie said that. "Used to play."

For the first time, Kelly wondered if she would actually be able to keep playing in the various sports leagues she participated in. She loved playing softball and teaching young junior high kids softball, plus teaching early teen boys and girls in her batting clinics. Kelly had always assumed she would continue her sports activities. What if she didn't have the time? Kelly concentrated on the blue and gray stitches accumulating on her knitting needles. She'd noticed years ago that whenever she was worrying about something, her knitting got faster. Stitches appeared on the needle more quickly.

Not being able to play was a disconcerting thought, but it was instantly followed by another one. Megan. Megan was still participating in all her sports activities. She'd only missed a few games right before and after Baby Molly's delivery. Kelly relaxed. If Megan could do it, surely she could, too.

"You said that golfer was Callahan's new wife. Did he and his first wife divorce, or did she pass away?"

"They divorced, then he remarried. But his first wife, Meredith, is no longer with us."

"Oh, I'm sorry to hear that," Kelly said sympathetically. "Does his second wife help him with the company business, too?"

"Hmmmmph!" Marie said. "She helps spend his money, that's all."

Kelly noticed that Marie's pleasant features had furrowed into a scowl. "Oh boy. We've all seen that before, haven't we? That seems to be an old story."

"Yes, and this is a sad, sad story, too." She suddenly stopped knitting and shoved her yarn into her fabric bag. "I knew his first wife as a dear friend, so I got to see what his rejection did to Meredith firsthand. She committed suicide because of it." Marie quickly rose from her chair. "I'll see you folks another time. Excuse me." She was out of the room and headed for the front entry in a matter of seconds.

Kelly was shocked by Marie's response and let her knitting drop to her lap. "Oh no! I feel awful now. I should never have started asking questions about her friend or that other woman."

"Don't beat yourself up, Kelly," Geraldine said in a reassuring tone. "It had nothing to do with you. You had no way of knowing about that family situation. It's clear Marie had an intense loyalty to that man's first wife. Consequently, she's developed equally intense feelings about the second wife."

Kelly felt herself relax a little inside. "You sound like you know them."

"Actually, no. But I've heard my friends talk. Gossip, really. I don't move in that golf club set, mainly because I don't play golf. Not anymore. I used to play a little, but I was never any good at it. So I never became addicted to it like some of my friends. For some of them, their weeks revolve around rounds of golf. My husband says it's no different with men. Some men become addicted to the game, mainly because you're constantly playing against yourself, to be honest. Managing your stance, your swing, your follow-through. All of that. One day you can play marvelously well. And the next day, you can mess up practically every shot. It doesn't matter how many lessons you've had, either. You're still competing against yourself, but you're doing it with a group of friends. Or at least fellow golfers." She gave an amused chuckle.

"You know, you've mirrored my feelings about the game, too. I feel the same way," Kelly admitted. "I grew up playing practically every sport. Either I learned on teams in junior or senior high school or in college. Softball, volleyball, tennis, soccer. Even basketball, but I didn't play basketball past junior high."

"Why was that?"

"Well, to be honest, whenever I was playing and got in that tight pack underneath the basket, someone would usually fall down," she said with a little smile.

"I have a feeling it wasn't you, Kelly," Geraldine teased.

Kelly nodded. "You're right. By junior high school, I was taller and stronger than most of the other junior high girls. So whenever I was trying to get free from that bunch under the basket, I wound up elbowing some delicate little girl in the ribs. She would either fall down or grab her ribs and cry. So I gave up basketball and stuck to the other sports. Which I enjoyed a lot more anyway."

Geraldine started to laugh softly. "I love that image, Kelly. It's you. Definitely you. And it sounds like you chose softball to concentrate on. I've heard you talk about playing on some mixed leagues and women's leagues in town."

"Yes, I found softball to be a good match for my abilities, plus you get to run as well as hit when you're playing. Every time you come to the plate to bat, there's a chance of making one of those great hits. A home run. And believe me, there's nothing like watching that ball sail high above and way, way, way out in the field." Kelly looked out toward the windows remembering ball games past. "Whenever that happens, you get to run around all the bases plus bring in all the other players who were already on the bases. It's a great feeling."

"Sounds like it," Geraldine said with a smile. "I think Mimi said you also teach young junior high girls batting classes as well."

"Oh yes. Not only girls, but young boys as well. If they can learn how to bat properly early on, they'll be good, reliable players. But you're right. I do coach a summer junior high girls softball team, too."

Geraldine glanced at her watch. "Oh goodness, I promised to meet someone at that café in Old Town, Coopersmith's." She pushed back her chair as she stuffed her knitting into her oversize purse. "I'll see you tomorrow, Kelly. And relax. You didn't do anything." She gave Kelly another maternal smile then reached out and patted her on the shoulder before walking away.

Kelly relaxed some more. Wow. You never knew what was going on in someone's life until you started asking questions. Asking questions was something Kelly just did naturally. One of these days maybe she could figure out which questions would rattle someone's cage so she could avoid those. Maybe. But she doubted it.

Kelly was simply pleased she could occasionally carry on a conversation and glance up from her knitting at the same time. Amazing. Maybe Mimi was right. Maybe she really had become a good knitter. *Shocking*, Kelly thought with a smile.

The entry doorbell tinkled again, and a very familiar young face appeared walking through the central yarn room. "Cassie!" Kelly exclaimed. "How great to see you! I thought you had softball practice after school."

Cassie's bright smile lit up her face. "It's game day, so no practice. We're playing at Longmont tonight." She leaned down to give Kelly a hug.

Kelly squeezed Cassie back. "Oh yeah. I forgot. How's school? You guys should be going into final semester exams this month."

"Ohhhhhh yeah," Cassie said as she settled into a chair on Kelly's side of the table. "We've already started reviewing subjects now. Humanities will be easy," she said, leaning back into the wooden chair in a relaxed teenage semi-sprawl. "Chemistry will be unreal, of course. Spanish will be easy. Our teacher is such a doll."

"Aren't you taking trigonometry, too?"

"Oh yeah. Forgot trig. It'll be a breeze." Cassie gave a little dismissive wave. "It's easy like geometry. Nothing at all like calculus." She screwed up her face.

Kelly laughed softly as she kept knitting. "That's because geometry and trig are both spatial. You can actually see it. Or picture the problem. Kind of hard to picture calculus."

"Who'd want to?" Cassie teased.

"Hey, it's still useful. You won't know why until you're taking some of those advanced courses in college."

"If you say so," Cassie said, then scooted forward. "How's Baby Jack doing today?" She placed her palm over Kelly's belly.

"Oh, he's playing soccer like usual. I figure it has to be soccer, because it feels like he's kicking the ball up and down the field. Scoring goals, of course."

Cassie gave one of her short, little half laughs. "Way to go, Jack. Down the field!"

"Where's Eric's team playing? Does he have a game tonight or just on the weekend?"

"He plays tomorrow, Saturday, at Rolland Moore. And we'll be playing there, too. We only overlap a little, so you guys can see both if you have time." She gave Kelly's belly a pat, then quickly rose from the chair. "I'll be working at the café early tomorrow morning, so if you feel like it, drop by."

"Oh, I probably will. Steve has started a new housing development in Wellesley, and he'll be working most of the day. He's trying to get a lot done so he can be around more once the baby comes."

Cassie nodded. "How's Lisa doing? I haven't seen her in over a week."

"She's still having morning sickness, poor thing," Kelly said. "Hopefully it won't last much longer."

Cassie screwed up her face. "Oooooo, that's too bad. Wonder why Lisa is having so many problems with it?"

"Everybody's different. Some women have an easy time with pregnancy, and others don't. But even if they have the nausea, it doesn't last long. And most of them cruise through the rest of their pregnancy."

Cassie nodded her head, clearly pondering what Kelly said. "That's good to hear. I'd sure like to think that Lisa would start showing up at the shop again."

Kelly gave her favorite teenager a smile. "Oh, I'm sure she will, Cassie. Lisa's tough. And don't forget, you'll be getting another new babysitting client just a few months after Baby Jack is born."

"Yay!" Cassie gave a cheer, then laughed.

• • •

Kelly closed the front door to the cottage and started down her front walkway, heading toward the café across the driveway. The May temps were getting warmer each day, and it was far more pleasant to work on her client accounts outside in the shaded patio than inside.

A large model black truck turned down the driveway then. Kelly recognized Curt Stackhouse, her dear friend and adviser on all things ranching related. She waved at Curt as he slowed down his Serious Truck and leaned out the window.

"Find us a table in the patio, why don't you? We've got to talk."

"Sure thing," Kelly said and walked over to the café patio while Curt parked the truck. She had just settled into a wrought iron chair at a shaded table beneath the cottonwood tree when Curt walked up.

"Hello there, Kelly-girl," Curt greeted her as he pulled out a chair on the other side of the table.

Kelly smiled at her mentor and trusted adviser as well as father figure. "Hello, yourself. What's up? Are those Wyoming gas wells still going strong?"

Curt signaled waitress Julie to catch her attention. "I'd appreciate it kindly, Julie, if you could get Kelly and me a couple of black coffees."

"Sure thing, Curt," Julie said as she finished clearing off a table. "Hot or iced?"

"Bite your tongue, girl. Hot, of course. Hot and black."

"You got it," Julie said with a laugh as she headed toward the café's back door.

"Actually, I've been drinking a lot of iced coffee now that it's gotten so much warmer."

"Travesty," Curt decreed with a raised brow.

Kelly laughed softly. "So are those wells doing okay?"

"Absolutely. All your properties are doing well. What we need to talk about is something way more important." Curt folded both arms on the patio table and leaned forward.

"Well, you've got my curiosity and my attention. What's up?"

"Both Jayleen and I want to know one thing. We've waited these last few months without saying a word, hoping that the issue would resolve itself. And it hasn't. So we decided it was time to speak up."

"Now you've really got my attention. What is it?"

Curt eyed her in that way he had. "When are you going to make an honest man out of Steve?"

Kelly stared at Curt for a second, then burst out laughing.

"I wasn't joking, Kelly. Neither is Jayleen. We both think it's high time you two tied the knot. You've got a baby coming in a month or less."

Kelly's laughter subsided slowly as Julie brought them their black coffees. "Thanks, Julie."

"You're welcome, Kelly. I made your coffee half-strength like Jennifer advised. And you'll have to tell me the joke later," Julie said with a grin before she walked away.

"Ohhh, Curt. I love you to death. You know that, don't you?"

"That's beside the point. You and Steve love each other,

and have been living together these last few years. Hell, you act married. You might as well be married!"

Kelly started laughing again. "You and Jayleen are something else."

"We sure are. We're married now. So it's time for you and Steve."

Kelly nearly spilled the coffee she'd just raised to her lips. Taking a sip, she stared at Curt. "Did I hear you right? You and Jayleen are married?"

"We sure are. And we both made out our wills, too, so our heirs had no doubt as to their inheritances. My property goes to my family and Jayleen's goes to hers."

Well, well, Kelly thought to herself. Who would have thought? Jayleen and Curt hadn't said a word.

"When did you two get hitched, as Jayleen would say?" she asked with a smile.

"Last year. We didn't want anybody to make a big to-do. I told my daughter and son-in-law and my older son who's in the military just a couple of months ago. They were really happy to hear it." He smiled his Cheshire cat smile.

"Well, Jayleen never let on, either." She wagged her head. "You two amaze me."

"Now it's time for you to amaze us all, Kelly-girl. You know that Steve hasn't even mentioned the word 'marriage' to you since that time you two broke up a few years ago. But you know full well Steve would jump at the chance to marry. And make this relationship legal at last."

Kelly laughed softly again. "Legal at last, huh?"

"Yes, indeed, Kelly-girl. You've already chosen a name. Finish this properly, so Baby Jack will actually have a legal last name." Curt gave an affirmative nod in emphasis. "It would sure make filling out the birth certificate easier."

"I promise I will give it some thought, Curt."

"Don't string me along, Kelly-girl." He frowned at her. "Jayleen and I are both dead serious. And if you want to know, all of your friends are dying for you two to tie the knot as well."

"You're kidding." Kelly grinned. "Who?"

"All of them. Megan and Marty. Greg and Lisa. Jennifer and Pete. They never bring it up because they don't want to make you mad."

Kelly blinked. "Greg and Lisa? They're not even married!"

Curt didn't answer; he simply leaned back into the chair and smiled his Cheshire cat smile. "You can ask Lisa yourself. She and Greg told Jayleen and me one night when they came over for dinner. I asked them both flat out if Greg's accident hadn't made them think seriously about the future. And they both confided that they had married about a month after Greg was out of the hospital and finished his rehab. And asked us to keep their secret. Of course, Jayleen and I swore we would."

Now Kelly stared out into the green of the patio garden. Early summer flowers coming into bloom. Good Lord! Greg and Lisa as well as Curt and Jayleen had really kept their marriages a secret. Whoa! Who would have thought? Greg and Lisa were married! It made sense. That scare with Greg's accident clearly made both of them think.

But why hadn't any of her friends mentioned marriage to her?

Kelly didn't have to wait long for an answer. Her reliable

instinct spoke up loud and clear. *Because you made it perfectly clear you didn't think marriage was important—or necessary.*

"Greg and Lisa also told us they made the decision after Greg got out of the hospital," Curt added. "They both realized that Greg could have been killed in that accident. And it made them think about the future."

"Wow, I had no idea," Kelly said at last.

"Well, now you do. And Greg and Lisa are going to have a baby later this year. They're clearly thinking about the future. Now it's your turn to do some thinking." He eyed her with that paternal look she was so fond of.

She smiled at him. "I promise I will give that suggestion serious consideration, Curt. You can tell Jayleen."

"Good. I'll tell her, and we'll both tell Mimi and Burt next time we see them. They've been thinking about the very same thing. That baby is coming, probably sooner rather than later. Time to get organized." He gave the table a firm smack.

"So you two have been conferring with Mimi and Burt about this?"

"Of course," Curt said matter-of-factly. "All four of us look at you couples like our own kids. So naturally we think about your futures even when you don't. Oh, and Mimi said to tell you that you and Steve don't have to worry about planning anything. She and Burt would love to have all of you in her backyard again. Just like they did for Jennifer and Pete. Keeping it simple."

Kelly had to laugh at that. Picturing Mimi and Burt in hushed conversations with Jayleen and Curt. Her instinct gave her a little jab. *Just think about it.*

"Keeping it simple, huh? Okay, Curt. I promise I will seriously consider it."

Curt arched a brow at Kelly again. "Don't string me along, Kelly-girl."

"I'm not. I promise I will give it serious consideration, Curt. Honest." Then she held up three fingers on her right hand. "Cross my heart," she said as she made the motion.

Five

"Wha-what?" Kelly said as she awoke. Steve was leaning over her while she lay in bed.

"Give me a kiss. I've gotta leave early," Steve said. "We have a lumber delivery at the site in half an hour."

"So early?" Kelly asked as she rubbed the sleep from her eyes.

Steve checked his watch and grinned. "Actually, it's seven o'clock. I wouldn't have awakened you, but I didn't want you to wake up and find me gone."

"Seven o'clock?" Kelly said, sitting up in bed. "I never sleep that late." She gave a big stretch.

"Enjoy it, Kelly. After Jack comes, we probably won't get to sleep through the night for a while." He backed toward the bedroom doorway. "Talk to you later. Promise to take it easy."

Taking it easy was the prime thing she was doing, in Kelly's mind. "Don't worry. I will. Drive safely." She flipped back the covers and stepped out of bed. Another huge yawn enveloped her. What she needed now was a nice hot shower. Well, not hot, hot. Nice and super warm.

Kelly rubbed her hair vigorously with the towel, trying to capture as much moisture as she could so her hair would air-dry faster. Loosely combing through it, she fluffed her damp hair then quickly applied her makeup. She was already dressed, and the tantalizing aroma of freshly brewed coffee tempted her out of the bedroom and into the open kitchen of one of Steve's ranch-style houses they had made their own a few short years ago. Located in the same development where friends Megan and Marty, Lisa and Greg, and Jennifer and Pete lived made it easy for all of their friends—or the Gang, as Kelly called them—to get together regularly.

Pouring a black stream into a ceramic mug, Kelly paged through the local newspaper until she reached the front page. Noticing the headline about an accidental house fire in the newer housing developments on the southeastern quadrant of Fort Connor, Kelly read several paragraphs before her eye was caught by a smaller side headline.

"Police report that an apparent murder was committed in the east central area of Fort Connor. No further details were available at time of publication."

Curiosity piqued, Kelly fetched her briefcase bag and withdrew her Day-Timer. Checking if she had any important phone calls scheduled, Kelly saw that she did not. Today was a simple day of client accounting. Easy, she thought with a smile as she took another sip of half-strength black coffee. That would give her plenty of time to head to Lambspun and catch up on gossip. Maybe someone around the knitting table knew something the newspaper didn't.

"Ahhhh, Geraldine. Just the woman I hoped I'd see here," Kelly announced as she walked into Lambspun's main knitting room.

Geraldine glanced up from the red, white, and blue afghan she was knitting and burst into a bright smile. "Well, hello, Kelly. So good to see you. Goodness me, Baby Jack looks like he's gotten bigger every time I see you."

"He's growing for sure," Kelly said, patting her bulging belly before she settled into a chair. "He's nine months. So all he's going to do from now on is gain weight."

"Ahhhh, yes, I remember. My daughter was my first child, and darned if she didn't grow to over nine pounds."

"Whoa, she was a big one," Kelly said as she removed the blue and gray wool hat she was knitting from her fiber bag. "Did she grow up to be tall?"

"Actually, she grew to medium height like me," Geraldine said. "So you never can tell how babies are going to turn out. It mostly depends on the genes that they inherit from their mothers and fathers. And all the grandparents, too." She continued to wrap the red, white, and blue yarn around her needles, adding to the colorful rows of the baby-sized afghan that gathered in Geraldine's lap.

Kelly focused on the blue and gray stitches forming on

her circular needles where the baby hat was slowly taking shape. Geraldine's last words still resonated in her mind.

"The genes that they inherit from their mothers and fathers. And all the grandparents, too."

Kelly knew all about her father's family. Her aunt Helen had told her a lot as well. Their family had been in Fort Connor for years. Descendants of some of the early settlers who had left the Midwest to come to the new Western states in the early days of the last century. They had settled in Colorado and become sugar beet farmers. Back in those days, that was a profitable crop. However, Kelly knew practically nothing about her mother's family except they, too, were longtime residents of Fort Connor, like her father. Her father didn't seem to know much about her mother's family, so Kelly simply stopped asking questions during her childhood.

"As long as the baby is healthy, that's the important thing," Kelly said, repeating what she and Steve had been saying out loud the entire time of her pregnancy.

"That's for sure. But if you're ever curious as to your family's genetic makeup, you can go to one of those websites that provide DNA testing. That way you can see where your ancestors came from. You know, they have several of those commercials on television. I did that last year, and it was fascinating. It turned out that I had mostly German ancestors with a few Irish thrown in for good measure. And a little spice, I guess." She chuckled.

Kelly pondered what Geraldine said. "You know, that does sound interesting. I may think about that. I know I've got a lot of Irish in my background because of my father. But who knows what else is there?"

The doorbell for Lambspun's entry door tinkled then, and Cassie walked into the main room, school backpack slung over one shoulder. "Hey there, Kelly. Geraldine," she said as she dropped the backpack to the library table and pulled out a chair across the table from both of them.

"Hello, Cassie," Geraldine said, smiling at the teenager.

"What are you doing with your school backpack? It's Saturday," Kelly asked, pointing to the backpack.

Cassie relaxed into the chair. "Exam time. I've had humanities and Spanish already. And next week I've got trig. So Pete and Jennifer suggested I come over here and find a quiet corner and study. They brought in part-time worker Bridget to work for me in the café."

Kelly smiled. "That's a good suggestion, considering you've got a trig exam. I bet you can use the back office to study."

"I take it 'trig' stands for trigonometry, correct?" Geraldine said, her fingers still working the red, white, and blue yarn.

Cassie grinned. "Oh yeah. And I've already studied for it. Plus, it'll be easy. Just lots of problems to solve."

Geraldine shook her head. "Goodness. That's the first time I've ever heard that something like trigonometry was easy. You must be a whiz at math."

Cassie shrugged. "I don't know. Trig seems easy to me. Just like you said, Kelly. It's kind of like geometry. What was that word?"

"Spatial," Kelly answered. "That means it takes up space and you can see it. Not like algebra or calculus where you have to solve lots of equations."

"Goodness, you two are speaking a foreign language," Geraldine said, chuckling.

Cassie popped up from the chair as fast as she'd sat down. "There were several stacks of magazines that I haven't had a chance to add to all the binders and bins." She scanned the room. "Oh, there they are." And she went to retrieve them.

"Do you have any more family here in Fort Connor, Kelly?" Geraldine asked as Cassie carried a large stack of magazines and stacked them at the end of the knitting table.

"No, it was just my dad, my aunt Helen, and Uncle Jim. Oh yeah, and my cousin Martha who used to live in Wyoming, then she moved to Landporte."

"What about your mother's family?" Geraldine asked.

Kelly noticed Cassie had looked up from the stack of magazines, her big brown eyes wide with obvious interest. Kelly gave Cassie a smile before she answered Geraldine's question. "Actually, I never knew my mother, because she left my dad when I was just a baby. So I don't know anything about her family here. Just what my father told me. They were longtime residents of Fort Connor like his family was."

Geraldine's face immediately registered concern. "Oh, I'm so sorry to hear that, Kelly. And I'm sorry I even mentioned it. I didn't know."

"Don't be sorry, Geraldine," Kelly said, in a reassuring tone. "I'm certainly not upset. I came to terms with my mother's decision long ago when I was still a teenager. I've often thought that some people simply aren't cut out to be parents. And it's understandable. Considering what a huge responsibility parenthood is."

"Well, that it is," Geraldine said, nodding as her fingers kept working the festive-colored yarn. "And I'm sure you'll be a great mother. You're caring and considerate, as well as sharp as a tack."

"My goodness," Kelly said, letting all those accolades sink in. "That was very flattering of you to say."

Geraldine glanced over at Kelly. "At my age, I no longer flatter anybody. I don't have time for it. If I say something, I mean it."

Kelly laughed softly. "Well, it's still kind of you to say that." Glancing over at Cassie, who was sorting through the stack of magazines, she added, "And here's an example of the fine parenting job Jennifer and Pete have done with Cassie. And neither of them had ever been a parent. But they turned out to be naturals."

Cassie grinned. "Absolutely. They're great."

Geraldine nodded. "I agree with you one hundred percent."

"Changing the subject, Geraldine, have you heard anything about that murder the newspaper mentioned today?" Kelly asked.

Cassie's head jerked up, and she stared at both Kelly and Geraldine, her big brown eyes even wider than usual. "There was a murder here in Fort Connor?"

"Apparently so," Kelly said. "The newspaper didn't print any details. So I'll bet we'll see more about it tomorrow. Or maybe on the television news tonight."

"Whoa . . ." Cassie said.

Shop clerk Rosa walked into the main room then, several bundles of candy cane red yarn in her hands. "Hi there, everyone," she said as she walked over to the yarn bins stacked on a side wall. "How are all of you doing? You still feeling good, Kelly?"

Kelly was about to answer when Cassie piped up. "Rosa! Did you know there was a murder here in Fort Connor?"

Rosa turned away from the yarn bins, her brown eyes almost as huge as Cassie's. "Yes. And it happened right over there on the golf course, too!" she said, pointing toward the golf course through the main room's windows. "I was here yesterday afternoon when a woman ran into the shop. She had just parked her car and was walking toward the front door when a guy came running off the golf course and asked if he could use her cell phone to call an ambulance. His phone was dead. She said she spotted a woman lying on the green and a guy kneeling beside her."

"Oh no," Geraldine murmured, hand to her breast.

"Then I heard the sirens, and the ambulance turned down the driveway. A team of paramedics ran over to the golf course with a stretcher. Then they carried the collapsed woman back to the ambulance on the stretcher. She was completely covered by a sheet, so I assumed she was dead. Marie said one of the golfers told her the woman wasn't breathing when he and his friend found her on the green earlier, and there was blood all over the front of her clothes. The guy even said he thought he knew who she was."

"Who was she?" Kelly couldn't help asking.

This entire drama was so alien to the normal, peaceful golf course setting, it was hard for her to imagine it happening. Golfers were usually quite docile, she thought. Especially compared to sometimes fiery tennis players. Maybe the slow pace of the game kept everything peaceful. The most violent action she'd ever seen a golfer commit on the course was tossing his entire golf bag into the Dumpster at the edge of the driveway, cursing the entire time.

"Marie said the golfer told her the woman was a local golf pro. Apparently, she was pretty well-known around the area," Rosa said as she leaned over the table. "Neither my husband nor I play golf, so we don't have any idea who she is."

"Oh my," Geraldine said as she stared out into the main knitting room. "I wonder if it was William Callahan's young wife. Apparently, she's won all kinds of local championships, so she was well-known in golf circles, I've heard."

Rosa shrugged. "Well, no one at the shop knows. I guess we'll find out when the police identify her."

"Whatever happened, it sounds like an awful way to die," Kelly said, glancing toward the peaceful greens once more.

"It certainly does," Geraldine agreed. "And now I'm curious. I think I'll make some phone calls when I get home this afternoon."

"Keep us posted," Kelly said, checking her cell phone, which gave a muted ring. Steve's name flashed on the screen. He sent a text saying he would be slightly delayed leaving the building site. She took a sip of her weakened black coffee.

Cassie returned to sorting the magazines as a somber mood engulfed the entire Lambspun knitting room. After a few moments, Cassie glanced up at Kelly. "Did your father ever tell you when his family came to Fort Connor? Pete said everybody's family came from somewhere else originally. And most of them moved here from cities and towns back in the East. Or farther West, like California."

"That's right, Cassie," Kelly said as she glanced up from

the blue and gray baby hat. "My father's family came from Ireland in the 1840s. There was a terrible famine in Ireland around that time, and many, many Irish immigrants arrived on the shores of the East Coast. I believe it was my great-great-grandfather who arrived at Ellis Island in New York City."

"Oh yeah. I remember learning that in history class back in elementary school."

"Actually, that entire area in New York is made up of small islands. The main one is Manhattan Island, which has New York City. That's the part of the city that has grown the largest, mostly because the immigrants settled there. But there are other smaller islands surrounding it. There's Staten Island, Long Island. And all of them are filled with people. But most of the immigrants arrived at Ellis Island when they arrived."

"Why'd they all settle in New York?"

"Mostly because the jobs were located in the city. New York City. Factories hired tons of people to run the machinery. There were all kinds of factories producing all sorts of products that people would buy. A lot of clothing manufacturers, too."

"Is that what your great-great-grandfather did?" Cassie asked.

"I think my dad told me his great-grandfather worked at a machinery factory making tools until he saved up some money. That's when he headed West and settled in Missouri. It was my dad's grandfather who finally got to Colorado. He raised cattle and slowly, slowly built up his herd."

"Like so many of our ancestors," Geraldine added with a smile.

"Most people moved from the East or the Midwest in the mid eighteen hundreds or early nineteen hundreds," Kelly continued. "Many of them came out here first in covered wagons. This was so-called open land here in the West. But the Native American tribes were living all over the Plains and the Rocky Mountains, too. So they weren't happy to see a whole lot of settlers moving in. The United States Congress actually passed a law called the Homestead Act. It said that an American citizen could stake a claim on over a hundred acres of open land starting in the Midwest. I can't remember exactly how many acres. But the important part was if they lived on that land for five years, then the land would legally belong to them."

"Yes!" Cassie said, eyes lighting up. "I remember learning that in our American history class earlier this school year."

"And there were other people scattered around the Southwest, too." Geraldine spoke up. "The Spanish explorers first came to Central America early on, back in the fifteen and sixteen hundreds. They explored around what we now call Mexico and even up into Colorado. Colorado actually means 'colored red,' roughly translated."

"Yes, indeed," Kelly agreed, enjoying this historical interlude around the Lambspun knitting table. She'd always loved learning about the early history of the United States. The country was made up of so many different people and cultures. "I think that was Cortés who explored Mexico. He was from Spain. Another Spaniard who sailed across the Atlantic to this new land was Ponce de León. He explored what is Florida today. There were more explorers, but I can't remember them all. Portuguese explorers, too. They traveled all the way to Japan."

"Wasn't Ponce de León searching for the Fountain of Youth?" Geraldine wondered out loud.

"I think you're right." Kelly nodded.

"There's a Fountain of Youth in Florida?" Cassie asked in surprise. "Where?"

"Actually, no. There is no Fountain of Youth," Geraldine said with a little laugh. "But people actually believed things like that back in those days. That was in the fifteen and sixteen hundreds and seventeen hundreds. And that was enough to send the early European explorers sailing to the New World to find the magic fountain."

"I wonder why the other European explorers didn't come looking for that fountain," Cassie said.

"Most came looking for gold like Cortés. The Portuguese actually started exploring in the fourteen hundreds," Kelly said. "They went all the way to China, if I recall my history correctly. And I think the other nations started later because they had not built the sturdier sailing ships that the Portuguese and the Spanish had."

"And the Spanish also had missionaries that settled in the land that became California," Geraldine added. "They established missions, and many of them helped the Native American tribes. But more settlers started coming, and once again, the Native Americans weren't too happy about all these new people coming into what had once been their hunting territories exclusively."

"In fact, Cassie, we had some early Russian settlers who came into the Pacific Northwest, too. So, there were many different people settling in these new lands," Kelly said.

"And they came across the Bering Strait," Cassie interjected. "They were able to walk across parts of it when it was frozen in the winter, right?"

"Apparently so," Kelly said. "Unless the history writers have revised all that," she added with a chuckle.

"Oh, and don't forget the French who came down from the Canadian territories into all those lands around Indiana and the Great Lakes," Geraldine said. "I remember visiting my sister in Indiana one fall, and we went to a wonderful weekend festival there near West Lafayette and Lafayette called the Feast of the Hunters' Moon. It took place in the fall when the moon moved into a certain alignment. I forget which. But there were celebrations of the French trappers and how much they had contributed to that area. They were the first European settlers there. There was a fort right near the city that was called Fort Ouiatenon. It was pronounced 'Wee-ott-non.'"

Cassie wrinkled her nose. "That's a funny name."

"I thought so, too, until my sister explained it was a rough pronunciation of the French words *oui* and *non*. That's French for yes and no."

"That's fascinating, Geraldine," Kelly said. "I just love learning bits of our early American history."

"I do, too, Kelly," Geraldine replied. "And I love sharing it with some young teenager with a sharp mind. Especially one who is naturally curious, like our Cassie."

"Thanks, Geraldine," Cassie said shyly.

"My pleasure, Cassie. My grandchildren are scattered all over the United States. No one lives here in Colorado. So, I love to 'adopt' grandchildren whenever I find a special one, like you." She gave Cassie a grandmotherly smile.

Cassie blushed slightly. “You’re sweet, Geraldine. I’d love to have another grandmother.”

“You can never have too many grandmothers, right, Cassie?” Kelly teased.

“Oh yeah,” Cassie said with a grin.

Six

Kelly climbed out of her car slowly. Now that she was full-term, Kelly found herself moving more deliberately than she was used to. Normally a fast walker, Kelly found herself laughing at this new pace she adopted. It was so unlike her.

She walked up the brick steps leading to Lambspun's front door. Having worked most of the morning on client Don Warner's Denver-area development accounts, Kelly had deliberately scheduled a peaceful afternoon of knitting and chatting with friends or whoever showed up at Lambspun. Cassie had a softball game that evening, and Kelly and Steve were going to join Megan and Marty and Jennifer and Pete so they could watch together. Lisa had mentioned she might attend, too. If so, Greg would surely show up.

Kelly paused in the covered front entry area of the Spanish Colonial 1930s-style farmhouse turned knitting shop and stared out toward the golf course. Since these spring days of May had suddenly heated up, she didn't spot many golfers on the course in the midday sun. That was smart. The heat would be intense soon. It was already in the nineties. Often the month of May would keep milder temps in the low to mideighties. Sometimes, however, summer's high temperatures would show up full force and continue to increase throughout summer. By August, the eighty degree temps would usually return and run through the end of the month. But then again, Coloradoans loved to say: "Every year is different. This is Colorado."

Escaping out of the high heat and into Lambspun's air-conditioned comfort, Kelly felt the difference as soon as she stepped inside. *Ahhhhhhhhh.*

"Hey there," a familiar voice called from the central yarn room.

Kelly glanced over and saw Lisa examining several yarns, hands full of Mimi's handspun. "Hey there. How're you feeling?"

"Much better. I think I'm finally through that early month's nausea. Let's hope." She held up two entwined fingers. She approached and gave Kelly a little hug. "How're you doing? Any of those low contractions Megan said were the warning signs?"

"Braxton Hicks? Nope. Not a one. So I think Baby Jack enjoys his comfy perch and isn't ready to leave anytime soon." She eyed Lisa. "Have you lost weight?"

"Yeah, a little," Lisa said with a shrug. "I'll gain it back this month, I'm sure."

"Let's go sit," Kelly said. "That nausea really worked you over. What are you able to eat now?"

"I'm doing the mild stuff like toast and soup. Greg made grilled cheese sandwiches last night, and they were yummy."

The image of Greg in the kitchen made Kelly laugh. "Hopefully he didn't set anything on fire," she said as they walked into the main room.

Lisa laughed, too. "No, he's gotten pretty good doing simple food. Lord knows he's had enough practice, what with this morning sickness stuff."

"Well, I predict you are moving out of that period, and it will be smooth sailing from here on." Kelly plopped her fiber knitting bag on the table and pulled out a chair.

Lisa settled into a chair beside Kelly, then pulled out a knitted piece from her oversize satchel. "I thought I'd start on a baby hat, so I chose this lemon yellow since we don't know the sex yet."

"Smart move," Kelly said, removing the light blue and gray baby hat from her knitting bag. "Steve and I didn't ask to know about Baby Jack until I was about five months along. I don't know why we waited that long. Other women are getting those results way earlier." She picked up her stitches where she left off on the circular needles.

"I think it's not a bad idea to wait. Just in case, you know . . ." Lisa didn't finish the sentence, but Kelly understood her meaning. Lisa had known several friends at the university who had also gotten pregnant in their late thirties, and a couple of them had miscarriages.

Kelly reached over and gave her friend's arm a pat. Reassuring by touch. "Don't worry, Lisa. You're going to be fine."

"Thanks, Kelly. That's a Mother Mimi pat." She smiled.

Kelly was about to reply when Geraldine walked into the room. "Hello there, ladies," she said as she pulled out the chair at the end of the table. "It's good to see you, Lisa. I hope you're feeling better."

"Thanks, Geraldine. I'm feeling fine now, and it's good to be back," Lisa said.

"I was hoping you'd be here, Kelly. I've learned more about that awful murder on the golf course." Geraldine searched inside her voluminous fiber bag and finally drew out some knitting needles and a lovely deep purple yarn.

Lisa's blue eyes flew wide open. "What? There was a murder on the golf course? When?"

"There was only a small article in the newspaper right after it occurred, so you probably missed it," Kelly replied. "It just said that there was a murder in east central Fort Connor. It was Rosa who told us all about it the other day. She was working at the shop the afternoon of the murder when a customer came in and told them that a woman had died on the golf course. And Rosa saw a woman lying on the ground on one of the greens. Then an ambulance came and took her away on a stretcher. There was blood on her clothes. Apparently, she was already dead."

"Good Lord!" Lisa exclaimed. "I can't believe it. Right next to our quiet little spot at Lambspun."

"Kelly and Cassie and I were listening to Rosa spellbound. We couldn't believe it, either," Geraldine added.

Glancing down the table, Kelly asked, "What else have you learned, Geraldine?"

Geraldine's fingers deftly moved, as new rows of purple yarn formed. "I called up three different friends of mine and asked what they had heard. One friend is an avid golfer and is a member of the Fort Connor Golf Club, so she knows practically everybody in town. And my friend said that gossip was buzzing about all this. After talking to her friends, she's convinced the murder victim really is William Callahan's young wife, Giselle."

Kelly looked over at Lisa and saw the same curious expression that must have been on her own face. "William Callahan is a successful businessman here in town, isn't that correct, Geraldine?"

Geraldine nodded. "Yes, indeed. He's president of that large, successful sports equipment company in town. So he cuts a broad swath in Fort Connor, shall we say. He's also in his sixties. Consequently, Callahan aroused a lot of attention when he divorced his wife of forty-plus years and married this young golf pro, Giselle Armstrong. Goodness, my friends really gave me an earful about her. They said this Giselle showed up on the Fort Connor golf scene about three years ago and began playing in and winning all the local women's tournaments. She was quite a skilled golfer. As a result, she attended all the golf club's social events. And since she was divorced, she always attended alone."

Geraldine's needles seemed to move a little faster, Kelly noticed, as she related the story.

"Anyway, they swear Giselle had her eyes set on William Callahan, and one friend said she often saw Giselle flirting with Callahan at these functions. Not brazenly, but unmistakably. Apparently, his wife of many years, Meredith, was devastated when her husband divorced her and married the young golf pro."

"That's such a sad story," Lisa said, not looking up from the lemon yellow yarn. More rows of stitches had appeared on her needles. "I hope the wife Meredith got some counseling during that whole process."

"I don't know if she did or not," Geraldine said with a slight shrug. "I didn't know Meredith Callahan well. Of course, I'd met her at several charitable fund-raisers around town over the years. She was a lovely woman." Geraldine's tone dropped.

"You said 'was,' just then. Do you mean that the first wife Meredith is no longer alive?" Lisa asked.

"Unfortunately, yes. She took her own life about a year ago, if I recall. The newspaper didn't say much, just when her funeral would be held. And I do remember the gossip going around hinted she had taken an overdose of sleeping pills." She wagged her head again. "So very sad."

Lisa's head jerked up again. "Oh no! That is so awful! Didn't she have any family here or nearby that could help her through that stressful time?"

"I asked the same thing, Lisa," Geraldine replied. "And my friends told me the Callahans' only child, a son, Henry, lived in a suburb of Denver. He was never around much, apparently. One friend told me Meredith started withdrawing from some of her social activities after the divorce. Of course, that didn't help, either."

"Didn't the poor woman have any other family in other parts of the country she could call on?" Kelly asked.

"Apparently not. One of my friends mentioned she thought Meredith had a sister who was out of state. And as I said, I didn't have a chance to get to know Meredith Callahan very well. Only through various charitable functions. And now that I'm thinking about it . . ." Geraldine paused and looked out into the main room. "I don't remember seeing her at the big charity fund-raiser for the Larimer County Food Bank last year. Or the fund-raiser for the Open Door Mission. So she had definitely pulled back from social engagements, it sounds like."

"So, businessman Callahan tossed away older first wife to marry cute young golf pro. Cast-off wife committed suicide. And now Callahan's young new wife is dead. Murdered." Kelly looked over at Lisa. "Hate to say it, but this story sounds like one of those convoluted daytime soap operas. Have you ever heard anything like this in one of your counseling sessions?"

Lisa looked at Kelly. "I wish I could say I haven't, Kelly. But unfortunately, sad stories like this are all too common."

"Good Lord," Kelly said softly.

"That's why they say truth is stranger than fiction, Kelly," Geraldine said. "Sad to say."

"And that's why it's so very important that both parties get counseling as they're going through a divorce. It's one of the most traumatic life events that can happen to people. Actual death is considered easier to handle than divorce."

"Easier?" Kelly asked, surprised.

Lisa nodded. "Yes. When someone has died, then family members can mourn and have end-of-life gatherings and talk about all of their memories. That helps with closure and allows people to deal with the fact that they won't have that person around anymore. But with divorce, that former family member is still around and often in the same city or community. So one party to the divorce who was most traumatized by the end of the relationship has to deal with seeing their former spouse with their 'new addition' right in the midst of family get-togethers. It's quite traumatic for some people. Often, they withdraw completely, which isn't healthy."

Kelly pictured all those scenarios. "Traumatic" would be putting it mildly for some people. "I'm glad you enjoy handling all those cases, Lisa. Because there's no way I would want to get into that kind of quagmire and try to solve problems. Give me accounting challenges anytime. Numbers are so much easier to deal with than demanding people."

Both Lisa and Geraldine laughed as Kelly took a big sip of weak coffee.

Kelly sipped the last spoonful of Pete's yummy cold potato soup. It was every bit as delicious as any French vichyssoise she'd ever tried. Taking a sip from her mug of now lukewarm coffee, Kelly decided it was time to switch to iced coffee. She relaxed into the chair as the café lunch crowd gradually thinned out.

Suddenly, Cassie hurried around the corner from the corridor. "Kelly? Are you busy right now? Can I borrow you for about an hour or so? Are you doing accounts or something?"

"Not at all. I'm simply relaxing after a yummy lunch. I already finished what few accounting entries I had for this morning. What do you need?"

"It's kind of a funny request, actually. Greg just called and asked if I'd like to try to solve one of those equations he's been showing me this last week. Now that school is actually over, I'm getting bored with no homework."

Kelly had to laugh at that. "Oh, Cassie. Do you know how many kids are celebrating no homework for three months? And you're missing it. I love it."

Cassie smiled and gave a self-deprecating shrug. "I'm weird, I guess. But I told Greg and Lisa that I would miss my math classes the most, and he said he had just the thing. Special equations I could learn how to solve. And the first one he showed me the other day was super cool. It went all the way across the blackboard. He had to help me solve that one. But now I want to try this new one and see if I can solve it by myself. But Greg can't leave the university all day, so I wondered if you could be the adult driver in the passenger seat while I drive over there."

Kelly laughed softly. "Equations across the blackboard. I remember those. Sure, Cassie. I'll be glad to be the designated passenger in the front seat. Nothing else is happening here, and the truth is, I'm starting to get bored."

Cassie's eyes lit up. "That's great, Kelly! Thanks so much. I'll be extra careful driving you and Baby Jack. I promise."

Kelly slowly rose from the chair. "Let me get a fill-up of iced coffee, and I'll be ready to go."

"Here, let me get it from Eduardo." Cassie snatched Kelly's mug from the table and scurried over to the grill counter. Eduardo was flipping a grilled cheese sandwich onto the grill, and the melted cheese oozed from the sides.

Cassie was back in a flash. "Here you go, Kelly. It's that weak kind you've been drinking. Let me grab your bag." She leaned over and had the bag in hand in seconds.

"Boy, you're fast," Kelly said admiringly. "I do everything slowly nowadays."

Cassie slipped her bag over her shoulder crosswise. "You're supposed to move slowly, Kelly. There's two of you," she said. "Just follow me. Don't worry. I'll go slow."

Go slow. Kelly had to smile as she walked toward the front door of the café. That was a first for her.

"Hey, Cassie. I see you got another number person to ride shotgun with you," Greg said as Kelly and Cassie entered the university classroom.

Since the university's spring semester had ended with final exams the previous week, this time period of empty classrooms was usually taken over by conferences and seminars with visiting speakers. Students were gone from the campus.

"Yeah, a super accountant," Cassie said with a grin.

"I welcomed the distraction, Greg. Baby Jack and I were getting really, really bored just sitting around."

Greg laughed. "I can imagine. You're not used to taking it easy, Kelly. So, let's see if Cassie and I can keep you and the precious cargo entertained."

Cassie hastened over to the blackboard. Kelly slowly walked closer to the front of the classroom where Greg stood. She zeroed in on the blackboard, which had a small graph drawn on one corner of the board and two lines of text describing an equation. "That does look interesting."

"You'll be able to watch us solve it. But no cheating. No asking Kelly questions, Cassie."

Cassie's smile vanished. She drew up taller and lifted her chin. "Of course not. That's the whole point, right? Giving me a chance to learn something new? So I want to solve it myself."

Kelly glanced to Greg with a smile. "Spoken like a true math geek."

Cassie walked past the blackboard, clearly concentrating on the long equation. "This is harder, that's for sure."

"That's the point, right?" Greg teased.

"Oh yeah. This is gonna take me a while," Cassie said, then paused. She pointed to the words at the bottom of the equation. "Wait a minute. We're missing something, aren't we?"

"Sharp girl," Greg said. "Yes, another measurement."

Cassie stared at the blackboard as Greg grabbed the chalk and wrote the missing part of the equation. Then the wooden and glass classroom door opened, and a tall, slender, dark-haired young man walked into the classroom. He looked about the same age as Greg, mid to late thirties.

"Hey there, Benjamin," Greg greeted him with a smile.

"Hey, Greg. Looks like you've got visitors. I can come back later. My class isn't for another hour."

"No, no." Greg beckoned him over. "Benjamin is a math professor here at the university," he explained to Kelly and Cassie. "I wanted you to meet some friends and fellow math geeks, Benjamin. Kelly Flynn is a corporate-level CPA, and Cassie just finished tenth grade in high school and is a lover of all things math, including equations that spread across the blackboard."

"Is she now?" Benjamin smiled at Cassie as he approached.

"Hey, Benjamin," Kelly greeted. "This is taking me back in time, for sure."

"Nice to meet you, Benjamin," Cassie said politely. "Greg's been giving me equations to solve ever since I told him I'd miss math classes the most this summer. The last equation was pretty tricky." She glanced toward the blackboard. "And this one definitely looks even trickier."

"That's Greg's specialty," Benjamin observed. "He's the king of tricky equations."

"The Trickster, that's me," Greg bragged with a grin. "I think I should have a cape. Able to leap tall buildings and differentiate equations at the same time." He held a classic profile pose while Cassie laughed out loud. Benjamin shook his head and chuckled.

Kelly laughed softly. "Oh Lord. I don't believe you folks have to put up with this guy all day. We've only got him nights and weekends, and he drives us nuts."

"Tell me about it," Benjamin said with a laugh. "We're all hoping fatherhood will mellow him."

"He's going to be more than mellow," Kelly said with a sly grin.

"Oh yeah," Benjamin agreed. "I told him the Universe has a sense of humor."

Kelly laughed. "I agree. Love it."

"They're ganging up on me, Cassie." Greg gave her a fake frown.

Cassie grinned. "You can handle it."

Greg laughed. "If you say so. Now, why don't you take a look at this equation? Benjamin loves to tutor, so you can ask him anything."

Greg walked over and stood beside Kelly, who had stepped back a little from the blackboard.

"Let's give these two geeks some room," she said with a smile, stepping back some more.

"I told Cassie I was gonna ramp it up, so to speak, with the equations. There's nothing like a challenge to keep kids interested," Greg said.

Kelly watched Cassie approach the blackboard and point to one of the numbers. Then she glanced to Benjamin and asked something. He turned to her and replied, pointing to another part of the long equation.

"You certainly came up with a challenging equation," Kelly said, admiringly. "I'm impressed."

"Thanks." Greg grinned. "But I had to make it interesting to capture Cassie's attention. And Benjamin is a born teacher. He loves nothing better than explaining stuff."

Kelly watched Benjamin point to another line in the equation. Cassie paid rapt attention. "He seems like a nice guy. He'd have to be to put up with you," she teased.

"And I kind of wanted to see them work together. They both approach an equation in a similar way, I've noticed."

That was an interesting thing to say, Kelly thought to herself, as she glanced to the blackboard again. Cassie was already figuring out one part of the equation along the side of the blackboard. Benjamin watched her efforts with interest. Cassie turned her head to ask him something, and Benjamin leaned over and pointed to another part of the equation.

Kelly stared at them, discussing higher-level equations, talking, listening. Then, from way in the back of her mind, she felt a little jab. A tiny jab. Not strong at all. Kelly kept watching the two math geeks at the blackboard, clearly enjoying solving the equation. Then both of them smiled. And Kelly blinked. She saw something.

"You saw it, didn't you?" Greg asked in a low voice.

Kelly turned to him. Greg had a little smile. "You saw it already?" she whispered.

He nodded. "I always thought Benjamin resembled someone I knew but couldn't place it. Then, one day Lisa met me at the student union café and she had Cassie with her. Benjamin passed by and dropped off a notebook I'd lent him. That's when it hit me. That's why I wanted to get the two of them together today. I wanted to see if someone else saw it. I knew Cassie would bring someone with her because of her learner's permit. So glad it was you. Hey . . . why don't you sit down?" He guided Kelly to the front row of tables and pulled out a separate chair for her. "We don't want Jack making his debut here in the classroom."

"Thanks, Greg. I needed to sit down after seeing this." She gestured toward Cassie and Benjamin.

Greg half sat on another desk close by. "Do you think I should say something to Benjamin? I mean, I'm making all these connections in my head, but . . . maybe they should just stay there."

Kelly glanced toward the student and the tutor again. "No. I wouldn't. It would be awkward. After all, all we have are circumstances, right? Pete's sister Tanya was the wild child college party girl who was partying in Old Town with fellow students every weekend. Pete said she was sleeping around with different guys." She shrugged. "Even she didn't know who Cassie's father was."

Greg nodded. "Yeah. But after I noticed their resemblance

to each other, I asked Pete if his sister ever said anything about who she thought the father might be. And Pete remembered Tanya once said she thought it might be a guy she spent several nights with. Totally different from her usual choices." Greg gave Kelly a sly smile. "She also said he was a grad student in math. And kind of a geek."

Kelly looked back into Greg's eyes and smiled. "Kind of a geek, huh?" She glanced back at the two math devotees. "Well, there are a lot of us geeks to go around, wouldn't you say?"

"Ohhhh yeah. Lots of us."

Seven

"Way to go, guys!" Steve stood up and cheered as Curt's grandson Eric's team trotted off the baseball field at City Park.

"Wooo-hooooo!" Megan yelled. Standing beside her, Marty waved his arms and let out a whoop after he swallowed a huge bite of hot dog.

"Boy, Eric's batting has improved. He's consistently hitting longer balls," Jennifer said as she reached into her oversize bag and drew out several packages of curly chips. "Anybody want some?"

"Way to begin the season, Eric!" Kelly congratulated the young teenager when he finally left the team huddle and headed for the bleachers where Kelly and friends sat.

"Good job!" Greg said, leaning over and giving Eric a high five.

"That was a great hit at the start of the inning," Pete said, giving Eric a slap on the back as he climbed the bleachers.

"You look like you could use some water," Jennifer said, offering Eric one of the bottles that sat on the bleachers. "It's cold."

"Hey, thanks, Jen," Eric said, his eyes lit up. "I was getting pretty thirsty." He glanced around. "There's Cassie's team. Looks like they're ready to take the field."

"I'll take one of those waters," Lisa said, fanning herself as she sat beside Greg, her drooping wide-brim hat successfully shading her face.

"Sure thing," Jen said, handing over one of the bottles.

"You okay? Do you want to get out of the sun?" Greg asked, a solicitous tone in his voice.

"No, I'm good. My hat is doing a great job. Jennifer's hat, rather."

"That's my Miz Scarlett hat," Jennifer said with a smile. "Remember that, Kelly?"

Memories started flooding from the back of Kelly's mind. "Yes, I do. It was years ago. That was when Jennifer, Megan, Jayleen, and I went up to Wyoming to check out the ranch my cousin Martha left me in her will. Curt and Steve came along in his truck to check out the cattle."

"You had a cattle ranch in Wyoming?" Eric asked, eyes popped wide. "Cool! What happened to it?"

"It's still there. But it's got gas wells pumping now instead of cattle. Your grandfather Curt took care of selling them off."

"Okay, but where does Miz Scarlett come in?" Pete asked, grinning.

Unable to resist, Kelly leaned back on the bleachers behind her. "You see, there was this cute ranch hand who was managing the property for me. Curt found him."

"Actually, Chet Brewster came to me because he was already taking care of everything at the ranch," Curt volunteered from his perch on the bleacher above them. "He was a good worker, that boy."

"Anyway, Chet took one look at Jennifer and fell all over himself. So, Jennifer couldn't resist teasing him."

"Of course," Steve said with a grin.

"So she went into this Southern belle drawl. Miz Scarlett. Like . . . 'Ah declare . . . I simply must have another mint julep,'" Kelly said, imitating a heavy Southern drawl.

Everyone started to laugh. "Don't forget when Megan jumped into the bull pen, and Steve had to rescue her," Jennifer said, grinning.

"Whoa!" Eric's eyes popped wide. "Did you really climb into the bull pen, Megan?"

"Not intentionally," Megan admitted sheepishly. "I just went in to fetch my hat, which had blown off."

"Cujo was the bull's name, right?" Jennifer said.

"Oh yeah," Steve interjected. "That was back when Kelly didn't like me, so I was doing everything I could to impress her. So I threw my hat into Cujo's pen to distract him while I jumped in and helped Megan get out. And me, too." He laughed.

"Big, bad Cujo stomped your hat flat, as I recall," Jennifer said.

"He sure did," Steve chuckled. "And it was a new Stetson, too."

"It was a fine-looking hat," Curt intoned from the bleacher above.

"Man, I would have loved to see all that," Eric said, before draining the water bottle.

Kelly continued, more memories flowing. "Another thing I remember is after all this Southern belle drama and Chet trying to impress Jennifer and Steve doing heroics in the bull pen, we walk back to the ranch house. Then Megan steps out on the porch, cute little apron on and holding a wooden spoon. She calls out that she's made hot biscuits with gravy and sausage and eggs if we were interested." Kelly gave Megan a wicked grin. "Steve and Chet and Curt just about knocked one another down running into the ranch house." Kelly laughed as her friends joined in.

"Hot biscuits? Damn right," Curt said.

"Oh yeah," Steve added. "Boy, a hot buttered biscuit would taste great about now."

"Now I'm getting hungry," Eric said. "Hungrier, actually." He dug into his back jeans pocket and pulled out a few dollar bills. "A hot dog would be good right now. Would any of you like something? I've got ten bucks."

Pete stood up then. "Save your money, Eric. My treat. You want that dog loaded?"

"Hey, thanks, Pete." Eric burst into a grin. "Yeah. Loaded, Kelly's way."

Pete laughed as he climbed down from the bleachers. "You got it. Anybody else?"

"One of those little ice cream things I like," Jennifer said. "Please."

"Now that you guys mention it, I'm getting hungry," Marty said and climbed down the bleachers from his perch beside Megan.

"When aren't you hungry?" Steve joked.

"Yeah, hot dogs à la Kelly sound tempting," Greg said as he rose from the bleachers and gave a big stretch before climbing down.

"Nothing for me, Greg," Lisa said, waving her hand. "I'm not risking ballpark food for a while."

Kelly shook her head. "No, thanks. I'll wait until post-game pizza."

"Me, too," echoed Megan behind her.

As the guys headed toward the concession stand, Kelly watched Cassie's team take the field, Cassie jogging out with her teammates.

Steve leaned back beside Kelly on the bleachers. "Hey, Eric, I was thinking since school's about over, maybe you'd like to work part-time over at my construction site out there on East Harmony Road. Just past the interstate. I know you work a lot for your folks in the summer, but maybe they'd let you free up some time."

Eric's light blue eyes lit up. "Wow! Are you serious?"

Steve grinned. "Dead serious. There's always extra work at a construction site. Carrying around lumber, cans of paint, ladders, tools. Tons of stuff. Plus helping the guys. We can always use an extra hand holding up drywall."

Eric twisted around on the bleachers. "What do you think, Grandpa?"

"I think it's a great opportunity, son. Grab it," Curt said from his spot higher up. "You'll learn a lot."

"Do you think Mom and Dad will let me do it?"

Curt gave his grandson a little smile. "I think they will. I'll talk to them."

"Cool!" Eric said. "Thanks, Steve. That'll be great. Mom or Dad will have to drive me into town, though. I only have my learner's permit. I can't drive unless there's an adult in the passenger seat."

"Oh man, I remember that," Megan said, grinning. "I couldn't wait to turn sixteen."

"When's your birthday, Eric?" Lisa asked.

"This August," he said.

"You and Cassie both have summer birthdays," Kelly observed. "She's in late August."

"You two are both turning sixteen," Megan mused out loud, leaning back on the bleachers, too. "Hard to believe you kids are growing up so fast."

"Doesn't feel fast," Eric said, before he drained another water bottle.

"Cassie signed up for drivers' training starting in June," Jennifer said. "Pete and I are thinking of letting her use my old sedan. There's a lot of metal in that old thing."

"That old tank?" Steve said. "I'd forgotten about that car. I thought you might have sold it."

"I was going to," Jennifer said. "But then Pete and I started thinking ahead. And figured that old monster would be a great car for Cassie. Lots of protection."

"Smart move," Kelly said. "My father did the same thing. He had this old Plymouth station wagon that I got to drive around once I got my license. It was huge. And sounded like a tank when I drove it." She laughed, remembering.

Eric joined the others in laughing, as Marty and Greg and Pete returned to the bleachers, their hands filled with hot dogs, soda cups, and other treats.

"Okay, folks. Food's here," Greg announced.

"Oh boy!"

"How many hot dogs did you eat on the way over, Marty?"

"Whatever it was, Greg probably matched him."

"Two or three. I forget," Marty joked. "Now, starving teenagers first." He handed Eric a huge, fully loaded hot dog and a can of soda. "I thought you might like something rather than water to wash it down."

"Hey, thanks, guys," Eric said with a grin. Accepting the frank totally loaded high with mustard, ketchup, relish, and chili, Eric took a huge bite.

"I always forget how enormous those things are," Lisa said, watching Eric close his eyes as he savored the snack.

"Okay, folks, help yourselves," Pete said as he and Marty and Greg handed out the various concession items.

"Hey, Kelly, what's this about a murder on the golf course?" Greg asked as he climbed back to his seat beside Lisa on the bleachers. "Pete told us as we walked over to the stand."

"Oh yeah, I remember seeing something in the newspaper. A woman golfer was found dead on the greens, I think," Steve said.

"I forgot to mention it to you," Kelly said. "Cassie and I were in the shop recently when Rosa told us that a woman was found dead on the golf greens the afternoon before. She said police cars were all over the golf course and the driveway. They even searched in that old garage and the shop storage building. Of course, they didn't find anybody."

"How could they be sure it was murder?" Greg asked. "Maybe she dropped dead from a heart attack."

"Someone at the shop said there was lots of blood on her clothes. Apparently, her throat was cut."

"Whoa!" Eric said, eyes wide as demitasse saucers.

"Excuse me," Jennifer said, holding up the half-finished ice cream bar. "Some of us are eating, here."

"Yeah, let's spare the details," Lisa said, hand on tummy. "That's pretty gruesome."

"Do police have any idea who might have done it?" Marty asked.

Kelly shrugged. "I don't know any more. I learned all that from this regular group of knitters who meet at the shop. They're all really connected to everything that's happening in Fort Connor. One of those knitters is especially chatty." Kelly grinned.

"Ahh, a chatty knitter. I love it," Jennifer said with a smile.

"She sure was," Kelly continued. "She told us about this businessman in town, Callahan, who divorced his wife of forty-plus years after meeting this young, flirtatious divorcée, Giselle, and marrying her."

"Oh boy," Megan said, shaking her head.

"We've all heard that story before, I'm afraid," Lisa added.

"Well, this one is sadder than most," Kelly continued. "Apparently, the older first wife committed suicide with sleeping pills after the divorce."

"Oh no!"

"That is so sad."

"Poor woman."

"And now this Giselle has been murdered. She was the one found dead on the golf course."

"What!"

"Damn!"

"Good Lord!"

Kelly glanced over to Eric, who had finished his huge hot dog and was listening to them all. "Sorry to be telling all these gruesome, sad stories, Eric."

"That's okay. You hear lots of stories back in the canyon. Last year something happened with one of the ranchers. His wife left him and ran off with this guy she knew from another state. The rancher didn't kill himself, though," Eric said, then drained his soda.

Jennifer gave Kelly a sardonic look. "Kids nowadays get to see a lot more than we did growing up."

"You know, that story brought back a memory fragment," Marty said, looking out toward the field, which was filling up with Cassie's softball team.

"Grab it before it disappears beneath a volume of case law," Greg joked.

Marty grinned. "Yeah. Now it's coming back. It was last year and I was pulling into a space at my office parking lot downtown. When I started walking toward the building, I noticed a man and a woman standing in the lot arguing loudly. As I walked past, I couldn't help overhearing some of it. The guy was all red-faced and he looked furious. He yelled at the woman, 'My mother killed herself because of you!' Then he called her a whole bunch of rotten names. The woman didn't say a word, just got in her car and drove off. The guy kept screaming until she drove away."

"Was this an older guy?" Steve asked.

Marty shook his head. "Naw. He looked about my age, midthirties."

"Ahem." Megan turned a wicked grin on her husband. "You're in your later thirties now. Just like the rest of us."

Kelly couldn't help but be intrigued, so naturally she had to ask a question. "This guy could have been that businessman William Callahan's son, Henry. So, what does this younger son do? Continuing in his father's business?"

"I think he has an investment firm, the last time I heard," Curt spoke up from the upper bleacher row where he and Jayleen had been sitting quietly. "Not sure."

"That sounds like a sleuthing question to me," Pete said with a smile.

"Oh Lord." Jennifer wagged her head.

"Hey, it's Kelly," Greg said with a wicked grin. "If she's breathing, she's asking questions. And sleuthing."

"Please promise us you won't go poking around the golf course, looking for clues," Megan said, arching a brow.

Kelly had to laugh. "Guys, calm down. I'm nine months pregnant. I'm not going poking around golf courses or anywhere else, okay?"

"Good. But we'll all be watching," Megan warned.

"And I just got a telepathic message from Baby Jack," Steve said, jerking his thumb toward Kelly's belly. "He says, 'Take it easy, Mom. I can come anytime.'"

Everybody laughed at that, and Kelly noticed Eric laughed the loudest.

Eight

Kelly tabbed through the columns on client Don Warner's expense spreadsheet. A mid-May spring shower had started outside this afternoon, which chased her inside Lambspun.

A rumble of thunder sounded then, rumbling louder than before. They needed the rain, for sure, so this shower was welcome. March had not brought any usual early spring snows, and April had only a few light rainstorms. Now that it was mid-May, the hotter spring temperatures and the sunny weather were creating lovely weekends for recreation but very dry conditions for all the trees, bushes, plants, and grass—unless they were regularly watered.

She took a sip of coffee from the mug beside her laptop. Kelly frowned at the weak brew. She couldn't wait until after Jack arrived and she could consume her normal black-as-tar coffee again.

The tinkling of the shop doorbell sounded as another loud rumble of thunder rattled the room, bouncing off the walls. Beverly, the snack vendor, walked into the main knitting room.

"Hi there, Kelly. I see you were smart enough to come inside before the rain started," Beverly said, as she fluffed out her graying hair.

"Well, you don't look wet, so you must have moved as soon as that thunder started. That's what I did." Kelly clicked her client spreadsheet closed.

"Yeah, I've learned to pay attention to that thunder. Living in the Midwest for a while did that to me," Beverly said with a smile. "If it wasn't raining, I'd ask you if you want a snack. Instead, I think I'll join you at the table and take out my long-forgotten knitting." She pulled out a chair at the other end of the table, then reached into her oversize purse and brought out a multicolored skein of yarn and some needles.

"That's a pretty yarn. Have you started anything yet?" Kelly asked, peering at the practically empty needles.

"Actually, I was going to make a scarf for next fall. Considering how busy my schedule is, I figure I'd better start early," she said with a good-natured chuckle.

"I know exactly how you feel," Kelly said. "It takes me a long time to finish a project because I simply don't have enough time to knit."

The sound of fast-approaching footsteps was quickly followed by Mimi walking through the doorway to the workroom.

"Hello, ladies," she greeted them with a smile. "Aren't you glad you're here in Lambspun rather than running errands outside? That sprinkle has turned into a spring shower." She pointed to the windows behind Kelly.

Kelly looked over her shoulder, and indeed the rain was coming down steadily now. "You're right. I think I'll just take my break now, here at Lambspun, rather than do errands."

Mimi walked over and gave her a pat on the shoulder. "Goodness, Kelly. You can ask us to do some of those errands, if you'd like. Burt just returned from the list of today's errands. It would have been no trouble at all to add a couple more."

"That's sweet of you to offer, Mimi. I'll keep that in mind," Kelly replied. "Actually, I don't mind the errands at all. I get bored if I'm sitting around too long. I'm simply not used to it."

Beverly gave her a smile. "In a few months, Kelly, you'll be grateful to have more time to sit down. If I were you, I'd enjoy this more relaxed time while you can."

"Absolutely, Kelly," Mimi affirmed with a nod.

Kelly gave in with a smile. "All right. I promise to inform Burt the very next time I have more than one errand on my to-do list. How's that?"

"I have a better idea. Why not give Burt a list of things you or Steve would need to do, and Burt will get it done. Believe me, he's very efficient," Mimi suggested, eyes alight with her new idea.

Kelly could see there was no arguing. So, once again, she surrendered willingly. "All right, Mimi. If you are sure Burt doesn't mind. Often my list contains groceries and things like that."

Mimi gave a dismissive wave of her hand. "Oh heavens, Kelly. That's right up Burt's alley. He prides himself on being an extremely efficient grocery shopper. And I have to admit, it does take me longer to get through the grocery aisles and to the register than it does when Burt shops for us. He's back from the store before I know it. Besides, Burt and I came back all refreshed from our long weekend up in the mountains."

"I'll bet you did," Beverly said, her fingers working the multicolored yarn. "Those mountains are beautiful."

Mimi rearranged several skeins of yarn, then moved to the next bin. "Yes, they are. And you can imagine how awful it was to return home to learn that something very ugly happened while we were gone."

Kelly didn't have to scan through her brain for the recent news events. She instantly knew what Mimi was referring to. "You mean the murder of that woman golfer, don't you? I can imagine how disturbing that was for you to hear, Mimi."

Mimi made a face. "Indeed, it was. A positively gruesome murder, too. And to think it happened right over there on our golf course." She gave a shudder.

"Yes, that definitely was unfortunate," Beverly said as she knitted. "Did you know the young woman, Mimi?"

Mimi walked over to the other shelves. "No, I did not. Neither Burt nor I are golfers, so we aren't out on the links every weekend like so many of our friends. And we don't go to the country club, either. So we don't meet a lot of people who are there."

"You and Burt are too busy running a successful business, Mimi. So neither of you has loads of free time to fill with social activities," Kelly said with a smile.

Mimi laughed. "You're right, Kelly. Our social life nowadays revolves around our friends and Burt's daughter and the grandkids."

"You may have some more 'adopted grandkids' to fuss over," Kelly teased. "You've got toddler Molly now, and pretty soon there will be Baby Jack."

Mimi beamed at her. "You are so right, Kelly. And I reserve the right to fuss over them as much as I want," she said with a little laugh.

Rosa leaned her head around the workroom corner then. "Mimi, there's a vendor on the phone who wants to talk with you."

"Oh goodness, back to business. Talk to you girls later," Mimi said as she scurried out of the room.

"You know, I haven't been called a 'girl' for a long time," Beverly said, grinning.

Kelly laughed. "That's why all my friends and I call her Mother Mimi. She still thinks of us as girls."

Beverly glanced over her shoulder toward the windows. "It looks like the shower has stopped. That means I'd better get back to business." She stuffed the multicolored yarn into her knitting bag and stood up. "I'm going up front to see if they want anything. Take care of yourself and Baby Jack, Kelly," she said, giving Kelly a maternal smile.

"Don't worry, I will," Kelly replied. "Happy selling."

"I hope," Beverly said as she walked into the central yarn room and toward the front of the shop.

Kelly settled into a peaceful knitting mode, as she started another circular row of the baby hat. Pretty soon she would be finishing off the crown. The front doorbell tinkled again, and another woman walked into the main knitting room. Kelly recognized Geraldine.

"Hello, Kelly," Geraldine said as she walked into the room.

"Hey there, Geraldine. Has it stopped raining yet? It looked like a typical May spring shower."

"Yes, it slowed down as I drove over here. How're you and that baby doing?" She set her fiber knitting bag on the table and pulled out a chair farther down from Kelly.

"We're doing great," Kelly said, giving yet another motherly knitter a warm smile. "I think Baby Jack has gotten comfortable in his perch. He kicks, but he hasn't made a move to leave yet."

Geraldine laughed softly. "He'll come when he's ready. Meanwhile, I hope you're taking it easy. Not doing any softball practice for a while. Also, not trying to solve crimes, either. I heard from Mimi about that." She pulled out the red, white, and blue yarn from her bag.

"No, no crime solving. All I do now is relay information. If I hear something interesting, I will tell Burt. He can take it from there." A memory surfaced in Kelly's mind. "That reminds me. Another thought just surfaced. Do you know if Meredith Callahan had any relatives other than a son? Someone mentioned a sister."

Geraldine paused knitting and furrowed her brow. "Yes, in addition to her son here in Colorado, I think I heard her mention a sister who lived out of state. She was a successful executive, I believe."

"That's interesting."

Geraldine smiled at her. "I bet you're going to tell Burt, right?"

Kelly grinned. "You're right, Geraldine. He'll pass it along if necessary."

"See, Kelly? You're still sleuthing. And I bet Baby Jack didn't mind a bit."

At that, Kelly had to laugh out loud.

"**Kelly,** I brought something for you," Mimi said as she walked up to the bleachers at City Park ball field. She reached into a colorful fabric bag and pulled out a cushion. "I completely forgot I had this. It was in the back of a closet. I used this cushion after I sprained some muscles in my hip a few years ago."

"Thanks, Mimi," Kelly said, accepting the print fabric–covered, doughnut-shaped cushion.

"Here, stand up and let me fix it for you," Steve said, taking the cushion.

Kelly stood up and watched Steve position the cushion exactly where she was seated on the bleacher row. "Okay, let me give it a try." She carefully sat down and was surprised when she sank into the softness. "Oooo, that's nice."

"Is it soft enough for you?" Mimi asked.

"Definitely. By the way, where's Burt?"

"He's over at his daughter's house because it's her birthday. The kids and Burt planned a surprise. I promised him I'd give him an update on the game and how the kids played."

The crack of a bat sounded then, and Kelly turned quickly

as bystanders cheered. She spied Cassie running like crazy for first base. Meanwhile, the other team's right fielder raced to snag the ball that landed behind her.

"Go, Cassie, go!" Megan shouted.

"Way to go!" Greg yelled.

"Woo-hoooo!" Lisa called.

"Great hit, Cassie!" Steve called out.

Then Marty let loose with one of his piercing whistles.

Kelly stuck her fingers into both ears. "Yeow! You're gonna make us all deaf, Marty!"

"Hey, that's my trademark!" Marty bragged. "Everybody does better after I whistle. Haven't you noticed?"

"Oh Lord. Don't tell me he's done a survey," Jennifer said, eyeing Marty skeptically.

"Only Marty," Lisa observed with a smile.

"Heads up, guys," Steve said. "That cleanup batter on Cassie's team is at bat. Let's hope she can knock it way out into left field so Cassie can make it around the rest of the bases."

"Yeah, we need some more runs. That Windsor team is up by two." Kelly shifted on the comfy cushion and leaned back onto the bleacher behind her.

The new batter stepped up to home plate and settled into a crouch. The pitcher wound up and let fly. The batter swung and missed.

"Steeerike one!" yelled the umpire behind home plate.

Megan scooted up onto Kelly and Steve's bleacher row and sat beside Kelly. "You feeling okay?"

Kelly nodded. "Yep. Still feeling good."

"Baby Jack has dropped. I can tell," Megan said with a grin.

"Oh yeah," Steve agreed. "I was surprised at the difference.

Kelly was carrying Jack up higher." Steve made a motion in front of his midsection. "Like you were, Megan. And all of a sudden, he was down lower."

"He's getting ready," Kelly said. "And I can't tell you how happy I'll be when I can have a cup of my regular strong coffee again. That weakened brew has nearly gagged me."

"Well, try to ease into the stronger brews," Megan advised. "You're going to nurse the baby for a while, aren't you?"

"Yes, for a few months. Until he's eating baby food."

"Get ready for all those little jars sitting in the fridge, Steve," Megan teased.

The crack of a bat caught everyone's attention then, and Kelly and friends cheered loudly as Cassie's team's cleanup batter rounded first base. Cassie was already racing toward home plate. The ball was way out in left field—gone.

"Can you pass over a slice of that Southwest chicken pizza, please?" Steve said, pointing to one of the open pizza boxes on Greg and Lisa's living room coffee table.

"Sure thing," Megan said, then used a spatula to lift a slice of that pizza onto a paper napkin. She handed it to Marty.

"For me? Why, thank you," he teased.

"No, it's for Steve. You've had so many I've lost count," Megan said. "And you've got two slices on your plate."

"Bite your tongue. There's no such thing as too much pizza," Marty said as he handed the pizza slice to Steve.

Jennifer laughed softly. "How're things over at your law firm, Marty? Any interesting cases?"

Marty took a sip of his soda before answering. "Not really. Just the normal civil lawsuits proceeding. I'm not in trial mode at all. Everything I'm handling has been settled before going to court."

"Smart," Steve spoke up. "I've heard those court fees add a whole lot to the legal bills."

"Oh yeah." Marty nodded before taking a huge bite of pizza.

"You know, Marty, you really ought to try taking smaller bites," Lisa suggested. "It's better for your digestion. Plus, there's less risk of choking."

"Lisa's right," Pete added as he scooped up a spoonful of chili beans. "A few years ago I had a customer at the café who choked on a big bite of burger."

"One of Eduardo's Wicked Burgers?" Megan asked with a grin.

"Oh yeah." Pete nodded his head. "Thank goodness, Julie was nearby. She saw him grab his throat and start wheezing, trying to catch a breath—"

"Ohhhhh Lord," Kelly said.

"I was away at the real estate office so I didn't see it," Jennifer said. "And I'm so glad. It must have been terrifying."

"Oh, it was," Pete continued. "I was trying to remember all those moves of that Heimlich maneuver, but Julie had it down cold. Thank God. She grabbed him around the chest and started doing that motion, and . . . in a few seconds, a chunk of meat shot out of his mouth."

"Oh, gross." Megan made a face.

"Well, better to be gross than dead," Greg said.

"True," Lisa agreed.

Kelly paused, pondering for a moment. "You know, I think it would be a good thing if we each learned that maneuver ourselves. Who knows? We may have to use it to save a family member's life sometime."

"That's a good idea," Steve added.

"Agreed," Lisa said. "But can we change the subject now, please? I keep picturing this guy in the café and chewed-up food flying out of his mouth. Yuck!" Lisa shut her eyes.

"Lisa's gotten really sensitive to anything that even borders on gross," Greg said with a grin.

"And she's still living with you?" Steve asked, an incredulous look on his face.

A loud chorus of groans echoed around the living room.

"Good one!" Jennifer said.

Megan laughed so hard, she was bent over and couldn't speak.

"That is so bad." Pete cackled.

"Man, I wish I'd said that," Marty said after a loud hoot of laughter.

"That . . . is so . . . funny," Lisa said when she could catch her breath.

Greg, for his part, was also bent over laughing, face beet red.

Kelly grinned at Steve. "That really was funny. And so unlike you. Marty and Greg are the usual comics."

"Every now and then I come up with a good line," Steve said with a wink.

"Boy, I need a Fat Tire after that. I'm thirsty," Pete said as he rose from the chair. "Lisa and Greg have quite a selection of beers and ales. Even some stout. Black-as-tar Guinness." He grinned. "Does anyone want one of them?"

"I'll take one of those ales, please," Jennifer said. "A Fat Tire is perfect."

"Well, I think I need one of those black-as-tar Guinness stouts," Greg said as he rose from where he sat on the sofa beside Lisa. Glancing to his wife, he asked, "Do you want some of that ginger ale? You said that was gentle on your stomach."

"Yes, as a matter of fact. After all that laughing, I'm thirsty, too."

"I can't wait until I can have a Fat Tire again," Kelly said.

"Not much longer now," Steve said, giving her a pat on the arm. "Meanwhile, do you want a ginger ale, a root beer, or a cola?"

"Hmmmmmm, I haven't had a root beer in a long time," Kelly said. "I'll take one of those, please."

"Why don't you turn it into a float with a scoop of ice cream?" Greg suggested. "We've got vanilla ice cream in the freezer. That's all Lisa could stand eating for a while."

Kelly pictured a dark root beer with a yummy scoop of vanilla ice cream. "I'd love one, Greg. That's a brilliant suggestion. Thank you."

"'Greg' and 'brilliant' in the same sentence?" Marty asked, seemingly incredulous. "Isn't that a higher-order grammatical error?"

"You're a higher-order grammatical error," Megan teased.

"And you're going to wait until last, or there won't be enough ice cream for all of us."

Marty assumed a look of horror. "Oh no!" he whispered. "Not that!"

Megan gave him a wave of her hand before joining the rest of her friends in the kitchen.

Nine

Kelly pulled herself off the floor following her exercises and headed toward the kitchen of the ranch-style home she and Steve had bought from his housing development in north Fort Connor. She took a deep drink from her mug that was on the kitchen counter. Making a little face at the weak brew, Kelly was about to head to the shower when the front doorbell chimed. She peeked out the peephole and saw Megan, holding something.

"Good morning," Kelly greeted her friend. Glancing down at the little red-haired toddler who was trying to peer through the frosted glass door panel, she added, "And good morning to you, Miss Molly!"

"I just finished getting these smaller baby clothes sorted, and I wanted to bring them over here before I forget," Megan said as she entered.

Kelly looked at the large pink plastic laundry basket that was completely filled with folded baby clothes. She spied pastel baby blankets, white baby T-shirts, tiny sleeper suits, and colorful shirts and pants.

"Wow, Megan. You didn't need to bring all these. I've already bought a lot of baby clothes."

"You'll be surprised how fast you go through blankets and clothes. And Molly has outgrown all of them." She set the large basket on the kitchen table.

Kelly watched toddler Molly speed across her great room and head straight for the cedar toy chest that sat in the corner.

"There she goes. Molly knows where the fun stuff is."

"Plus Molly knows you've already got toys in it so she could play."

"I couldn't resist it. Real cedar wood with that wonderful aroma, and it's been sitting for years in Mimi's upstairs guest room. I was so glad Mimi gave it to me. She said she'd forgotten all about it."

"Well, you can definitely use it, and Mother Mimi knows that. Plus, we're all like daughters to her, so that makes it extra special." Megan grinned.

"You're right. We're all like her kids." Turning back to the kitchen, she offered, "Do you have time for coffee? I've finished my exercises and was about to fire up the laptop and get on my accounting."

"Oh yes. Business as usual beckons. I wish I could stay, but believe it or not, I have to go to a funeral with Marty this morning. The entire law firm is attending. Then, I get back to work."

"Whoa, was it an older client of Marty's that died?" Kelly asked as she poured another cup of blah coffee.

"No, actually this funeral is for William Callahan's younger wife, Giselle. You know, the one we talked about who was murdered." Then Megan looked straight at Kelly. "Now don't you go getting any ideas about sleuthing, Kelly."

"Don't worry. I'm just asking questions nowadays," Kelly replied with a laugh. She decided to keep the rest of her questions to herself. Otherwise, Megan would be convinced Kelly was sleuthing. She pondered. She probably was, Kelly thought with a smile. What was it Greg said? "It's Kelly. If she's breathing, she's sleuthing." So true.

Megan walked toward the front door, then she turned to Molly who was play-walking a spotted giraffe across the floor. "Come along, Molly," she said. "We have to go to the grocery store."

"No," Molly said, shaking her head as she kept walking the giraffe along the floor.

Megan sighed. "And we're now entering the phase where we don't want to do anything that Mommy suggests. It's 'no, this' and 'no, that.'"

"Clearly, Miss Molly has a mind of her own," Kelly said with a grin. "Not unlike someone else I know."

"Yeah, yeah, yeah. I hear you," Megan said as she walked over and scooped up a reluctant Molly from the floor.

Molly began fussing and protesting loudly, chubby toddler legs kicking.

Megan reached into the back pocket of her shorts and brought out a large, colorful key ring with several oversize plastic keys on it. She dangled them in front of Molly's red face. "Look! Here are Mommy's special keys." She shook the keys again, and they made a little musical sound.

Molly's crying stopped immediately as she gazed at the keys. Then she dropped the giraffe and grasped them and shook them. Another little musical sound escaped.

"What a great idea," Kelly said. "Musical keys. Where did you find them?"

"One of Marty's clients gave them to us after Molly was born. She was Swiss and didn't say where she bought them. They're safe for toddlers. I checked out the company's name online. It was on the back of one of the keys in raised lettering."

Kelly chuckled. "I'm impressed with your sleuthing, Megan."

Megan simply rolled her eyes as she opened the front door. "I'll send you a text with the website of the company."

Kelly gave a wide stretch and yawned. Uh-oh. She was getting sleepy. But she needed to get this last expense spreadsheet finished for the Don Warner account. Warner had told her on the phone he was planning on buying a couple of pieces of equipment for his new construction site in the Denver suburb of Lakewood. It was a small strip mall with specialty foods and a café.

Another yawn escaped, and Kelly stood up from her spot along Lambspun's knitting table where she sat alone. Enough with the yawning. She was going to have a cup of Eduardo's strong black coffee. Period. And she would ignore any raised eyebrows or fussing. She was tired of drinking the weak brew. No more!

Filled with rebellious fire, Kelly headed toward the back of the café. She spotted Eduardo at the grill and leaned over the counter. "Eduardo, could you please pour me a cup of your full-strength coffee? I need to stay awake."

Eduardo looked over his shoulder. "And I need to stay out of trouble. You know what Jennifer would say." His brown eyes were wide. "She'll tell Megan, then Megan will come in here and fuss at you. Then she'll be annoyed with me because I gave you the coffee." He shook his head. "That Megan is something else."

"Well, then, don't tell anyone," Kelly said with a little smile. "What Megan and Jennifer don't know won't hurt them." Kelly glimpsed a little smile start at Eduardo's mouth.

"Crazy Kelly. Only you would try this. Okay, but don't mention my name." Eduardo grabbed a ceramic mug and poured a black stream into it.

Kelly gratefully accepted the cup with both hands. "Thank you, thank you, Eduardo. You're a doll." She inhaled the dark coffee aroma and took a small sip.

Ahhhhhhhhh, she thought as the rich, strong flavor teased her taste buds. Savoring, Kelly took another small sip and enjoyed. How she had missed this treat. Surely Baby Jack didn't mind, she thought, noticing his soccer practice had already started for the day.

"Bless you, Eduardo," she said as she headed toward the corridor again. Walking back to the knitting table, Kelly shoved her laptop and files back into her briefcase bag and took her coffee and her accounting work outside. Beautiful weather beckoned once more.

Halfway finished with the coffee, she headed toward the sun-dappled and shaded patio. She spotted that the far table was empty and claimed it. Plopping her briefcase bag on the wrought iron table, she settled into a chair. Only a few more revenue streams to enter, and she could then find out what the latest expenses were. Knowing Don Warner, Kelly figured there would always be some extra expense tucked away in the records.

She had just popped open her laptop when she heard a very familiar voice.

"Hey there, Kelly. How's my favorite mom-to-be doing?"

Kelly looked up to see Burt walking toward her along the flagstone path that wound through the garden patio. "Hey, Burt. I'm doing fine, and so is Baby Jack because he's playing a lot of soccer."

"That's great, Kelly. You look good," Burt said as he walked up to the table and pulled out a chair. "Healthy and happy."

"Thanks, Burt. I feel good, and so far there are no signs Baby Jack wants to leave yet. I think he's gotten very comfortable where he is."

Burt chuckled. "I hope you're not planning to continue the accounting work much longer. I'm sure both your clients, Housemann and Warner, would definitely understand if you took it easier before Jack comes."

"Don't worry, Burt," Kelly said, clicking her laptop into Sleep mode. "Accounting spreadsheets are easy work. No exertion whatsoever. How was your mini vacation in the mountains?"

"Relaxing," he said, leaning back into a wrought iron chair. "Just what we needed. It's going to be a busy summer, what with all the grandkids and Cassie and Eric playing in various leagues. It's all Mimi and I can do to keep track of everybody's schedule."

A stray thought poked up from the back of Kelly's mind. "I guess you've heard that there was a murder while you two were gone. Right over there on the golf course." She pointed toward the grassy greens bordering the Lambspun driveway.

Burt's smile disappeared. "Yes, I did. A particularly gruesome killing from what I've heard. Neither Mimi nor I knew the young woman. It's a damn shame someone chose to end her life."

"I figure you've probably talked to Dan since you returned. How's the police investigation going?"

The corner of Burt's mouth crooked up. "I swear, Kelly, even pregnant and almost ready to deliver, you're still poking into murders."

Kelly gave a good-natured shrug. "I can't help it. It's in my DNA, I think. Natural curiosity."

"It must be. And yes, I did talk with Dan when we returned. He told me that police have no suspects. Apparently, the murder took place late in the afternoon, and they haven't found anyone yet who was in the vicinity to witness it."

"No golfers were around? We've got such beautiful weather."

"Since it was a Friday afternoon, he figures a lot of the

golfers were getting ready for Friday night activities and had already left the course. Traveling up into the High Country, most probably. You should have seen how many people were at Estes Park and Rocky Mountain National Park."

"I can imagine. And it's not even summer yet." Kelly paused, another thought nibbling at the edges of her mind. "Have they questioned the families? Some of the knitters here at Lambspun told me all about the divorce of that successful businessman William Callahan and his remarriage to this younger woman, Giselle. And she was the one who was killed."

"Dan said they are planning to." He peered at Kelly. "Sounds like some of the knitters have been keeping up with the local gossip."

"I'd say it's more than gossip. They also told me about Callahan's first wife of over forty years and her suicide. That's so sad."

"Tragic, simply tragic. Meredith Callahan's suicide hit many people in this community hard. Mimi was one of them. She said Meredith was a dear person, generous and kind and very much involved in charity work. I think I remember meeting her at a fund-raiser for the local food bank once. Can't remember William Callahan, though. Maybe he wasn't there."

"Well, I hope the police find someone who was in the vicinity, so they can get some leads into who committed that vicious murder." Kelly stared out toward the golf course. "I mean, slitting someone's throat is particularly brutal in my opinion. Any idea what kind of knife the killer used?"

"You really can't stop sleuthing, can you?" Burt said, smiling. "Dan said the medical examiner's report determined it was a very thin blade, thinner than most pocket knives, even Swiss Army knives."

"Thinner than those? What on earth did they use, Burt? Any ideas?"

Now it was Burt's turn to shrug. "The only thing I can think of is a razor blade. Those are super sharp and thin. I remember hearing years ago how some street gangs had homemade knives made out of razor blades. Easier to get rid of, too."

"Whoa . . . that is brutal. You have to get up close and personal to do that."

"Dan also said the medical examiner's report showed that it wasn't one clean cut across the victim's throat. Rather, there were two deep shorter strokes."

Kelly looked back at him. "That is vicious. I sure hope they find someone who was in the vicinity and can give the cops a clue."

"Amen to that."

Suddenly, the niggling little thought in the back of Kelly's mind moved front and center. "Oh yeah. Tell Dan he may want to talk to some of our knitters who knew Meredith Callahan. Geraldine said she knew her slightly from charity work and was at various business functions that Callahan attended with his former wife. She also told me that another of the knitters, Marie, and Meredith Callahan were best friends."

Burt's eyebrows shot up, a sure sign he was interested in something she'd said. "Oh really. I'll make sure to tell Dan."

"Good. I had a chance to talk with Marie in the shop one

day and mentioned the murder, which had just happened. Boy, did she have a strong reaction. Her animosity toward Giselle Callahan was really evident. She got so upset she actually walked out of the shop."

"Really?" Burt's eyebrows shot up again. "I will definitely be giving Dan a call. And I'll make sure I tell Dan that pregnancy hasn't slowed down your sleuthing. Not at all." He gave her a wink.

Kelly turned the corner into the café. The scent of Eduardo's Wicked Burgers floated in the air. That scent had teased her all the way from the central yarn room where she was admiring some of the new yarns Mimi and Rosa had added to the center round table.

Jennifer was standing at the grill counter. "Hey there, Kelly. Perfect timing. It's lunchtime. Can we tempt you with one of Eduardo's Wicked Burgers?"

Kelly paused at a nearby table in the alcove and pondered. She'd dearly love one of those burgers with all the trimmings. But she was trying to keep her pregnancy weight in line. She'd been successful so far, having gained just twenty-one pounds. *Hmmmmmmm.* Should she or shouldn't she?

Jennifer grinned. "Well? What would you like? We have some Chicken Tortilla soup, too. What sounds good?"

"Decisions, decisions," Kelly debated out loud. "How about a bowl of that Chicken Tortilla soup. I'm trying to keep my weight in line, you know." She dropped her briefcase bag on a nearby table and approached her friend at the counter.

"Eduardo, let's get her a bowl of your delicious soup for today," Jennifer advised. "Then why don't you make her one of your super yummy grilled cheese sandwiches. You know, just the way Kelly likes it with lots of cheese inside so it oozes over the sides when it's on the grill."

Eduardo grinned at Kelly over his shoulder. "You got it, Kelly."

"Oh brother. I can see the extra pounds waiting to jump on the scale with me."

"And I can almost see Baby Jack cheering for the grilled cheese and soup. He needs nourishment to keep up his soccer practice," Jennifer countered.

"Okay, okay." Kelly raised her hands in surrender. "You convinced me."

Kelly watched Eduardo go for the sliced bread and spread both sides of the sandwich, inside and out, with real butter. Then he reached into a nearby fridge and brought out the packages of sliced cheese. He added American cheese, Jack cheese, and Gouda. Then Eduardo placed the top slice of buttered bread, grabbed his ever-present spatula, and pressed the sandwich down on the grill. It sizzled and, sure enough, within a few seconds, melted cheese began to ooze out of the sides of the sandwich. Kelly's mouth started to water.

"I swear, Eduardo, anyone who's trying to lose weight should absolutely stay out of this café. You are deadly."

Eduardo cackled. "Crazy Kelly."

"Oh, we have regulars who are constantly trying one diet after another. But they order salads, and they don't come near the grill counter," Jennifer teased. "Or they'd all order burgers."

"Oh yeah. This counter is deadly," Kelly agreed, as she stepped away and settled into a chair at the café table where she'd dropped her briefcase bag.

"Don't worry. It won't go to waste. I'll box up whatever you can't finish. Even the soup. And you can take it home," Jennifer said as she filled a glass with water and brought it over to the table. "Or you can nibble on it this afternoon if you're still here."

Kelly laughed softly. "Thanks, Jen, I appreciate it. I have found myself nibbling in the afternoons."

"I told you. That's Baby Jack asking for more nourishment. He's saying, 'Feed me, Mom. I'm hungry!'"

This time Kelly laughed out loud.

"I swear, Kelly, I keep worrying that Baby Jack will suddenly decide that he wants to arrive early and those contractions will start off with a bang. Not gradual, like everyone always says they do. That doesn't happen every time. Otherwise there wouldn't be women giving birth in taxis on the way to the hospital!"

Kelly grinned up at her friend who was standing over her, and saw the actual worry that hid behind Jennifer's teasing words. "Now it's your turn not to worry. I won't be delivering Jack here in the shop beside the yarn bins or outside in the patio garden beneath the trees." She pictured herself lying amidst the green vines and the summer flowers that had burst into bloom. It would be picturesque and in keeping with all those early settler stories. But not what she envisioned. "The hospital is only ten minutes away down the street. And both Mimi and Burt have gassed up their cars and are ready to go. There's even an extra driver with Cassie, now that school is finishing."

Jennifer let out a long breath. "Okay. But I'm holding you to your promise. No Lambspun deliveries."

Kelly gave her a mock salute. "No Lambspun deliveries of babies. Yarns, yes. Babies, no."

Ten

Kelly gave Rottweiler Carl a good head rub and behind-the-ear scratch. Carl started his "sing-along" with several ecstatic noises. "Good boy. Good dog, Carl," Kelly crooned.

Carl sang a little more then did his characteristic head shake, ears flapping.

"Okay, that's enough for now, Carl. I've got work to do."

Kelly grabbed her shoulder briefcase bag and headed across the driveway separating the Lambspun shop from her cottage. She wanted to get started on those Arthur Housemann expense spreadsheets. It was another gorgeous late spring day—warm with brilliant sunshine. She'd just reached the sidewalk leading up to the Lambspun front entry when she recognized a familiar truck coming down the driveway. Jayleen. Kelly stopped where she was and waved at her friend.

Jayleen pulled into a parking space and climbed down

from the truck. "Hey there, Kelly-girl!" she called. "Why don't you join me out here in the patio? I've got a hankering for one of Pete's good breakfasts."

"Sure thing, Jayleen. I may even snitch a piece of bacon when you're not looking," Kelly teased as she followed Jayleen down the flagstone pathway into the café patio garden.

"I'll make sure to order enough then," Jayleen said with a grin. "Anything left over can go to Carl." She headed toward an empty table that sat half in the morning sun and half in the shade of a nearby cottonwood tree and pulled out a chair.

Kelly set her briefcase bag on the ground and settled into a chair on the other side of the round table. "I've been working out here practically every day unless it's raining. I just love this weather. I escape outside whenever I can."

"I know what you mean, Kelly. And once he comes, you'll probably be taking Baby Jack outside pretty soon. It'll be warm enough."

"You think so?" Kelly asked, with a concerned look. "I guess I could wrap him up in lots of blankets, so any chilly breeze won't bother him."

Mother of two grown children, Jayleen threw back her head and laughed, silvered blond curls falling over her shoulder. "Lordy, Lordy, Kelly . . . you don't have to worry. It will be June before you know it. And our Colorado weather is acting exactly as it should. Bright sunshine, warm temps, and occasional showers. You and Baby Jack will be fine. Believe me."

"If you say so," Kelly said. "I always like to hear input from women who actually raised children. All the baby and birthing books are great, but there's nothing like firsthand knowledge."

"Remember, women have been giving birth to babies out in the forest and in deserts for thousands of years. And those women had to wrap up their babies in whatever they had available and be ready to run with the rest of the tribe whenever they had to leave camp."

Kelly pictured the primitive images Jayleen brought up, glad she wasn't born centuries ago. "You're right, you're right. We new mothers-to-be are just anxious, that's all."

"I predict Baby Jack will be strong and healthy, just like his mother and father. So you can stop worrying." She winked at Kelly.

"Thank you, Jayleen. That's reassuring to hear."

Julie walked over to their table then and gave them her usual bright smile. "Hey, Jayleen and Kelly, what can I get for you?"

"I'll take a glass of orange juice, please, Julie," Kelly said.

"No coffee?" Julie asked, clearly surprised.

Kelly made a face. "That weak brew I've been drinking for these last few months is about to make me gag. I don't think I can stand another cup."

"Oh yeah," Jayleen said. "I heard about Megan's proclamations from Curt. I like to have died laughing. If there was something wrong with drinking strong coffee, my two kids wouldn't have come out as healthy and strong as they did."

"I hear you, Jayleen. But believe me, you don't want to have to listen to Megan fuss." Kelly rolled her eyes.

Julie grinned. "She's world-class, I agree. Listen, Kelly,

let me try something you might like. My mom went to Japan on a cruise and came back with some matcha green tea. It's strong and tastes very good. If you like it, then you can tell Megan you're drinking green tea."

Kelly pondered for a split second. "Why not? I'll give it a try. Thanks, Julie."

"How about for you, Jayleen?" Julie asked, pen poised over her notepad.

"I'm going to have one of those big breakfasts Eduardo does so well, and black coffee, of course," she said with a grin. "Scrambled eggs and bacon and hot biscuits. I'm hungry as a she-bear."

"Love it," Kelly said with a laugh. "And you can bring me a couple of strips of bacon, too. I had flaxseed cereal, coconut milk, and banana for breakfast. I can always find room for some bacon."

"You got it. I'll be right back with that green tea and coffee," Julie said as she scribbled then headed toward another table of customers.

"While we're waiting for breakfast, why don't we get some business done," Jayleen said, digging in the back pocket of her jeans. Pulling out a small notebook and pen, she said, "In case you've forgotten, you promised Curt a week or so ago that you would 'make an honest man out of Steve' before the baby gets here. And as far as Curt and I are concerned, a promise is a promise."

Kelly couldn't resist teasing her good friend. "I believe I told Curt that I would think about it."

Jayleen eyed Kelly. "Enough beating around the bush, Kelly-girl. Curt and I are scheduling the ceremony. So if you want to cancel the proceedings, you'll have to do it in front of Steve and all your friends and family alike. And the pastor." She gave a firm "And that's that!" nod of her head.

Kelly had to laugh. "Jayleen, if you and Curt schedule the ceremony, I'll be there."

"All righty, then. That's a yes in my book. So, we've been looking at the calendar, and this next Saturday looks like a perfect time. Curt and I have already checked with Mimi and Burt and all of your friends. And everyone is free or can be. Even Cassie and Eric's ball teams are playing earlier in the day."

"Really?" Kelly blinked. "That's surprising."

"Yes, it is, so we'd better grab it." Jayleen opened the small notebook on the table in front of Kelly and turned a page.

Kelly looked at the calendar. That next Saturday would work perfectly.

"Mimi and Burt were thinking about having the ceremony in their pretty backyard like Jennifer and Pete's wedding. Curt and I agree. And all of your friends, too. As much as I'd love to have you folks out to my ranch, like we did for Megan and Marty, we're all afraid to hold it there in case you go into labor."

Kelly laughed softly. "That's a good point. And Mimi's backyard is simply lovely. That's a wonderful idea."

Jayleen's bright smile returned. "We all thought so, too. I checked with some of my friends I've been working with at the Mission and asked them for suggestions as to ministers around town who could perform the ceremony. They gave me a couple of names, and Curt and I have already spoken to both of them. One is younger and a lot more relaxed acting than the other, so I figure he'd be good. Pastor Frank Quinlan. He also said he performs a lot of different weddings for folks who are not traditional churchgoers."

Kelly laughed out loud at that. "I'm impressed, Jayleen. You folks have done a lot of work. And organizing."

"Thank you, ma'am," Jayleen said. "So, it's settled. I'm going to write in here this next Saturday is Kelly and Steve's Wedding Day." She started writing on the small calendar.

Suddenly, another thought came blazing through from the back of Kelly's mind. "Oh my Lord! Steve! Did you check with Steve? He's stopped working Saturdays, so I think his schedule is free, but we need to check." She shook her head. "Good Lord. It must be what Megan calls Pregnancy Brain. I'm forgetting things."

Jayleen chuckled. "Don't worry. Curt and I checked with Steve first thing. Believe me, Steve is dying for a chance to get married. He was waiting for you to give a hint. So, Curt and I decided to give you a little push. Or a shove, actually."

Kelly laughed again. "After all, what are good friends for?"

"That's right."

Another thought came out of the back of Kelly's mind—a memory more than a thought. "Tell me, Jayleen. How is Felix Marsted doing? Your mention of the people you work with over at the Mission brought that memory back. How's he holding up, now that his daughter, Nancy, is in prison?"

Jayleen's expression turned solemn. "Well, she's not actually in prison yet. She's still in Larimer County Correctional Facility in the women's section since last year. There was no trial because she confessed to police. Nancy was brought before a judge and charged with second-degree murder, and she pled guilty. Then she was sentenced to approximately twenty years in prison in Cañon City, Colorado."

"Second-degree murder?" Kelly asked in surprise. "Why's that? I'm afraid I didn't follow up with all the proceedings like you did. Burt told me Nancy was going to be charged with murder because she admitted she deliberately ran into Neil Smith, her old boyfriend."

"And the father of her child," Jayleen said in a judgmental tone.

"That's right. But I assumed she was charged with first-degree murder because she admitted she drove into Smith. How come the charge came down to second-degree?"

"That was because she said she didn't plan to kill Neil Smith. Just hurt him. Like break his leg or something. That's why she panicked when she saw what she'd done."

"Well, that makes sense. We sure don't want Nancy spending her entire life in prison for a rash spur-of-the-moment decision. And now I remember something else. Isn't she due to deliver a baby pretty soon?"

Jayleen's big smile spread across her face once again. "She's already delivered a beautiful baby girl. Felix brought her over to show all of us at Alcoholics Anonymous. She's a little sweetheart, that's for sure."

"Ohhh, that's wonderful. Does Felix have custody, I hope?"

"He certainly does. Curt and I made sure Felix had a good lawyer. Since he was the only living blood relation family member within the state, he was awarded custody. After all, he's the baby's grandfather. Susie is her name. Nancy wanted to name her after her mother who'd died years ago."

"Ohhhh, I'm so glad Felix will be able to raise her. He was such a nice, gentle man as I remember. He'll make sure Baby Susie has a good home."

"Yes, he will. And Felix will have all of us helping him, too," Jayleen said with a firm nod.

"I'm sorry I didn't keep up with them. I should have asked you how Felix was doing."

"No need for you to apologize, Kelly. No need at all. You have had plenty on your plate. If I remember correctly, Jennifer and Pete's wedding was right after that. And you and Steve had a big announcement yourselves." She grinned.

"That's true. It has been a busy year."

"That's putting it mildly, Kelly-girl," Jayleen said with a chuckle.

Kelly walked down the corridor between the Lambspun shop and Pete's Café. Spotting the extra large Mother Loom near the front of the shop, she paused to admire the pretty yarns someone was weaving. It was a lovely combination of soft gray, white, and light blue yarns.

"How pretty," Kelly said as Rosa turned the corner into the room.

"Yes, it is. She's a new weaver who's been taking Mimi's weaving classes for several months. And she's graduated from using those smaller portable looms to the middle size and now the Mother Loom."

Kelly lightly touched the weaving, just once. "Well, tell her she's doing a great job."

"I'll make sure to tell her," Rosa said with a smile as she plucked two skeins of cotton multicolored sock yarn from a bin. "Oh, and I just heard from Mimi that Jayleen got you to commit to a date for the wedding. I'm so glad, Kelly. All of us are really looking forward to it."

"Boy, word certainly traveled fast. Why am I not surprised? It's the Lambspun network," Kelly joked as she walked into the adjacent central yarn room. She spied Cassie ahead at the library table, sorting through several skeins of yarn. "Hey there, Cassie," she said as she entered the main room. "Are you completely finished with school now?"

Cassie glanced up. "Almost. I finished all my exams, so I don't have to go back until tomorrow and the general closing assembly."

Kelly set her bag and coffee mug on the library table and settled into a chair. "Wow, it's hard to believe the school year is finished. It flew by this year. You'll be working here at the café this summer like you did last year, right?"

"Absolutely," Cassie said with her trademark grin. "Pete and Jennifer really do need the help. Summer's a busy season."

Kelly pulled out the almost-finished baby hat from her bag. "Well, it'll be nice to see more of you during the daytime. Summer is always super busy around here. Even in the shop. So many people come to Colorado to vacation, and a lot of them drop in here. Either accidentally or because friends told them about Lambspun."

"You're right. Practically every day last summer some newcomer walked into the shop. It was fun, actually." Cassie shoved back her chair and returned the several skeins of firecracker red yarn to their bins. "Oh yes, Kelly. What flowers do you want in your bridal bouquet for this Saturday? I'm going to arrange it." She grabbed a notepad and pen in the middle of the table as she settled back into her chair. "Eric and I are going to decorate Mimi's backyard on Friday night like we did for Jennifer and Pete's wedding last fall."

"Oh my goodness, are you really? Don't go to any trouble. I haven't even thought about a bouquet." Kelly picked up her stitches where she left off on the baby hat.

"Don't be silly," Cassie said. "You're a bride, and all brides need a wedding bouquet. So, what kind of flowers would you like in it?"

Realizing she was facing teenage conviction, Kelly gave in. "All right. Hmmmmmm. Let me see. I like practically every flower. Especially the bright summer annuals. And roses, of course."

Kelly scribbled away on the notepad. "Okay. Mimi's roses have just opened this week, and they're a pretty coral color. What else?"

"Let's see. You know, I really love some of the annuals and perennials that grow out in the café patio flower beds. They're bright and pretty. How about using some of them?"

"Okay," Cassie said, writing it down. "I know you like red, so I'll look at Mimi's and other gardens for some pretty red flowers. Roses for sure. Oh, do you like those orange daisies?"

Kelly had to smile. In fact, orange daisies always made her smile. "Yes, I do. Why don't you simply fill in the bouquet with whatever flower you think is pretty? I trust your taste, Cassie."

"Okay, Kelly," Cassie said, scribbling some more. "I'll be able to check Mimi's gardens again later today. And Eric said his mom had told him he could pick any of her flowers in the garden for your bouquet."

"Ohhh, that's so sweet of her."

"Don't worry about flowers, Kelly. Eric can help Friday night. We'll get most of it done then because both Eric and I have games on Saturday morning. We can finish off Saturday afternoon before the ceremony." She gave Kelly a big smile.

Kelly laughed softly. "I have no doubt you two will do a great job. You're both amazing in my book."

"Why, thank you," Cassie said with a grin. "I'll tell Eric you said that. He'll laugh."

Kelly remembered something she'd wanted to ask Cassie when it was a relaxed time. "Changing the subject, there's something I keep forgetting to ask you, Cassie. How is your college savings fund coming along? College is only two years off."

"Oh, it's building slowly. And I'll be able to save money every week because I'll be working at the café every day now that school has finished."

"Forgive me for being the nosy accountant, but I can't help it. That's how my mind works, and I can't turn it off." Kelly gave a good-natured shrug.

"That's okay, Kelly. I don't mind. You're a CPA, so you can't help being curious about money," Cassie teased. "Besides, I'm kind of proud of how much I've saved. I have some friends who worked in fast-food restaurants last summer, but they didn't save their money. They spent most of it every week. A lot of it on junk food, too." She made a face.

"Well, they're probably expecting their parents to foot the entire bill for their college education," Kelly said. "It was the same when I went to college, believe it or not. Some kids totally freeloaded off their parents and didn't contribute a dime to their college bills. Others, like me, had to work every summer at whatever job we could to pay college bills."

"I know what you mean. Half of my friends have to work like I do. And the other half of them are expecting their parents to pay everything. But I don't expect that from Jennifer and Uncle Pete. I'm just so glad I've had that extra babysitting money from Megan and Marty. That has added a lot to my savings. I've got over three thousand dollars now."

"That's great, Cassie. I'm proud of you."

"Thanks, Kelly. Both Eric and I are saving as much as we can. Colorado State raised their tuition again last year, you know."

"Oh yes. At least state colleges' and universities' tuition rates are more reasonable," Kelly added. "I swear, some of the private colleges' tuition rates have skyrocketed these last few years. It's gotten to the point that a whole lot of kids are graduating from college with large student loans still hanging over their heads. That's why it's so great that you're working hard and saving as much money as you can."

"Eric and I are pretty proud of how much we're earning each summer. Of course, he'll earn a whole lot more after he works the entire summer at Steve's Wellesley building site."

"That's for sure. But wait until you see how much you'll earn babysitting both Molly and Baby Jack on Saturday nights during this coming school year. That's when the Gang gets together. By October I'm pretty sure Steve and I will be ready to let you babysit Jack. Certainly by November. Jack will be six months old, and he'll be sleeping. Molly should be getting to bed around that same time, too. So, you'll be getting paid by Megan and Marty and Steve and me."

"Yay!" Cassie cheered. "Then my account will really grow. I kind of thought you'd combine the payment or something."

Kelly shook her head. "No, no. You're taking care of the most precious things any parent has—our children. So, you deserve to be paid well. Quite well, in my opinion."

Cassie grinned. "As the nosy family accountant, right?"

"Yes, indeed."

"Lisa told me that she and Greg were going to use student nurses from the University of Northern Colorado School of Nursing as babysitters at first. After all, both she and Greg have to go back to work at the university a couple of weeks after the baby is born."

"Oh, that's right. Neither Lisa nor Greg have tenured faculty positions with the university. Lisa is an instructor, and Greg is an IT specialist. So they can't afford to be away from their jobs for too long."

Cassie gazed off into the central yarn room. "You know, Eric and I talked about this once. He and I thought that when all of the kids are a little older, not babies anymore, maybe he and I could babysit all of them on a Saturday night when the Gang goes out. Molly and Jack, and Greg and Lisa's baby, too."

That image immediately formed in Kelly's mind. Cassie and Eric riding herd on a roomful of toddlers and preschoolers. "Wow, now that you mention it, I can picture it. Boy, you two would surely have your hands full."

"Ohhhhhhhh yeah," Cassie agreed with a smile. "Hey, have Greg and Lisa decided on a name for the baby yet?"

"They've come up with all sorts of names but haven't been able to decide on anything yet." Kelly grinned. "No surprise. Greg has to ponder over all the names. Of course."

"Of course," Cassie agreed, then laughed out loud.

Eleven

"**Do** you see what I see?" Kelly asked her dog, Carl. "There's a bushy-tailed critter that's sitting very still on the side fence." Kelly paused in the cottage patio doorway. Having spotted Carl's nemesis, Brazen Squirrel, she wondered how long it would take Carl to notice.

Carl ignored Kelly's observation and returned to slurp more water from his oversize water dish on the concrete patio. There were still scents to sniff in the backyard grass, and he had to figure out what animal intruder ventured into the cottage backyard last night. More importantly—there were naps to take.

Just then, Kelly's cell phone rang on the kitchen counter with a popular song from her playlist. Brazen Squirrel immediately started racing along the top rail of the fence. That quick movement caught Carl's attention, and he gave an

"Intruder Alert!" bark and ran for the back fence. Brazen was already tearing along the upper rail. He leaped into the air toward an overhanging cottonwood branch just as Carl threw himself into the fence, barking nonstop.

Kelly held her breath. No matter how many times she'd witnessed this little backyard drama, she was always afraid that Brazen Squirrel would mess up his frantic leap and land—oh no! Right in front of Carl. Kelly figured if that ever happened, she would run into the yard yelling and trying to distract Carl before he could chomp down on the little varmint. Even out the odds between Big Dog and Little Squirrel. But Brazen continued to be fleet of foot and escaped Big Dog yet again.

Kelly retrieved her cell phone and noticed Steve's name on the screen. "Hey there. What's up? It's only been an hour since you left."

"I got a call from the concrete supplier. He's going to be delayed and won't start to pour the foundation on one of the houses until this afternoon. So, I'm afraid I'll be home late."

"That's okay. I'll use it as an excuse to invite myself to dinner at Megan and Marty's tonight." She took a sip from her coffee mug.

"That's a great idea. I'll grab something to eat out here. So don't bother fixing anything for me. Besides, there are a bunch of leftovers in the fridge."

"That sounds like a plan. Enjoy the concrete pour," Kelly teased.

"I'll enjoy it a lot more when it's done. Gotta watch carefully to make sure everything is done right. Can't have one side of the basement too thick and another side too thin. Hey, how're you feeling?"

"Just fine. Nothing unusual happening. Jack alternates playing soccer and sleeping."

"So no beginning pains or contractions?"

Kelly could hear the anxious tone of Steve's voice. "Not a bit. Don't worry. I'll call you if anything exciting happens."

She slipped her fabric briefcase bag over her shoulder then headed toward the cottage front door, cell phone to her ear.

"Okay, that makes me feel better. I have my phone with me, as usual, if you need me."

"Got it. Stay away from the concrete pour. We don't want you stuck in the concrete foundation if Jack decides to come," she joked.

Steve laughed. "You got it. Talk to you later." His phone clicked off.

Kelly grabbed her coffee mug—complete with weakened brew—and headed out the front door. Another beautiful Colorado spring day. Temps had moderated and would make it into the low eighties today. With brilliant sunshine, of course. For the umpteenth time, Kelly gave thanks for being able to live in Colorado.

Yanking open the heavy wooden front door, Kelly walked inside the Lambspun shop. She was immediately treated to new yarns and new colors filling the foyer. The Lambspun elves had been at it again. All of the lighter and pastel spring colors were replaced by vibrant reds, velvet blues, blazing yellows, and jungle greens. Yarns were stacked on the antique dry sink in the foyer and spilling out of a well-traveled steamer trunk. Shawls and baby-sized sweaters dangled from the ceiling.

Rosa stepped around the corner then, holding several fat skeins of butter yellow yarn. "Hey there, Kelly. How're you feeling?"

Having adjusted to everyone asking her if she felt all right months ago, Kelly had decided that she was extremely lucky to be around so many people who cared about her. "I'm doing great, Rosa. Thanks for asking. Jack plays a little soccer then takes a nap. I hope he keeps that regular schedule after he's born." She fingered a soft royal blue yarn. Merino wool mixed with cotton. "I've got an appointment with my obstetrician this afternoon. Now that I'm in the ninth month, I have to check in weekly."

"That's excellent. Your obstetrician is being extra careful, which is really important in the last month. That's when a lot of women's blood pressure readings get elevated," Rosa said. "You have to be careful of that. Also, lab tests need to be run weekly on urine to guard against any hint of toxemia that might occur."

"I remember Megan saying that. But I didn't think toxemia was a threat nowadays with all the testing doctors do."

"Well, it can still happen. Especially with women who don't have regular OB checkups. Some women still show up in the emergency room just in time for delivery."

"I know that happens, but I'd like to think it's not that frequent," Kelly said, running her fingers over the butter yellow yarns in Rosa's arms. Soft, cottony soft.

"You'd be surprised, Kelly," Rosa said as she stacked the butter yellow yarns beside skeins of bright jungle green wool on the shelf of the antique dry sink that sat in the corner of the foyer. Right next to the butter yellow yarn, they made a brilliant contrast. "Geraldine is already in the knitting room, if you're looking for company."

"Good, I haven't seen her for a few days," Kelly said as she headed into the central yarn room. She spied Geraldine sitting at the end of the table, her lap covered with fire-engine red yarn. "Hey there, Geraldine. You're here earlier than usual."

Geraldine looked up and gave Kelly a big smile. "Hello, yourself, Kelly. You're looking good. That's always good news for the baby. A healthy mother usually leads to a healthy baby."

Kelly settled into a chair on the other side of the table. "I just had an interesting conversation with Rosa as she was putting out some new yummy yarns in the foyer. I mentioned that I was going to the obstetrician weekly now since I'm in the ninth month of pregnancy. That way the doctor can keep track of all those vital readings like blood pressure."

"That's very important. As well as urine tests for protein. Doctors need to keep track of that level as well," Geraldine said. "There are a lot of women out there, unfortunately, who are not able to see a doctor regularly. Some are in the urban areas but simply do not have the money for visits. And they do not know about any of the local clinics that provide free and reduced-rate health care visits. Then, there are many people who live away from the urban areas. If there are no doctors close by or they don't have access to a car, trying to see a doctor regularly is much harder."

"You're right, Geraldine," Kelly said. "I don't think most

of us realize how lucky we are to live where we do. Fort Connor has great doctors in every specialty, and excellent hospitals that rate at the top. We're all spoiled with excellent medical care." She pulled out the nearly finished baby hat from her knitting bag. "I'm hoping to finish this hat before Baby Jack arrives. Who knows? He may be able to wear it home from the hospital nursery. It's one hundred percent cotton, so there are no scratchy fibers to bother sensitive baby skin."

Geraldine eyed the baby hat from where she sat farther down from Kelly. "You should be able to, Kelly. It looks like you're nearly there. You've already transferred the stitches to the finishing needles."

A stray thought skipped through Kelly's mind, reminding her of something. "By the way, Geraldine, did you notice that short mention of Giselle Callahan's funeral in the paper a couple of days ago?"

"Yes, I did," Geraldine said, nodding as her fingers swiftly worked the yarn.

"There was no mention of how Giselle Callahan died. Simply the time and place of the funeral. My friend and her husband attended because William Callahan was a business associate."

"Yes, I noticed that. Callahan probably put in a call to the newspaper office and asked them to be discreet. My husband and I also attended the funeral. I must say, William Callahan looked positively awful. His face was gray, and there were lines and creases that had never appeared before."

Kelly remembered something else. "Was Callahan's son,

Henry, there? Considering how he may have felt about his father's younger wife, I would be surprised if he came."

Geraldine glanced up with a wry smile. "You're right, Callahan Junior wasn't there. None of us who knew the couples were surprised." She knitted another row of fire-engine red stitches then looked at Kelly. "You know, someone else wasn't there. Our fellow knitter friend, Marie. Of course, her absence was totally understandable, considering she was Meredith Callahan's closest friend."

Kelly remembered Marie's emotional response to Kelly's questions a couple of weeks ago. "That's not surprising, considering the depth of her feelings when I spoke with her."

The sound of a clock chiming came from Geraldine's direction. "It still startles me when my phone rings," she said as she reached for the cell phone.

Kelly tuned out Geraldine's conversation for a couple of minutes, then decided now was a good time for some of that strange but drinkable green tea Julie suggested she try the other day. Kelly left the baby hat on the table and headed through the central yarn room toward the corridor. As soon as she entered the café, she spotted Burt standing beside the grill counter.

"Hey, Burt. How're you doing this morning?"

"Doing fine, Kelly, but more importantly, how are you feeling?"

Kelly laughed softly. "Everybody asks that every day. I'm still doing fine and so is Baby Jack." Then she signaled Julie, who was approaching from the front of the café. "Julie, can I have a cup of that weird, strong green tea you have, please?"

Julie's face lit up. "The matcha green? Sure thing, Kelly. I'm so glad you liked it enough to try again."

"'Liked' is too strong a word. 'Tolerate' is more like it. But I'm in an adventurous mood today."

Julie laughed as she walked away. Then Burt appeared from the corridor leading to the knitting shop, a take-out cup of coffee in his hand. He gestured to Kelly. "Why don't we have a little morning sit-down and catch up?" He pulled out a chair for Kelly at an empty table then sat across from her.

"Sounds good," Kelly said as she settled into the wooden chair. Baby Jack chose that moment to kick a goal, one foot pushing up. "Jack's at it again. Goal!"

Burt chuckled. "What can you expect? Both his parents are excellent athletes." He sipped his coffee.

Her recent conversation popped into Kelly's mind then. "Did you and Mimi go to Giselle Callahan's funeral? I was just talking with Geraldine at the knitting table, and she told me William Callahan looked awful. Not surprising."

"No, Mimi refused to go. Which is not surprising considering Meredith was Mimi's friend."

"Do police have any clues yet? You said they were going to question the local businesses across from the golf course. As well as the managers of the course."

"Yes, Dan said they have questioned all the neighboring businesses situated around the course. And some of the golf course managers. They're still trying to contact people. But so far, no one saw anything or even noticed anything unusual. That's understandable because the office is way down the course on the far side. So even if someone was staring toward the golf course, they wouldn't be able to see what happened. And, of course, they came to question the staff here at Lambspun first thing since the shop borders the golf course. It has the best view. And the staff all told me that none of them saw anything."

"And none of the brewery employees saw anything?"

"Apparently not. I'm afraid Dan and the guys have run into a brick wall. But there may be some other employees they haven't contacted yet."

"I wonder if they've questioned Callahan's son, Henry."

"I asked Dan, and he said they did question him, but he supposedly has an alibi. He was driving back from Denver at the time. Alone."

"Hmmmmmmm," Kelly pondered. "That's not much of an alibi. Everything depends on when he drove back, and if he has any proof he was in Denver. Like gas receipts or something."

Burt smiled. "Spoken like a sleuth. I'm sure Dan and the other detectives will follow up."

Julie walked up to the table then, ceramic mug in her hand. "One cup of matcha green tea. Enjoy." She placed the mug in front of Kelly.

"Thanks, Julie," Kelly said as the young waitress turned to a beckoning customer.

Burt chuckled. "I never thought I'd see the day when you actually chose to drink tea instead of coffee. Will wonders never cease?"

Kelly lifted the mug and blew on the hot liquid. "Believe me, it's not a choice, really. It's simply gotten to the point that I can barely gag down that weak coffee." She made a face while Burt laughed. Then she took a sip of the matcha green tea and then another. "It's not as bad as I thought it would be at first." She took another sip. "Tolerable. Not good, but tolerable."

"Damning with faint praise once again. Now I've seen everything," Burt said with a grin.

Kelly slipped the blue and white patterned maternity dress over her head, then stepped into her sandals once again. Her obstetrician's nurse poked her head around the exam room door. "Dr. Jefferson will be with you in a moment."

"Okay," Kelly said and settled into a chair beside the doctor's desk. A few moments later, a knock sounded at the exam room door.

"All clear," Kelly said with a smile.

Dr. Jefferson opened the door and stepped inside. "The lab tests are finished, and all your levels look good, Kelly. Urine levels are good. Blood pressure is still good. Everything looks great. I can't tell you how glad I am that you're an athlete and are so healthy. Exercising every day is such an important part of a healthy lifestyle, but so many women simply don't make it a habit." He pushed his glasses to the top of his nose then sat down in the desk chair. "We encourage them as much as we can, but we sure can't do it for them."

"I've noticed the same thing, Doctor. People will listen to your advice, but they don't follow through. Some are able to change, but not everyone. The owner of Lambspun knitting and fiber shop, Mimi, and her husband, Burt, started jogging a few years ago, and they've made it a habit. They both lost weight and are in much better shape now than they were before."

Dr. Jefferson closed the file folder in front of him. "As you mentioned once before, Baby Jack seems pretty comfortable where he is for now. Heartbeat is strong. And you've said he's kicking a lot."

"Playing soccer is more like it," Kelly joked.

Dr. Jefferson chuckled. "I can picture that. But he's bound to make a move sometime this month. Until then, we'll keep weekly tabs on you. Are you still taking your pregnancy vitamins?"

"Absolutely," Kelly answered with a smile, then followed it with a little salute.

Dr. Jefferson smiled. "All righty, then. Check with my nurse and the appointment desk in the front, and we'll schedule next week's appointment."

"Sounds like a plan," Kelly said.

Dr. Jefferson rose from his chair. "And let us know whenever you experience regularly recurring contractions. That's important."

Kelly slowly rose from her chair. "Don't worry, Doc. I will. I can't wait until Jack moves out and I can start moving normally again. I've felt like I'm walking through molasses this month. Especially since the baby dropped."

Dr. Jefferson paused with his hand on the doorknob of the examining room. "Jack is getting ready, that's for sure," he said with a smile. "Take care of yourself, Kelly. And Baby Jack. I'll see you next week."

"See you next week," Kelly said as he disappeared out the door.

• • •

Kelly pulled into Megan and Marty's driveway as her cell phone rang. She turned off the ignition before answering. "How was the doctor visit?" Steve's voice came over the line. A loud banging in the distance echoed in the background.

"He said I'm doing great. All the lab tests are normal. Blood pressure is still good. He said Jack's heartbeat was strong. So, we're all just waiting for Jack to move out."

"Any pains? Any signs of the contractions?"

Kelly could hear the worry in Steve's voice even with all the construction background noise. "Nope. Nary a one. So we're still in Waiting Mode. Nothing happening. How's it going over there?"

"We're good. The guys are starting to pour now. So I'd better get over there. Take it easy and say 'hi' to Marty and Megan for me."

"Will do. See you later."

"Love you."

"Love you, too," Kelly said, then clicked off her cell phone as she slowly climbed out of her car. She reached inside for the bouquet of coral roses Mimi had given her this afternoon. "Early bloomers," Mimi had called them.

"Hey there," Marty called from their open front door. "Let me take those, Kelly." He hastened down the front sidewalk and took the bouquet from her hands. He also took hold of Kelly's arm. "You're looking a little tired. Are you feeling okay?"

"Oh yeah. I just went over to the obstetrician's office this afternoon. Everything's fine. All vital signs are normal. Lab tests, too. So, I'm good."

"Just tired, right?" Marty smiled at her solicitously.

"Yeah, kind of."

"I recognize that look. Megan looked tired those last couple of weeks, too. It won't be long, Kelly."

"I sure hope not," Kelly said with a little laugh.

Twelve

"These are really pretty, Cassie. Thank you so much," Kelly said as she looked at the colorful bouquet of blooming spring flowers—coral-colored roses, red roses, bright orange daisies, and yellow-as-butter daffodils.

"You're welcome," Cassie said. "I found the coral roses and the red rose blossoms in Mimi's front yard where it gets sunshine all day. Eric brought the daffodils and daisies. His mom has a big flower garden with a ton of daffodils and daisies. She told Eric he could have as many as we needed."

"You did a great job. Thank you so much. I love it."

"I'll keep it in the fridge so it'll stay fresh until Saturday," Cassie said as she took the bouquet and placed it in the fridge at the rear of the kitchen area.

Kelly settled into a chair at one of the café tables in the

back alcove. "How's it feel to be out of school and working at the café again?"

"Great. I actually like meeting lots of people," Cassie said as she wiped an empty tabletop.

"Steve says Eric's doing real well. Steve and the construction crew keep him busy."

"Oh, Eric loves working there. He told me so. Just watching an entire house being built is cool, he said. He watched his uncle's crew build an extension to the end of the stables once. But that's not the same as a house with all the plumbing and wiring."

Burt entered the back of the café then. "Hey, you two," he greeted them.

"Hey, Burt. You want me to get you some more coffee for that empty mug?" Cassie asked as Burt walked over to Kelly's table.

"How could you tell it's empty?" Burt asked with a wry smile.

"By the way you're holding it," Cassie said with a grin. "Sit down with Kelly, while I take care of the coffee." She took the ceramic mug from Burt's outstretched hand and walked over to the grill counter.

"She's observant. That's good," Kelly said, glancing to Burt as he settled into a chair across the table from her.

"That's for sure," Burt agreed. "Listen, Kelly, I remembered something as Mimi and I were driving to the shop this morning, and I wanted to ask you. Have you and Steve got a marriage license yet? If not, you'd better get it done. Ceremony is the day after tomorrow, Saturday."

"Don't worry. Steve's already done it. He showed it to me

last week. He wanted to have it in case we did something spur-of-the-moment."

Burt visibly relaxed in the chair. "Oh good. That was bedeviling me all the way into the shop this morning."

Cassie reappeared at their table and offered Burt his mug. "All done. Nice and full, Burt. With two creams."

"Now that's what I call service."

"Gotta get back to my customers. Jennifer's working outside this morning."

Kelly saluted Cassie with her mug. "Talk to you later."

"That girl is a jewel. I swear she is," Burt said, then blew on his coffee.

"She sure is," Kelly said. She sipped her coffee. "By the way, have the police found any more clues to that Giselle Callahan murder?"

Burt's brow furrowed. "No, I'm afraid they haven't. They've come to a dead end, Dan says. No one at the brewery saw anything. And none of the employees of the golf course noticed anything, either. Of course, the golf course office is far down at the other end of the course, so that's understandable." He took another sip of his coffee. "Not many people are around in the late afternoon. The café is closed, and the Lambspun windows only have a good view of half of the golf course. Those thick bushes block the other half."

Kelly gave Burt a skeptical look. "But still . . . a woman gets her throat cut right out there on the golf course, and no one sees anything?" She shook her head in obvious disbelief.

"It's not that hard to imagine," Burt said. "If the killer had the razor blade in one hand and quickly stepped up behind Giselle Callahan, he could have slashed the blade across her throat in a couple of seconds. Then he could simply have stepped away as she fell to the ground, dead."

The image of that moment formed in Kelly's mind. Burt was right. It wouldn't take long. One swift movement, and it would be done. *Gruesome*, Kelly thought, feeling a little shiver.

"You're right," she admitted. "Gruesome as it is, it wouldn't take long. Without anyone else around on the course to see anything, no one could rush to the victim's aid."

"And it only takes two to three minutes for someone to bleed out from a massive wound like that. I asked one of the emergency room doctors that question once. And I was amazed by his answer."

"I think I heard that once before, too. It's always surprised me that it's so quick. How could anyone be rescued?"

"It would be almost impossible. Unless someone was attacked inside the emergency room of a hospital." He gave her a wry smile. "And that would be highly unlikely."

Kelly pondered for a second. "Well, no wonder police haven't found any witnesses. Someone would have to be right there on the golf course close to that exact location in order to see anything. And if someone did see something, I'm sure they'd contact police straightaway."

"Precisely."

"Brother, I wonder if Dan and his detectives will ever find the murderer."

"Time will tell, Kelly. It's amazing how bits and pieces of information appear here and there. It's like solving a puzzle." Burt glanced at his watch. "I've got to do some spinning today, or we won't have enough to display in the front entry.

Someone came in yesterday and bought five skeins of that merino wool and cotton blend Mimi created. Cream-colored."

"Goodness, that's a lot. Who bought it? One of our regulars?"

"No, neither Mimi nor I have ever seen her before. She told Mimi she was from Johnstown."

"That's just down the interstate. Maybe she heard about Lambspun and decided to check out the shop for herself. And fell in love, of course," Kelly said with a little laugh.

Burt chuckled. "Our biggest fan. Come on, join me in the main room while I spin. You always say it's restful watching the spinners." He rose from his chair.

"That it is, Burt. I think I'll take your advice." Kelly picked up her empty mug and followed after him as he headed toward the corridor.

"Hey there, Burt. Kelly," Rosa said as they entered the central yarn room. She looked up from stacking more skeins of butter yellow yarn on the shelves.

"Hey, Rosa," Burt said. "I'm going to start spinning in the main room. Trying to catch up with customer demand for Mimi's handspun mohair and cotton combination."

"Maybe we should call it Burt's Handspun," Rosa teased.

"Hey, Rosa," Kelly said, raising her hand in greeting as she followed Burt to the main knitting room.

"Oh goodness, Kelly." Rosa wagged her head. "You've come back to put us all on the edge of our seats. Waiting for Baby Jack to make a move."

Kelly laughed as she pulled out a chair at the knitting table. "Jack hasn't made a move in over an hour. So I think he's taking a nap. This morning he had soccer practice. Running up and down the field." She settled into the chair.

"Here, Kelly. I was going to pull out your chair, but you beat me to it," Burt said. "Oh well. At least I can get you something comfy to sit on. How about a couple of skeins of alpaca yarn?"

Kelly looked up in surprise. "What?" she said, trying not to laugh. "You want me to sit on those nice skeins fresh out of the yarn bins? I'll squash them flat. I've gained twenty-one pounds with Baby Jack."

"That's okay. The alpaca will bounce right back," he said with a grin. He reached into the yarn bins and drew out two large skeins of cream-colored yarn. "Here we go. Baby alpaca. Softest of the soft," Burt said as he placed the two skeins on the seat of Kelly's chair.

Kelly smiled at her old friend, mentor, and father figure. Her dear friend. "Burt, you're a hoot and a half, as Jayleen would say."

Burt chuckled. "That does sound familiar. And I bet Jayleen would laugh herself senseless if she saw me putting the yarn on your chair."

"You're right about that, Burt. In Jayleen's words, she would 'bust a gut' laughing."

Both Kelly and Burt laughed out loud, picturing another dear friend's reaction to the comfy yarn seat.

As Burt was checking the spinning wheel, Megan walked into the main room. "Ah, ha! Here you are," she said as she strode over to Kelly and Burt.

"Hey, Megan, what's up?" Kelly asked her friend, recognizing Megan had a determined look on her face.

"You've got one of those looks on your face, Megan," Burt said with a grin. "What's up?"

"You took the words right out of my mouth, Burt," Kelly teased.

Megan cocked her head to the side. "You're going to have to take a break from the accounting spreadsheets, Kelly, because you and I are going shopping." She gave Kelly a big smile.

"Shopping?" Kelly said, clearly surprised at the suggestion. "For what?"

"For a pretty maternity dress. A dressy one, I hope."

"Why? I've got plenty of maternity dresses in the closet. Jack's about ready to move out anyway," she joked.

Megan rolled her eyes, causing Burt to start laughing. "You need something special for Saturday," she declared, using her "And that's that!" tone of voice, Kelly noticed.

"Just go along with her, Kelly," Burt advised with a sly smile. "You won't be able to talk her out of it. This is Megan, remember?"

Kelly joined in Burt's laughter. "Okay, okay, where are we going?" Kelly pushed back her chair and rose.

"Oh, I've seen a new place open up, and it has a line of very stylish maternity clothes. I went in earlier this morning to check them out. So, c'mon." She beckoned as she headed toward the corridor. "Follow me."

"It's better to just give in and go along," Burt advised with a wink. "Arguing with Megan is not productive."

"Yes, I know. I've tried it in the past," Kelly joked as she grabbed her shoulder bag and obediently followed Megan into the corridor.

• • •

Kelly turned sideways and looked into the dressing room's full-length mirror. "This is actually pretty," she said, checking the frontal view again.

"Yes, and that sky blue shade is very flattering on you," Megan said, observing Kelly's image in the mirror.

Kelly captured the dangling price tag and checked the price. "And it's not outrageously expensive. Maybe I can have it altered after Jack, so I can wear it again."

"That's a good idea. I had several of those lacy blouses I wore while I was carrying Molly altered. I can give you the name of my seamstress if you need it," Megan offered.

"Remind me in a couple of months," Kelly teased. "I've got so many things already on my To-Do Before Baby list."

Megan laughed out loud at that. "Will do."

"Mimi's keeping me updated on how the plans for Saturday are coming along. And Cassie, of course. She's fantastic. She asked me a couple days ago what kind of fresh flowers I liked so she could make a bouquet. And today she showed me this beautiful bouquet of roses, daisies, and daffodils. All are from Mimi's yard or Eric's mother's garden. I just love it. Red, coral, yellow, and orange. All fresh."

"Cassie is a real 'doer,' that's for sure. Most kids her age aren't involved in as much as she is, and she handles it easily." She motioned at Kelly. "Turn around and I'll unzip you."

Kelly turned her back to Megan. "I know. She's working six days a week in the café with Pete and Jennifer, handling both breakfast and lunch. Then she's going to softball practice and playing games two or three times a week. Most kids aren't half that busy."

"I know. Most kids work a few hours a week at a fast-food restaurant and call it good." Megan unzipped the back of the dress. "Here, I'll hold it while you step out."

Kelly carefully stepped out of the dress. Her protruding tummy had caused her to alter her balance somewhat. "And the same is true for Eric. He's working all day either on his mom and dad's ranch or over at Steve's building site. Carrying lumber, hammering nails, fetching whatever the builders and construction crew need."

"Boy, that is valuable experience," Megan said as she arranged the dress back on its hanger. "I'll take this up front while you finish getting dressed, okay? I feel a little nervous having you out here at the shopping mall. Just in case Baby Jack gets antsy." She gave Kelly a smile.

"Got it. I think he's sleeping right now, so we're safe." Then, Kelly remembered something. A stray thought that was way in the back of her mind. "Hold on a minute, Megan. I've been wanting to ask you something that's been lurking in the back of my mind, and Pregnancy Brain keeps forgetting it."

"Sure," Megan said as she leaned against the dressing room wall. "What is it?"

"What is the status of Pete and Jennifer's official attempt to legally adopt Cassie? I know they asked Marty to handle it," Kelly said as she slipped on the maternity dress she wore to the shop.

Megan sighed. "It's moving along, but slowly. Legal proceedings like that can take a long time. There are only so many slots on a family court judge's calendar each month. And some cases tie up several days when both parties want to argue."

"But I didn't think that would happen in this case," Kelly said in concern. "After all, Tanya has willingly agreed to let her brother, Pete, be awarded legal custody of Cassie. Pete has assured Tanya she can see Cassie anytime. So, there's no disagreement at all."

"Mainly I think it's the slowness of the family court's schedule," Megan said. "That's been compounded by the illness of one of the court's judges. Judge Jane Seaworth was off the bench for six months for breast cancer treatment. She was operated on, went through chemotherapy, and is exercising now to regain her strength. She's slowly recuperating, her husband says. Hopefully, she will return sometime next month, and then the court's schedule should move faster. We hope." She held up two crossed fingers. "But as far as legal proceedings go, we all know how slowly some cases move along."

Kelly straightened her dress and fastened the front buttons. "Has Cassie had to show up in court yet? I know that older kids are often asked questions to make sure they are in favor of the new arrangement."

Megan smiled. "Yes, she did. Cassie did great, too. She was very composed and told the judge she wanted to stay with her uncle Pete and Jennifer."

"Excellent."

"A couple of months before, Cassie was interviewed at the Judicial Center downtown by the family court's counselor and questioned about her decision. She told Marty afterwards that she told the counselor straight out that her mother would have to come here to Fort Connor to see her. Cassie refused to go to Denver and stay over with her mother again. And she told the counselor exactly what Tanya's boyfriend tried to do and how she had to leave the apartment at night to get away from him."

Kelly grinned. "Good for her."

"Yeah, Marty was real proud of her for standing up," Megan said with a nod. "So all we have to do now is wait for the family court schedule to move along."

"That's encouraging news, in my opinion," Kelly said. "I've got a good feeling about all of this, Megan. Let's hope that things get resolved in Cassie's favor sometime this summer. That would be great."

"That's what we're all hoping," Megan said before she disappeared behind the dressing room curtain.

Kelly glanced at the familiar jazz trio playing at the front of the Jazz Bistro's bar and lounge as she sipped her glass of orange juice. A pianist, string bass player, and drummer created a smooth melody that still had a jazz bounce to it. "You know, those three guys have such a smooth, harmonious sound. They must have played together for years," she observed.

"Probably," Steve said with a nod, then sipped his glass of amber ale. "Then again, I've heard some musicians say they will actually put a group together right before they play a gig." He shrugged. "It's gotta be a learned skill." He took another sip.

"Would you like another Fat Tire, sir?" a waiter asked when he approached their table.

"No, thanks. We'll be heading back home in a few minutes. Jack's mom needs her rest."

The young waiter looked puzzled for a second and peered at Steve, then Kelly. "I'm guessing Jack is someone else, because you're not old enough to be his mom." The waiter jerked his thumb at Steve.

Kelly smiled at him as Steve chuckled beside her. "You're right. Jack's the baby," he said, glancing toward Kelly.

The young waiter laughed. "That explains it."

"You'll have to excuse our playfulness. The baby will be coming any day now, and we're getting excited," she said.

"That's understandable," the waiter said with a smile. "You folks enjoy the rest of your evening. And just signal me if you'd like something else from the bar." The waiter moved to another table in the lounge.

Kelly set her glass on the white cloth–covered table and leaned back against the comfortable cushioned seat. The trio was playing a familiar song but with a totally new jazzed-up rhythm. "I'm so glad we took the time to come here tonight. It's so relaxing."

"I know. And we can both use the relaxation when we can get it," Steve said.

Kelly laughed softly. "You make it sound like we're not going to get here after Jack is born."

Steve shrugged. "Well, those first few months will be pretty intense, from what everyone says."

She grinned. "Are those guys on your construction crew still trying to scare you?"

He chuckled. "They're doing their best. Telling me to 'kiss my free time good-bye' and all that."

"Well, we'll simply have to make sure we take time for

ourselves. Mimi and Burt have been telling me that over and over. They say that you and I have to regularly schedule time for ourselves. Have date nights and stuff like that."

Steve smiled. "Date nights, huh? That sounds like a good idea."

"And they offer themselves as willing babysitters, too," Kelly added.

"Really? Well, we may take them up on it. But we'll be using that nursing student for the early weeks, right? The one who babysat for Megan and Marty."

Kelly nodded. "Yes, that's right. Megan gave me her phone number, and I confirmed with her a month ago that we would be able to use her services this summer. I think Molly was four months old when Megan and Marty came to their first game alone together."

"Oh yeah, I remember," Steve said. "They took turns coming to games before that. One stayed home with Molly and the other one would come out to a game."

Kelly shrugged. "Let's see how we like doing that. After a while, we may start taking Jack out to the games, too. We can sit in the shady part of the back bleachers. That never gets any sun."

Steve nodded. "Yeah. It'll be summertime, too, so no one should have the flu and start sneezing."

Kelly laughed. "Good point. As long as we wrap enough blankets around him, he won't get cold."

"Get cold in July and August?" Steve teased. "I don't think so."

"Don't you remember how many blankets Megan wrapped around Molly?"

"Okay, we'll pack extra blankets and stuff in that baby bag or diaper bag, so we'll have it covered." Steve leaned back into the booth seat and gave Kelly a wry smile. "Boy, it'll be like packing for an excursion every time we go out the door."

"You got it," Kelly agreed, joining his laughter.

Steve reached into his pocket and brought out a small black velvet box. "I think this is a good time," he said with a smile. Then he opened the little box and held it out for Kelly to see.

Kelly caught her breath. A gorgeous diamond ring sparkled back at her, flashing fire in the café's table light. "Oh, Steve," she breathed. She had no other words.

"Do you like it?" he asked, almost sounding concerned that she might not.

"Oh yes . . . yes . . ." she whispered. She looked into his eyes. "It's beautiful . . . I . . . I don't know what to say . . ."

Steve's smile lit his face. "Just say 'yes.'" He lifted her hand and slipped the ring on her finger. "Say you will be my wife."

Kelly looked back into his eyes, her heart overflowing with pure joy. "Yes . . . of course . . . a thousand times 'yes.'"

He grinned. "Just one will do." Then he reached over the table and brought her face closer for a lingering kiss.

Thirteen

Steve held out his open palm and gave Kelly a big grin. "You ready?"

Kelly smiled into Steve's eyes and placed her hand in his. "Absolutely."

"Let's do it," Steve said, then glanced around the cluster of friends surrounding them and spoke to the young man wearing a dark blue suit. "Ready, Pastor Quinlan?"

"You bet," Pastor Quinlan said, his round face spread even wider with a smile. "All you folks want to make a semicircle around the three of us? That way you can gather close."

"Sure thing," Marty said, then gestured to the others. "C'mon, guys. Let's circle up."

Kelly watched as Jennifer and Pete, Mimi and Burt, Megan and Marty, Lisa and Greg, and Jayleen and Curt dutifully moved into position, forming an expanded semicircle surrounding Kelly and Steve. Pete wrapped his arm around Cassie's shoulders as she stood beside him, while Eric went to his grandfather Curt's side.

"Good job, folks," Pastor Quinlan praised, his smile spreading. "You follow directions well."

"First time for everything, Pastor," Curt spoke up in a dry voice.

Kelly and Steve joined their friends' laughter, which rippled around the semicircle as Pastor Quinlan began speaking, holding his arms wide open. Kelly recognized words and phrases she'd heard for a lifetime whenever she'd attended other wedding ceremonies.

"Do you take this woman to be your lawfully wedded wife?" Pastor Quinlan asked Steve.

"You bet I do," Steve said, his grin spread wide.

Pastor Quinlan turned to Kelly. "And do you take this man to be your lawfully wedded husband?"

Kelly shifted her gaze to Steve's, and she smiled as wide as her face would allow. "Yes, I do. Absolutely, yes."

"Then I pronounce you husband and wife." Pastor Quinlan held up his hands in a sign of blessing. "God bless you both."

"Hallelujah!" Jayleen called out.

"It's about time!" Curt added.

Kelly barely heard her friends' laughter. She threw both arms around Steve's neck as he swept her up in a deep kiss and embrace.

"Here, Kelly, sit down," Burt said, patting the lawn chair beside him.

"Actually, it feels good to stand up," Kelly said, giving a little stretch. "I've been sitting so much."

"Take my advice and sit more now," Burt said with a grin. "You and Steve may be walking the floor pretty soon." He patted the chair beside him again.

Kelly laughed softly as she followed Burt's advice. She was surprised how tired her back was getting, carrying around twenty pounds of extra weight. "Oooooo, that does feel good," she admitted, sinking back against the cushioned chair.

"I knew it would," Burt said, laughing softly. "You're not the first pregnant lass I've been around."

"Nor the last," Kelly said with a smile. "Lisa is due sometime in late November or early December, she thinks."

"That's a gorgeous ring, Kelly," Burt said, pointing to her sparkling diamond on the gold band around her finger.

"It sure is," Kelly said softly, staring at the new adornment. She wasn't used to wearing much jewelry. "My hand almost feels heavier now."

Burt chuckled, then gazed off to the side of the yard, where Mimi planted her flower garden. Colorful spring annuals were blooming, and the yellow sunflowers and bright orange zinnias flaunted their colors. Mimi's rosebushes were filled with bright coral-colored and red blossoms.

"It's hard to believe so much has happened these past few years. It's been wonderful to watch all of you girls as you built your lives. I feel privileged to have been able to witness it all and occasionally participate. You girls are like daughters to me, you know." He turned to Kelly, a smile warming his gaze.

"We know, Burt." Kelly returned the warmth. "And all of us treasure that. And you, too."

"And I'll repeat the standing offer to bring Baby Jack over as soon as you and Steve start going out with friends again. Mimi and I love to babysit."

Kelly laughed softly. "Don't worry. We've got you at the top of our list."

"Good. Megan and Marty said they will bring Molly over starting this month as Molly turns one year old. Mimi and I are looking forward to the little redhead's visit."

"You'll have to let us know how it goes. Molly can be a little terror, I've heard."

"Oh yes. Mimi and I have heard all the stories. Plus, other folks' tales from the knitting shop."

"Then you'll be properly forewarned and prepared with lots of toys and some good cookies, too. Megan-approved, of course."

"Of course," Burt said with a twinkle in his eye. "Whatever would we all do without Megan shepherding us around?"

Kelly laughed out loud at that.

Steve walked up to them then, a bottle of Fat Tire ale in his hand. "What's so funny, you two?"

"Ohhh, we were simply sharing Megan the Shepherd stories," Burt chortled.

Steve pulled up a lawn chair beside Kelly. "How're you feeling?"

Kelly spotted the slight concern in his eyes. "I'm fine. I was just getting a little tired. Baby Jack is getting heavier by the day, I think."

Steve placed his open palm over Kelly's belly. "Hey there, Slugger. Take it easy on your mom, okay?"

Baby Jack gave a kick in reply, his foot pushing up. "I

think he's ignoring you. He just kicked another goal," Kelly said.

Burt chuckled then called out as Eric approached them. "Hey, Eric. It's good to see you."

"Thanks. It's good to see all of you, too," Eric said as he walked up. "I get to see Steve every day at the building site over in Wellesley. But I don't get to see everyone else unless they come to our ball games."

"Steve says you're doing a good job over at the construction site," Kelly said, watching Eric's face light up.

"We're keeping him busy, that's for sure," Steve said, leaning back into his chair, arm still around Kelly's shoulders.

"That's a great opportunity, Eric," Burt added. "You're getting a chance to learn some of the construction business. That always comes in handy."

"That's what Grandpa Curt says," Eric said with a grin. "And I like working there, too. It's cool to watch a hole in the ground turn into a finished house."

Steve chuckled. "It sure is."

"Are you two going on a honeymoon or something?" Eric asked, gesturing to both Kelly and Steve.

"We already took a vacation last fall down in the sunny Caribbean," Kelly said, remembering the warm temps and beautiful beaches. "We figured this summer would be taken up with Baby Jack."

"You figured right, you two," Burt said.

"You're going to bring him to some of our games this summer, aren't you?" Eric asked. "Megan and Marty used to take turns coming to games after Molly was born."

"We may do that. Or we may just use one of those nursing students to babysit so we can come out and see you guys play," Steve promised with a smile.

Eric grinned. "Good. We miss all that extra cheering."

Baby Jack gave another strong kick just then, so Kelly said, "Put your hand over here, Eric. Jack is kicking soccer goals."

Eric reached out, and Kelly took his outstretched hand, then placed it right where Baby Jack had last kicked. Jack wiggled a bit then let fly a big kick that caused Kelly's stomach to bulge as a baby foot pushed upward.

Eric laughed as his eyes lit up. "Whoa! That is so cool!"

"It sure is," Steve agreed with a smile, "but right now, Jack's mom is getting real tired of lugging him around. So we're all hoping he'll get a move on and come out to greet us pretty soon."

Eric glanced up at Kelly's face. "Yeah. He's gotten bigger, and it looks like he's down lower, somehow. I don't know."

"You're absolutely right, Eric," Kelly said, smiling into the sharp teenager's face. "That's pretty observant of you to notice, too. Babies shift lower in their mothers' bellies before they're ready to come."

Eric pondered for a couple of seconds. "I don't remember noticing that with my mom when my younger sister was born five years ago. But I do remember Mom looking kind of tired or sleepy afterwards in the hospital."

"I'll bet she was," Burt agreed.

Cassie walked up then, a bottle of iced tea in her hand. "Hey, guys. Is Kelly feeling all right?"

"She sure is," Steve said, giving Cassie a wink.

Cassie looked relieved. "Oh good. Eric and I have been

reading about all kinds of situations that might happen. His mom has this huge book that goes through everything that can happen in pregnancies."

"Good Lord," Burt said, shaking his head. "Don't get yourselves all wound up with all those emergency situations. Kelly's going to be just fine. She's healthy as that proverbial horse. Apologies to the bride, of course."

Kelly started to laugh, watching Father Figure Burt explaining.

"Now I'm curious," Eric said, cocking his head to the side, a slight smile forming. "What the heck is a 'proverbial horse'?"

At that, everyone burst out laughing.

Fourteen

Kelly took a deep sip from her ceramic mug of matcha green tea—the strange but tolerable hot beverage she'd adopted to take her through the last weeks of her pregnancy. She also noticed she was no longer falling asleep as much in the afternoons. Tabbing through client Don Warner's expenses spreadsheet on her laptop computer, Kelly added the few expenses yet to be included in the column totals.

Cassie looked up from the winding table in the front room of Lambspun where she was turning a skein of the butter yellow yarn into a round, fat ball. "You know, I always think it's funny to be selling wool yarns once our temperatures have risen to summertime hot."

"I agree with you, Cassie," Kelly said, totaling another column of expenses.

Rosa glanced around the empty front room as she rearranged items on the counter. "I feel the same way. That's why I switch to wet felting decorative pieces in the summer. It may not make sense, but that's what I do."

"Your wet felting pieces are beautiful, Rosa. And I'm so glad Mimi convinced you to let her sell some of them in the shop." Kelly pointed to the opposite wall where a dramatic combination of greens, blues, and purples was displayed.

"And Rosa has already sold one of them this month," Cassie said, her left hand busily turning the yarn winder while her right hand steadied the ever-fattening ball of butter yellow yarn.

"Thanks for the compliments, you two. I really enjoy wet felting. It's such a unique process."

"I made one wet felted piece a few years ago, and it's hanging over in the cottage. But lacking Rosa's talent, I simply switch to knitting with cotton yarns in the summer," Kelly joked.

Mimi appeared then, as she stepped down into the front room. Gesturing around the room, she continued what was obviously her conversation with someone. "This is where we have all the extras, 'the notions' as my mother and grandmother used to call them. The buttons, zippers, and decorative items we use on our knitted and crocheted garments."

Kelly noticed the young woman appeared to be pregnant. Not as far along as Kelly, but it was obvious. Kelly had learned long ago not to assume until it was abundantly clear that a woman was going to give birth. "Better safe than sorry," she remembered Aunt Helen saying in situations like that.

"Kelly, Cassie. This is Dee Dee. She's a new student in my beginner sweater class," Mimi introduced.

"Hi, Dee Dee," Kelly said. "That sweater must be coming along nicely if you're looking at buttons."

"Mimi thinks it is," Dee Dee said with a little laugh. "I still think it looks kind of weird."

"Don't worry. It'll look much better after blocking," Mimi reassured her. "Meanwhile, you can think about what kind of buttons you want to use."

Dee Dee glanced around the notions area. "Oh wow, there really is a large selection here. This is going to take me a while to decide," she said, her face lighting up. "Is it all right if I take some time to browse?"

Mimi gave her what Kelly recognized as a Mother Mimi smile. "Of course you can, dear. Browse away to your heart's content." At that, Mimi returned to her usual spot behind the front counter.

Just then, Baby Jack started soccer practice, and Kelly watched a familiar bulge appear. "Jack's playing soccer again," she said. "And he just scored another goal."

Cassie giggled. "Go, Jack, go!"

"Soccer goals, huh?" Dee Dee said as she browsed the buttons. "I have to remember that. I started playing soccer at six years old. I even went to university on a soccer scholarship. So, Emma will probably start doing the same thing as she gets further along."

Cassie stopped winding and turned to Dee Dee. "You went to university on a soccer scholarship? That's cool! Did it pay for your bills?"

"Oh no, it only paid for a portion of the tuition. But it sure helped."

"I had a similar experience, Cassie. I got a small softball scholarship years ago when I went to the University of Virginia. My father had saved up a little for my college, but I had to work part-time jobs and summer jobs plus use student loans for the rest of the fees. Softball and soccer aren't big enough sports to rate a full scholarship at some universities. Those usually go to the students who play football, basketball, and volleyball."

Cassie pondered for a few seconds. "Okay. I understand. Those football and basketball games always have a lot of fans coming to the stadiums. Volleyball, too. So that makes sense."

"Absolutely, and a lot of those games get broadcast on television, too," Kelly added. "That means sometimes the universities get paid by advertising companies. They know there will be a large audience because so many people enjoy watching."

"That's for sure," Dee Dee agreed. "You can see volleyball games on television that are being played all over the country and even in other countries around the world."

Cassie pondered again. "The YMCA gym is full of guys playing basketball games every night. And lots of volleyball games going on, too. Several teams are coed. I've seen them. Not as many people play football, though."

"Probably because tackle football requires wearing pads or you can break a shoulder. They'll play tag football instead," Kelly said.

"They should switch to soccer," Cassie decreed as she returned to winding yarn.

Kelly grinned. "You've made a good point, Cassie. They'd get a ton more exercise playing soccer, too. You are running that field back and forth, back and forth."

"Tell me about it," Dee Dee said with a little laugh. "Not much running these days, though."

A funny memory tickled the back of Kelly's mind, then. She decided to share it since it would make Cassie laugh. "You know, several of us played on coed volleyball teams a few years ago. Megan and I were both playing on one team. And Steve and Marty were playing on another coed team."

"That sounds like fun," Cassie said, as she continued to wind the yellow yarn.

More memories surged forward, and Kelly grinned. "That was during a weird time when Steve and I were not talking to each other; not going out together, either. In fact, we didn't see each other at all. Whenever I'd go over to see Megan and Marty, Lisa and Greg, and Jennifer and Pete, Steve wasn't there. And the reverse would happen whenever Steve went to visit them. I wouldn't be there."

The yarn winder stopped turning immediately. Cassie turned in her chair instead. "What! Why?"

Kelly laughed. "Like I said, it was a weird time. I'd said something to Steve that he didn't like, and he got mad. I came back to the cottage where we were both living together, and Steve had moved out completely. His clothes were gone, everything. Even his toothbrush." Kelly shook her head, thinking back now over the incident that caused their breakup.

Cassie stared back at Kelly, her eyes wide, clearly incredulous at what she was hearing. "I can't believe that. What did you say?"

Kelly let out a sigh, realizing she would have to explain more for the story to make sense to Cassie. "Well, let me back up some and try to explain. The recession had hit Northern Colorado like it did everywhere in the country, and builders and developers either shut down their housing developments or slowed them to a crawl. Some builders went out of business completely. No one was buying houses. Steve was hanging on by his fingernails. Everything he'd worked so hard for was slipping through his fingers, and he couldn't stop it. He'd even had to sell his properties in Old Town. Anyway, one night we'd come from being with the Gang, and Marty and Megan announced they were going to get married. Later, when Steve and I were back at the cottage, he suddenly, out of the blue, asked me if I wanted to get married, too."

Cassie was listening attentively, Kelly noticed. And Dee Dee was looking over at them from across the room where she was checking buttons. Even Rosa glanced over from her spot behind the front counter.

"You said 'yes,' didn't you?" Cassie demanded.

"Well . . ." Kelly started, wondering how to begin.

"No, she didn't!" Mimi's voice interjected. The smiling shop owner had suddenly appeared from around the corridor where she'd obviously been listening.

Cassie blinked, clearly astonished. "What!"

"Well . . ." Kelly tried again. "I didn't really say anything at first. I was so shocked that he even asked, I just stared at him. Then, I blurted out something like, 'Steve! You're barely holding on, and you want to get married?'"

Cassie's brown eyes got even wider. "Oh no . . ." she whispered.

"You didn't," Dee Dee ventured, looking as surprised as Cassie.

"Yeah, I did," Kelly confessed. "And I could tell from the look on his face that I'd said the wrong thing. The very worst thing. I could see that Steve was looking for reassurance. Everything else in his life was falling apart. And I acted like I was rejecting him. So, he walked away. The next day when I was at a client's office, he came and cleared out all his things. I was going to apologize and try to make up, but I never got the chance. Steve was gone." Kelly looked around at her transfixed audience.

"What happened then?" Cassie asked. "How'd you two get back together?"

"Yeah, this is a great story," Dee Dee said with a laugh. She gestured toward Kelly. "I take it this Steve is the father, right?"

Kelly laughed out loud at that. "Yes. Yes, he is. And we did get back together, but not right away. It took about a year—"

"What!"

"Didn't you two see each other around town or something?"

"Nope," Kelly said, shaking her head. "I was either working in the cottage across the driveway, here in Lambspun, or going to see my client in Denver or my other client's properties in Fort Connor. I kind of burrowed into my work. And so did Steve. Because the housing situation was so bad, he actually joined with a builder in Northern Colorado who had a commercial development he was working on along with some other commercial sites around Denver. So Steve was out of town all the time. He said he would often bunk at a friend's place in Denver or sleep in his car."

"Ohhhhhhhh, poor Steve," Cassie sympathized.

"Yes, poor Steve," Mimi echoed in a teasing tone from behind the counter. Rosa giggled.

"Hey, you two. I didn't make Steve sleep in his car," Kelly countered with a laugh. "All our friends said he just dropped out of everyone's lives for about six months and squirreled himself away in Denver."

"Squirreled away," Cassie snickered. "Never heard that before."

"Carl taught me that word," Kelly teased. "Anyway, about six months after he walked out, we accidentally ran into each other at this big real estate developers' conference at a hotel in Denver. Steve's boss asked him to attend and pick up any new ideas developers were tossing around. I attended because my Denver client was there, and he wanted me there as his financial adviser."

"And . . ." Dee Dee encouraged.

"And Steve and I nearly ran into each other at the coffee machine." Kelly laughed softly, remembering. "He just stared at me, his mouth open. After a moment I said to him, 'Are you just gonna stare at me or say something?' Anyway, that got us talking at least. Work stuff mostly, then we both went back to our seats. That's all."

Cassie looked puzzled. "That's all? Something else must have happened."

"Yeah," Dee Dee prodded. "How'd you two get to that volleyball game?"

"Oh yeah," Kelly said with another laugh. "Sorry. Pregnancy Brain. Since we at least broke the ice, we would say 'hello' to each other at the conference. Then a couple of weeks later, Megan and I started playing in a coed volleyball league in Northern Colorado. Believe it or not, Steve and Marty were playing on one of the other teams. And we had to play them one time. Well, I was playing front line one night and Steve was right across from me. We were both getting into the game, and one shot came over the net and I . . . well, I stuffed it. Right in Steve's face."

Cassie looked shocked at first, then burst out laughing. "You didn't!"

"Ohhhhhh yes, I did," Kelly said with a grin. "And I enjoyed every minute of it."

"What'd Steve do?"

"Yeah, what'd he do?" Dee Dee asked with a laugh.

"He shook his head to clear it, then he looked across the net at me and said, 'You didn't just do that.' And I said, "Yeah, I did,' and laughed. Then he said, 'Coming back at ya!' And a couple of shots later he stuffed me right in my face. Really rang my bell." Kelly laughed out loud, remembering. "Payback."

"Love it," Dee Dee said as she returned to the buttons.

"Yay, Steve," Cassie teased and returned to the butter yellow yarn on the winder.

"Changing the subject, when is the baby due, Dee Dee?" Kelly asked, sensing the question was safe to ask.

"In September, most probably."

"Well, I will gladly bequeath this comfy armchair to you after Jack arrives. I abandoned those hard wooden chairs in the knitting room for this comfy one a few days ago." Kelly examined some of the stitches circling the crown of the hat. So far, so good. She glanced back to Dee Dee. "You're going to name the baby Emma?"

"Yes, it was my grandmother's name, and she lived with us as I was growing up. She used to tell my sister and me stories. She had lots and lots of stories."

Kelly pictured that lovely scene. She wished she'd had a grandmother as she grew up. But she did have Aunt Helen and Uncle Jim. They were the only family Kelly ever knew, aside from her father.

"I think it's a pretty name," Cassie spoke up from the winding table.

"Mimi, I'm going to open that box from the Nebraska vendor. I'm hoping it's that shipment of red, white, and blue yarns we ordered," Rosa said as she stood in the archway to the central yarn room.

"That's an excellent idea, Rosa. Thank you," Mimi said as she returned her attention to the papers in her hand. They looked like inventory sheets to Kelly.

Kelly went back to her blue and gray baby hat. She was circling the center, narrowing in. She'd be finished soon.

Burt stepped from around the far corner that led to the back of the café and also to the basement. "Mimi, did you have any electrical work done while we were gone? I just saw the bill from a local electrician. It says he was here nearly six hours."

"Yes, Pete was talking about fixing some lights in the café, and I remembered we had a couple of lights in the knitting room that started flickering last month. So I called up our regular electrician and he's retired now, but he recommended someone else." Just then, the phone beside her elbow interrupted Mimi. "I'll check the calendar after I get this. Lambspun of Colorado," she said in a cheerful voice as she answered.

Burt walked from behind the counter, sorting through various pieces of paper. The unmistakable look of bills, Kelly recognized.

"Ahhhh yes. Time to pay the bills," she teased. "So much fun, isn't it, Burt?"

"Spoken by an accountant." Burt gave her a wry smile.

Kelly looked around the front room. Dee Dee appeared to be still entranced with all the buttons surrounding her. Even so, Kelly lowered her voice.

"How much longer before you and Mimi will have paid off that loan to the real estate investor?"

Burt glanced to Cassie, who had stopped her yarn winding and was listening intently. He gave her a smile. "It's a sign that you've gotten old enough to have adults discuss financial matters in front of you, Cassie. Mimi and I are almost finished paying off a mortgage loan on this shop. In another three years, Lambspun will be ours. We will own it."

Cassie's big brown eyes widened. "I thought you and Mimi already owned the shop."

Burt chuckled. "Oh no. Mimi had been paying monthly

rent for years to a real estate investor who owned the property. But after Mimi and I married a few years ago, we started planning how we could buy Lambspun. That was before you came into our lives."

Kelly watched as Cassie processed the new information. "Mimi and Burt had a beautiful wedding, Cassie. Her backyard was just perfect, filled with flowers just like it was last Saturday. And I'm convinced that's when Jennifer decided she wanted to be married there, too." Kelly then leaned forward and whispered, "But don't tell her I said so."

Cassie grinned. "Don't worry. I won't." And she returned to her yarn winding.

Rosa walked back into the front room then, arms filled with skeins of fire-engine red yarn. "I just love this shade of red," she said. "I think I'll put some patriotic piles of red, white, and blue yarns all over that table in the middle of the yarn room."

"Rosa, did an electrician come to the shop while Mimi and I were away on vacation? I've got a bill." Burt waved the paper.

"Yes, he did, Burt. Mimi said she called him to fix some lights in the café that Pete said weren't working properly. Oh, and he fixed a couple of those lights that were flickering in the knitting room, too."

"Do you remember how long he was here? His bill said he worked for nearly six hours." Burt frowned at the bill again.

Rosa pondered for a moment. "Well, he was working in the café most of the time. I think he mentioned he had to rewire something. But it took him quite a while as I recall. He came in the afternoon after the café was closed, too."

"Oh, well, then, I guess he was here nearly six hours if he had to rewire those kitchen ceiling lights," Burt said as he headed behind the counter and disappeared around the corner again. Mimi had gone into the central yarn room, still on the phone with a customer.

"Burt's in the midst of paying bills, Rosa. But I think your patriotic piles are a great idea," Kelly said.

"Patriotic piles. That'll be perfect for the Fourth of July, Rosa," Cassie added.

Beverly stepped down into the front room then. "Well, Lambspun is a busy place this afternoon," she said. Looking toward Dee Dee, browsing the wonderland of buttons and decorative items, she observed, "Goodness. It looks like we've got two expectant moms here today."

Dee Dee looked over and gave Beverly a smile. "Hi there. You must be the snack vendor. I think I've seen you at my hair salon, the Ultimate Cut. The stylists there say you have all sorts of tempting stuff."

"Well, that's nice to hear. That salon certainly has a lot of customers. I check in with lots of shops every week to see if they'd like some of my healthy organic snacks."

Clearly, Beverly said the magic word—"organic"—because Dee Dee's head popped up again and the buttons were momentarily forgotten. "Organic? That's great. What do you have?"

"What doesn't she have?" Kelly couldn't resist tempting. "Tell her about those scrumptious pecan bars, Beverly."

"Ohhhh, those sound yummy."

Beverly smiled. "We've got several organic and natural snack bars, cookies, and candies. And chips made from sesame seeds. I can bring in a card listing all of our products from the truck, if you'd like."

"Yes, I'd love to see a menu, please."

"And don't forget to show her those natural and organic chocolate-covered cherries," Kelly tempted with a smile.

Dee Dee's eyes widened. "Oh yes. Please!"

"Kelly, you are wasted being an accountant," Beverly said with a grin. "You are a natural-born salesman."

"Only when it comes to chocolate," Kelly teased.

"I'll be right back," Beverly said and walked toward the front entry.

Dee Dee glanced toward Kelly. "Goodness, it looks like you're nearly full-term. When are you due?"

Kelly paused in her knitting. "Actually, pretty soon. I reached nine full months last week, so my doctor says it could be anytime now."

"Oh my. Have you got all the baby supplies and all that ready? I'm just starting to accumulate stuff. My husband and I bought a crib last weekend." She gave a little laugh.

"Well, that's the best place to start. And it looks like you'll have plenty of time," Kelly said. "I've got tons of stuff, what with the things I've bought and what our friends gave us."

"That's nice to hear. I hope our friends do the same."

"Have one of your friends drop a hint."

"Good idea," Dee Dee said.

"I always like to learn how people found out about Lambspun. Did a knitting friend tell you about the shop? Is that how you learned about the knitting group meetings?" Kelly glanced up.

"Well, kind of," Dee Dee said as she lifted a package of buttons to examine. "We moved here six months ago, and the girl at the condo apartment next door told me about the shop. I'd noticed she had some knitting stuff on her sofa."

"Well, we're glad you found us," Kelly said as Beverly hurried through the central yarn room and into the front of the shop again.

"Here you go, Dee Dee," Beverly said as she handed over a menu and a small box.

Dee Dee accepted the items eagerly, ripping the end of the box open. Then she poured a small handful of chocolate candies into her hand. "Wow, chocolate-covered cherries." She popped one into her mouth and savored. "Ummmm-mmm," she decreed as Kelly laughed softly.

"Where did you move from?" Cassie asked as she stopped winding. The yarn had fattened into a butter yellow ball.

"From Ohio. My husband and I both grew up there."

"Really? I grew up in Ohio, too. Near Columbus," Beverly said. "I even went to Ohio State."

"Did you get a sports scholarship?" Cassie asked, clearly interested. "Both Kelly and Dee Dee got athletic scholarships."

Beverly gave a little laugh. "No, Cassie. I'm afraid I have two left feet. I was awful at sports. I'd trip every time I tried to run to a base in school."

"Ohhh, it couldn't have been that bad." Kelly couldn't resist.

"Oh, it was. Believe me. One time, I even knocked over the first baseman. Or woman. Whatever," Beverly said with a laugh.

Cassie, Dee Dee, Rosa, and Kelly joined in as hearty laughter bounced around the room.

Fifteen

"Oooooo, such a good boy," Kelly said, rubbing behind both of Carl's velvet-soft black ears.

Carl, for his part, was beyond doggie speech at this point. A double ear rub! Ecstasy! He simply tilted his head and closed his eyes, enjoying the moment.

"You silly boy," Kelly said, finishing with a rub to the top of Carl's smooth black head. "What are you going to do when Baby Jack is old enough to crawl around on the floor? We'll have to put your toys outside so Jack can't chew on them." Carl simply shook his head in reply and went over to his water bowl where he slurped several large gulps.

Kelly gathered up her oversize bag, grabbed her empty metal coffee mug, and headed out of the cottage. Checking the flower boxes that lined her walkway to the driveway running between her cottage and Lambspun shop, she admired the bright yellow marigolds, red and white impatiens, and purple and pink petunias. Cheerful colors greeted her every morning.

As she walked over to Lambspun, she recognized Burt's truck coming around the café corner and pulling into a parking space. "Hey, Burt, how're you doing?" she greeted when he stepped down from the truck.

"I'm doing fine, Kelly," Burt said as he walked up. "More importantly, how are you feeling?"

"I'm feeling huge, but Jack still seems content to stay where he is," Kelly said as they walked toward the entrance to the café patio garden.

"No hints or twinges or anything?" Burt asked, peering at her.

Kelly shook her head. "Nope. Nary a one."

"Why don't we sit over here?" Burt indicated an empty wrought iron table along the edge of the patio garden. He pulled out a chair for Kelly.

"Thanks, Burt," she said as she sank into the wrought iron chair. "I seem to be moving a little slower since Jack dropped. Dr. Jefferson said it's normal, though."

"And all your vitals are good? Blood pressure and everything?"

Kelly couldn't miss the concern in his voice. "Absolutely. I'm still as healthy as that proverbial horse. Albeit a pregnant horse." She watched Burt relax back into his chair.

"Well, that's good to hear. We're all watching you like a bunch of hawks, you know."

"I've noticed," Kelly said with a wry smile. "Changing the

subject, how's the investigation into Giselle Callahan's murder going?"

"It's going nowhere at the moment. Dan says they're still questioning neighboring businesses. A couple of detectives came over to the shop again yesterday afternoon to ask all of the café and shop workers if anyone remembered seeing anything the day Giselle Callahan was killed. They questioned each of us separately this time. But we still weren't much help. Mimi and I had already left on our weekend trip, and none of the others saw anything."

"Nobody saw anything? Nothing at all?"

Burt shook his head. "Lambspun staff are usually too busy to look out the windows, Kelly. But Dan said they're now trying to contact all of the café workers to see if any of them saw something."

Julie walked up to them and smiled. "Can I get you some of that matcha green tea, Kelly? You seem to be tolerating it pretty well."

Kelly had to laugh. "Tolerate is right, Julie. But at least it's drinkable. The weak coffee makes me gag."

"You know, we could try the tea iced, if you want," Julie suggested.

"Uhhhh, maybe we'd better not. It's tolerable right now when it's hot. Let's just keep it that way, okay?"

Julie grinned. "You got it. I'll be back in a minute." She started to walk away then turned back to them. "Oh yeah, Burt. Mimi came into the café a few minutes ago and asked me to tell you that some other lights in the shop are flickering now."

Burt screwed up his face. "What? I don't believe it."

"Yeah, I know. I almost hated to tell you," she said before walking away.

"Maintenance issues. They're a constant problem for shop owners as well as home owners," Kelly observed.

Burt reached inside his pocket and withdrew his cell phone. "You're right about that," he said as he punched in a number. "And they're giving me even more gray hair."

Kelly relaxed back into the wrought iron chair. It was a beautiful late May morning. The temperatures had moderated, and the Colorado sun was shining behind the cottonwood trees bordering the golf course. All was peaceful and quiet. Only a few golfers were on the course. It was hard to believe that only a couple of weeks ago a woman was brutally murdered right there on the golf course. In broad open daylight, as her aunt Helen would say.

"Mimi? I'm sitting out here on the patio with Kelly. Julie just told me we're having problems with the lights again."

Julie came up and silently set a mug of matcha green tea in front of Kelly then hurried away to take care of the other customers who were enjoying a late breakfast.

"The lights in the yarn room and the front room?" Burt said. "Oh boy. It sounds like the wiring is starting to go bad all over the shop."

Kelly gave Burt a sympathetic look. Rewiring the entire Lambspun shop and the café would be expensive. The building was nearly one hundred years old, having been built in the 1930s.

"I agree. You'd better call up the electrician and tell him to come back. Otherwise, we may find ourselves in the dark some evening. I'll call him if you're busy. I'm coming inside now anyway." He scooted back the patio chair and clicked off his phone.

"I'm sorry to hear that, Burt. That does sound expensive."

"Yeah, I'm afraid it will be, Kelly," Burt said as he stood. "It's a good thing that Mimi and I have been regularly putting away money for shop maintenance."

"I love you two. You're the perfect accounting clients. You're organized and you keep great records. Plus, you're thrifty." Kelly gave him a smile.

"'Thrifty,' now there's a word we don't hear very often nowadays. Talk to you later, Kelly," he said before walking away.

Kelly was about to signal Julie when Jennifer walked up to the table then. "Hey there. Can I get you anything other than the matcha tea? Some scrambled eggs? Your favorite bacon and sausage?"

"No, I'm good. I had a nutritious breakfast sandwich earlier this morning." Kelly glanced around the garden patio. "I haven't seen Cassie checking tables. Is she working inside?"

Jennifer nodded as she pulled out a chair on the other side of the patio table. "Yes. Pete and I thought it would be a good idea to rotate Cassie, Julie, and me so we'd have equal time inside and outside. We don't want anyone getting bored," she said with a smile.

"You guys are too busy to get bored," Kelly observed. "You're all rushing around taking care of customers, running to the kitchen, carrying trays, racing back and forth."

"Wow, no wonder I'm tired," Jennifer teased with a smile. "To be honest, it's been a great help ever since Cassie started working. She's taken care of a lot of the patio work this spring. In fact, Pete and I are going to raise her part-time wages because Julie and Bridget got raises in their last paycheck. As well as Eduardo and the extra grill cooks. Eduardo is the genius in the kitchen."

"Genius is right," Kelly said. "And the café's monthly revenues have increased over last year's, so that makes the raises easier to justify."

Jennifer grinned at her. "You're such an accountant. I love it. I bet you'll be computing revenues and expenses when you're in labor."

Kelly had to laugh. "Now that is a new one. I'll have to share it with my maternity exercise class. What an image."

Kelly savored the last bite of her lunch, a delicious chicken salad sandwich. "Julie, make sure you tell Eduardo his recipe for chicken salad is the best I have ever tasted."

"I'll be sure to, Kelly," Julie said as she wiped down one of the café tables in the alcove where Kelly sat.

Cassie walked up from the kitchen area. "I've cleaned all the tables in the front. Only one table is still occupied, but it looks like they're finishing."

"That's good news. I've got a ton of errands to run this afternoon," Julie said as she straightened chairs around tables. "Why don't you take off now and start enjoying the afternoon."

"Hey, thanks, Julie. Jennifer left a half hour ago for a dentist appointment, and Pete went with her. He had an appointment, too."

Julie grinned. "Double dentals, what fun. Go on, enjoy the rest of the afternoon."

Cassie walked toward Kelly in the alcove. "Hey, Kelly. How's Jack doing today?"

"I had Eduardo's yummy chicken salad sandwich, so I think Jack is napping now." She slowly rose from the wooden chair. "Come on, let's go back into the shop and see what they're up to."

"I'll get your bag," Cassie offered and swiftly retrieved Kelly's briefcase bag from the end of the table. "Hey, it feels lighter than usual." Cassie hefted the over-the-shoulder fiber bag up and down, as she and Kelly walked into the corridor separating the café from the knitting shop.

"That's because I left my laptop back at the cottage. I finished checking my accounts earlier," Kelly said as she and Cassie turned down the corridor.

A middle-aged woman with light brown hair sat on a chair at the end of the corridor toward the entrance to the workroom. She was winding strands of bright shamrock green yarn around wooden pegs on a square-shaped board attached to the wall. Kelly thought she'd seen the woman at the shop before but wasn't sure.

"Hi there," she greeted the woman as she and Cassie drew closer. "I think I've seen you here at the shop before. I'm Kelly, and this is Cassie."

"This is Penelope, Kelly," Cassie said, gesturing to the woman winding yarn. "She's been here a few times, right?"

"Right you are, Cassie," Penelope said with a smile. "And I'm impressed that you remembered my name."

"Do you go by Penelope or Penny?" Kelly asked, watching the woman continue to wind the shamrock green yarn.

"I've always liked using Penelope," she replied. "It's an

old-fashioned name, and we don't hear it much anymore. Most everyone has a nickname."

"You're right," Kelly agreed. "My first name, Kelly, is really an Irish surname. There're a lot of Kellys in the phone book."

"That's for sure," Penelope said with a smile.

"I like those old-fashioned names. Pe-NEL-oh-pee," Cassie pronounced.

"You have an old-fashioned name yourself, Cassie," Penelope observed, still winding the green yarn. Over some pegs and under other pegs. "You use a nickname, Cassie, but Cassandra is your full name. And there's quite a story attached to your name. Did you know that?"

Cassie cocked her head to the side, obviously trying to recall. "I think I read something in my humanities class about the ancient Greek times and the myths, but I forgot exactly what."

Kelly tried to remember as well. "I barely remember reading about it, too. High school was many years ago. But I bet you know what it is, Penelope."

Penelope smiled as she wound the yarn. "Yes, I do. According to Greek mythology, Cassandra was a clairvoyant back in the days of ancient Greece. More than two thousand years ago. In those days, clairvoyants were highly revered, and kings and queens asked their guidance on what they 'saw' in the future. Did you learn about Greek mythology in your humanities class?"

Cassie nodded. "A little. I remember some of the names of the Greek gods and goddesses they worshipped. Like Athena, the goddess of wisdom, and Aphrodite, goddess of beauty and love. And Poseidon. He was god of the sea. And Zeus. He was the leader. The most powerful."

"Good job, Cassie," Kelly commended, giving Cassie a pat on the shoulder.

"Excellent, Cassie," Penelope added. "According to Greek mythology, Cassandra was given the gift of prophecy by the sun god, Apollo, in exchange for, ah . . . shall we say, sharing her favors with him."

Cassie slowly smiled. "I get it."

"The tricky thing is, Cassandra received the gift of prophecy but did not share herself. Well, Apollo got mad—"

"Those gods and goddesses were always getting mad about something," Kelly teased.

"You're right," Penelope agreed. "Well, Apollo punished Cassandra by saying no one would ever believe her prophecies. And according to the legends, Cassandra predicted the fall of Troy." She stopped winding. "Perfect timing. I've got the lengths of yarn I need. Now I have to measure and tie off the yarn lengths so I can thread the heddles on one of the table looms."

"You call all this wrapping yarn around the pegs 'warping the loom,' right?" Cassie asked her.

"Right you are, Cassie," Penelope replied. "I see you've been paying attention to more than your humanities class."

"That's a beautiful shade of green, Penelope. What do you want to weave?" Kelly asked.

"I'd like to weave four holiday place mats to use as gifts. I figure if I start now, I'll have a fighting chance to get all four woven before November. I hope." She laughed lightly.

"Oh, I think you will definitely reach that goal, Penelope."

A tiny little thought wiggled from the back of Kelly's mind. "You know, you're also named for someone in Greek mythology, Penelope. I've forgotten the story, but why don't you tell Cassie."

"Well, all right," Penelope agreed as she leaned back into her chair. "According to Greek myths Penelope was the wife of the Greek hero Odysseus. He went to fight in the Trojan War and was gone twenty years."

"Whoa! That's a long time," Cassie observed.

"I'll say," Kelly agreed.

"It certainly was. And during that time, Penelope was constantly asked by different men to marry. After all, everyone assumed Odysseus was dead and would never return. Well, Penelope refused every one of the men. And when they kept insisting, she told them all she would marry one of them once she finished weaving the shroud she was weaving for her husband. Do you know what a shroud is, Cassie?"

"Yeah, people use it in burials. They wrap the body in it, I think."

"Smart girl," Penelope said with a twinkle in her eye.

"You're going to be in good shape for those SAT exams," Kelly teased.

Cassie laughed. "So, Penelope was a weaver. Did she finish weaving that shroud?"

"Not for years and years," Penelope replied. "She'd sit at the loom every day and weave. Everyone saw her. But then, when she was alone at night, she would unravel everything she'd woven during the day." Penelope gave Cassie a wink.

"Oh wow!" Cassie said. "She tricked them. That was so smart. Did those guys ever figure it out?"

"Eventually. But to make a long story short, her husband finally came home from the war. But she didn't recognize him, so he had to win an archery contest and tell her a secret before she knew who he was."

"Whoa," Cassie said, shaking her head. "Those ancient Greek relationships were really messed up."

Both Kelly and Penelope laughed so hard that Julie came out of the café to find out what was going on.

Steve settled Kelly's cushion on the bleachers then held out his hand. "Here you go," he said to her.

"Thanks," Kelly said as she slowly sat down. "Wow, everything looks so different from the front row," she said as she scanned the City Park ball field.

"Got to admit, I'm surprised to see you here, Kelly-girl," Jayleen said from a bleacher row above. "I thought you'd be home taking it easy before the main event."

"This is Kelly. She never does anything the easy way," Curt observed in a wry voice. He popped another kernel of popcorn into his mouth.

"Amen to that," Steve said with a grin as he settled beside Kelly.

Kelly couldn't miss the slight concern in Jayleen's gaze. "Well, I thought I'd come out for one more ball game before the spring season was over. Baby Jack hasn't made a move yet."

"Well, I parked closer than usual, just in case," Steve said. "I figure he's gotta make a move sometime."

Kelly spotted Cassie in center field throwing the softball to a teammate. "Cassie keeps telling Jack that his rent is up," she laughed softly. "It's so funny. She leans over my belly and talks to him."

"Love that girl," Jayleen said, waving high over her head. "Hey, hey, Cassie!" she called.

Curt gave a loud whistle, more melodious than Marty's earsplitting version. "Who're they playing?"

"I think Cassie told me it was Loveland. Either that or Longmont," Kelly answered. She noticed Mimi and Burt approaching the bleachers. "Hey there, you two," she greeted.

"Hey there, yourself, Kelly," Burt replied. "And I'm surprised to see you here. Cutting it a little close, aren't you?"

"The ball fields aren't far from the hospital," Steve said as he waved toward Cassie. "Otherwise, I'd have hidden the car keys."

Kelly gave a soft laugh. "You misplaced them this morning."

Steve shook his head. "Naw, I had them in my pocket. I told you I misplaced them so you wouldn't be tempted to run out on an errand right before we came here."

"Smart move," Curt opined from the upper bleachers. "You gotta be quick to outsmart Kelly."

"Tell me about it," Steve said with a laugh.

Kelly joined the laughter that floated around the bleachers. Her reputation preceded her.

Sixteen

Kelly stepped inside the Lambspun foyer. The fresh coolness of the air-conditioning enveloped her. After driving around most of the morning doing errands, she welcomed that cool embrace. *Ahhhhhhhhhh*, she sighed. *Escape.*

She headed toward the front of the shop, hoping no visiting knitter had claimed the comfy armchair. All the staff and local knitters had kindly given Kelly first dibs on the armchair whenever she was in the shop—which was every day nowadays. She preferred being around familiar faces during the day, just in case Baby Jack decided to come. Plus, the Lambspun shop was much closer to the Fort Connor Hospital than the house north of town in Wellesley.

Cassie turned around the corner from the hallway into the central yarn room. Spying Kelly, she broke into a smile. "Hey there, Kelly. Do you want some of the matcha green tea you've been drinking? I can bring it to you in the front room where you like to sit."

Kelly paused in the archway into the Loom Room. "You're a mind reader, Cassie. Yes, I would love some of that tea. Thank you."

"No problem. It will only take a couple of minutes. Pete keeps that teakettle boiling for you now."

Kelly had to laugh. "I never thought I'd see the day when someone, anyone, kept a teakettle going for me. Will wonders never cease?"

Cassie laughed her familiar laugh and turned back toward the corridor.

Kelly stepped down into the front room and spied the comfy armchair, empty. She gave a grateful sigh and set her shoulder bag on the floor and sank into the chair. A deep feeling of relaxation settled over her. *Ahhhhhhhhhhhhhhhhh!*

"You're looking a little tired, Kelly," Rosa commented, peering at her.

Kelly sighed out loud this time. "You're right about that, Rosa. I made the mistake of doing four errands this morning. I'd promised myself I would cut back, but I didn't."

Rosa shook her head. "Kelly, errands can wait until Steve gets home, and he can do them. You need your rest."

"I know, I know." Kelly nodded dutifully.

"One errand a day in the morning. Period."

Kelly laughed softly as she reached for her shoulder bag and brought out the baby hat. Only a couple of rows were left before she could tie off the crown and make a small cotton pom-pom for the top.

Rosa eyed her with a decidedly maternal look. "I'm not

kidding, Kelly. One errand. Or I'll inform Megan what you've been doing, and she'll be over here in a heartbeat. Then she'll fuss at you up one side and down the other."

At that, Kelly laughed out loud. She hadn't heard that expression since her aunt Helen was alive. It was a perfect description for Megan, however. Megan wouldn't leave any part of Kelly "unfussed."

"I promise, Rosa. Really."

"Okay, I'll be watching."

Just then, a man wearing dark blue pants and a white uniform shirt stepped down into the front room. He was carrying a ladder. "Pardon me, ladies, but I'm going to have to get in between you two. Stay right where you are, and I promise I won't hit you with the ladder."

"Oh goodness," Rosa said as the man walked closer to the end of the front counter. "Be careful of our expectant mom over there." She pointed to Kelly, comfortably ensconced in the comfy armchair in the corner beside the front window.

He glanced toward Kelly. "Don't worry, ma'am. I'll be extra careful."

Hearing the man call her "ma'am" made Kelly smile. "You must be the electrician."

"Yes, I am, and this is the second time I've come to this shop in the last couple of weeks. Seems you folks are having more trouble with the lights," he said as he opened the ladder and set it in place.

"I'm afraid we are," Rosa said.

"It's certainly a pretty building. Mrs. Parker says it's not on the Historic Register, but it's had quite a history." He moved the ladder back and forth a couple of times, clearly checking to see if it was securely set on the wooden floor.

"Yes, it has. It was built in the 1930s by a sheep farmer, I believe," Rosa said as she rearranged display items on the front counter. Two small metal stands held custom handmade earrings, created by Lambspun regulars.

Kelly returned to knitting the baby hat. Only two small rows to go before tying off. "I heard someone won the land in a card game. Poker, I guess."

"That story sounds about right," the man said as he climbed the ladder. "And that makes the house nearly one hundred years old. So it's no wonder the wiring is going bad."

"Surely the wiring has been replaced before now," Kelly said, watching the electrician unscrew the overhead light fixture.

"It hasn't been replaced in the ten years I've been working here," Rosa observed. "We'll have to ask Mimi."

"Well, we may be in for a surprise, then," the man said as he unscrewed several bolts holding the light fixture in place.

Cassie stepped down into the front room then, carrying a mug. "Here you go, Kelly. Matcha hot tea," she said, offering the mug. Glancing above, she added, "Looks like he's working up front now. This morning he was in the workroom."

"Wow, it sounds like the repairs are moving room to room," Kelly said, then blew on the hot liquid. Taking a small sip, she was surprised that she was growing used to the flavor. Amazing.

The electrician removed the light fixture from the ceiling, then carefully carried it down the ladder. "It's certainly a pretty little corner here. Kind of peaceful looking out on the golf course over there," he said, pointing out the large front window.

"I think so, too," Kelly agreed. "That's why I like to come over here every day." Only one more row to finish and she could tie off the crown.

"Well, it wasn't so peaceful a couple of weeks ago," Rosa spoke up. "That's where the lady golf pro was murdered." She pointed out the window toward the golf course. No golfers were in sight.

The man's eyes grew wide. "Really? Damn, I remember reading about that in the paper. And it happened right over there?" He followed Rosa's lead and pointed toward the golf course.

Kelly didn't say a thing. She concentrated on finishing the final row of knitting the baby hat. Clearly, Rosa was playing the role of town crier, spreading the local news.

"Yes, right over there," Rosa said, nodding. "And the police still have no idea who did it. They even came back the other day to interview us for a second time. But none of us saw anything. We're so busy in here. We don't have time to look out the window. Police went over to the brewery and café across the street and interviewed them, too."

"Well, I'll be. This sounds like one of those television cop shows. What sorts of questions did they ask?"

Burt leaned around the corner from the Loom Room then. "Hey, Kelly. You want to bring that mug and join me in the café for a coffee break?"

"Sure thing, Burt," Kelly said, placing her knitting on the wide arm of the comfy chair as she slowly stood up. "I'll be right back, Rosa. Don't give away the chair."

"Don't worry, I won't," Rosa said with a grin.

Burt glanced toward the ceiling. "Did you have any trouble getting that fixture off?" he addressed the electrician.

"Nope. Not really," the electrician replied, then blew on the fixture. A small cloud of dust wafted off. "It's been up there a long time."

"I think Mimi said the former owner told her the fixtures were changed in the early nineties," Burt said as he stepped aside for Kelly. "How're you doing?" he asked as they walked toward the corridor leading to the café. "You look a little tired to me."

Kelly gave a little laugh. "Well, you're right. I did a few too many errands this morning. But don't fuss at me. Rosa has already done that. And made me promise only one errand per morning, or she'll tell Megan."

"Good for Rosa," Burt said, chuckling. "The threat of a Megan Fussing works wonders."

"That it does," Kelly said as she headed for a smaller table in a corner of the café. Not as many lunch customers inside the café. Everyone was outside in the pretty weather.

"Welcome, you two. I was about to call you, Kelly, and see how you're doing. I missed you yesterday," Jennifer said as she approached.

"I'm doing fine, Jennifer," Kelly said as she settled into the wooden table chair. "The doctor yesterday said I'm in good shape. We're all simply waiting for Baby Jack to show up."

"He'll come when he's good and ready," Burt said with a fatherly smile.

Kelly took a sip of the matcha tea. "Well, I'm good and ready right now. So Baby Jack can get a move on any day."

Jennifer grabbed a clean mug from the table and filled it

with Eduardo's Black Gold. "Burt, what can I get you? Lunchtime has already started."

"I'll take one of Pete's Wicked Burgers with all the trimmings. Except raw onions. And please cut it in half. I think Kelly needs some nourishment. She's looking pretty peaked, as Jayleen would say."

"That's a great idea. I'll tell Eduardo that our expectant mom here needs sustenance," Jennifer said as she walked off.

"Actually, I am feeling a little hungry," Kelly admitted.

"Well, Pete's Wicked Burger will be just the thing you need to give you some energy. You've got to take care of yourself, Kelly. Busy days are coming up."

Kelly took another sip of tea. "So, what's happening with Dan's investigation into Giselle Callahan's murder?"

Burt stirred some cream into his coffee before taking a sip. "I think I mentioned that they had already questioned Callahan's son, Henry, earlier. When I talked to Dan today he told me that they questioned Henry Callahan again, and he was extremely nervous this time during the interview. Dan said sweat was forming on his forehead, and he stammered a couple of times. So that made Dan very suspicious."

"I bet it did. I remember Marty said he'd witnessed Henry Callahan yelling at Giselle in a parking lot. Apparently, he blamed her for his mother's decision to take her life."

"Yes. So, you can see how it would look if his statement that he drove to Denver doesn't hold up. If he has no gas records or fast-food or restaurant checks to prove his whereabouts, then Henry Callahan will become Suspect Number One."

Kelly took another sip of the matcha tea. "And did you

question Marie? Was she able to prove that she had gone to the library all the way across town at that time?"

Burt sipped his coffee. "Yes, I did speak with her. She was with other people at the library, and they could corroborate. So now it's up to Henry Callahan to prove he's innocent."

Kelly stared off into the busy interior of the café, swiftly filling up with customers. "Dan may have found the guilty party already. That's pretty efficient. Keep me posted, Burt."

"I sure will, Kelly."

Kelly knitted another shorter strand of blue yarn on her needles. She'd already tied off the crown of the baby hat. All she had to do now was to make the little pom-pom and sew it to the top.

The electrician walked back into the front room, holding what looked like a new light fixture. "Sorry to keep disturbing you folks with this ladder, but this old wiring needed a lot of repairs."

"Don't worry. It's not in my way," Kelly said from her comfy spot in the armchair.

Just then, Beverly walked into the front room. "Hello, everyone. It looks like you are having some repairs done."

"Major repairs," Rosa said from behind the front counter. "The old wiring was in bad shape. Lights were going off all over the shop."

"Oh my. That's expensive," Beverly commented, glancing toward the ceiling. "I think you folks deserve a treat. I'll give you snacks for half price. How's that?"

"Ooooo, that sounds good." Rosa's eyes lit up. "I'll take those special banana chips, please."

"You got it. How about you, Kelly? Can I tempt you with some of your favorite chocolate-covered cherries?" She gave Kelly a smile.

"Indeed, you can, Beverly. Even though I had a big juicy burger lunch, I can always find an excuse for chocolate."

Beverly chuckled. "And what about you, sir? Would you like some chips or some crackers or candies?"

The electrician shook his head. "I wish I could. But I promised my wife I'd stay on my diet this time. Doctor said I had to lose weight." He slowly started to climb the ladder.

Beverly spoke up. "Do you want me to hold this light fixture while you climb? We don't want you tumbling off." She reached over.

"That's really helpful, ma'am," he said as he handed the fixture to Beverly. "I appreciate it."

"No problem," Beverly replied.

Kelly watched the electrician climb up to his perch near the top and reach for the fixture. Then, he slowly fit it into place on the ceiling above his head.

"I'll be right back with those snacks, folks," Beverly said as she walked out of the room.

Kelly glanced outside and saw Beverly open the back of her vendor truck. Boxes of different snacks and goodies were neatly stacked inside. Beverly gathered several, slammed the door shut, and was back inside the shop in a moment.

"Boy, you are efficient," Kelly observed. "Rosa, can you add this snack to my shop tab, please?"

"Sure thing, Kelly," Rosa said as she accepted the package of chips.

"Here you go, Kelly. Enjoy," Beverly said with a big smile.

"Thanks, Beverly. These are too yummy."

Beverly glanced over her shoulder. "Well, it looks like there are some customers in the main room now. It was empty a few minutes ago. I'll see you folks again soon, and thanks so much." With that, she headed toward the other side of the shop.

Kelly knitted another couple of short rows of blue yarn that would make the pom-pom. It would look nice against the blue and gray hat. She watched the electrician slowly climb down the ladder and glance above.

"Well, that will make a big difference in here, folks," he said. "There will be a lot more light."

"That will be nice," Rosa commented.

The electrician leaned on the ladder and glanced outside again. "Now I remember where I've seen that truck before."

Kelly glanced out the wide front window and watched Beverly open the back of the vendor truck again.

"Probably at another shop," Rosa offered. "She covers a lot of shops in town."

"Actually, no, it was here," he said. "I saw that truck parked on the other side of the building near the café steps. I was working in the café behind the shop one afternoon. The café was empty of customers so I was able to get a lot of wiring repair done. And I recognize that woman. She got out of the truck and walked into the garden."

Kelly's instinct gave her a little jab, and she paused her knitting.

"Beverly must have been bringing more snacks," Rosa joked.

The electrician shrugged as he slowly closed up the ladder. "Funny thing is, I remember a man getting into the truck later and driving away. I thought that was strange."

This time, Kelly's instinct gave her a buzz. A big buzz. She looked up from the knitting. "Do you remember what day that was?"

The electrician looked over Kelly's head, where colorful knitted sweaters and shawls hung on the wall. "I think it was a couple of weeks ago. Let me look at my scheduler." He dug into his back pocket and withdrew a small black notebook. He paged through it and read. "It was May eleventh. I came in at twelve noon and worked until past five."

Kelly immediately recognized that date. It was the day Giselle Callahan was murdered on the golf course. Her little buzzer was going off nonstop now.

You need to tell Burt about this guy. Police don't even know about him. And he was here the day that Giselle Callahan was killed. Police will want to talk to him. Why was Beverly's vendor truck parked around the front of the café after it was closed for the day? And who was the guy that got into the truck and drove away? Did someone take her truck? And where was Beverly?

"Okay, thanks. I was just wondering," Kelly said in a nonchalant tone and returned to her knitting.

"You folks should be in good shape now," the electrician said. "I've replaced that old fixture with a new one. Plus I've repaired all the wiring I saw that needed it. So, let me know if the lights start acting up again, okay?"

"We will. Thank you so much," Rosa said with her big smile.

"Take care," Kelly said. "You're certainly efficient."

"I try to be. And you take care, too," he told her as he lifted the ladder and headed into the Loom Room toward the front door.

Kelly dug her cell phone out of her shoulder bag and rose from the chair. "I'll be outside for a few minutes, Rosa. Gotta make some calls."

Rosa simply shook her head and scolded gently. "Only a few minutes, all right? Then back in here to take it easy. You have to learn how to slow down."

"Yes, ma'am," Kelly teased. Walking through the Loom Room, she scrolled through her phone's directory to Burt's name and number and clicked it. Clearly, her idea of slowing down differed from everyone else's.

She pushed open the wooden front entry door and walked over to the quiet little corner Mimi and the shop elves had created for fiber workers who wanted to be outside. Burt's phone rang several times then switched into voice mail. Kelly quickly left a message relaying what she had learned and asked Burt to give her a call whenever he and Mimi returned.

Seventeen

Kelly slowly climbed out of bed and gave a big stretch, followed by an even bigger yawn. Steve walked into the bedroom holding a large mug.

"Here's some coffee," he said.

"Thank you. It will help me wake up," Kelly said, eagerly accepting the mug. She took a deep drink. Weak but tolerable.

"I've got to run over to the site early," Steve said, reaching into his jeans pocket. "We're having some trouble with that last shipment of drywall. The lumber company switched suppliers. And I'm not happy with this new product. Damn!" He stared at the cell phone's black screen.

"What's the matter?"

"I can't believe I forgot to charge my phone last night. It's dead." He frowned at the phone. "I can't believe I did that."

"Well, you've got a lot on your mind. Plug it in while you drive over." Kelly kissed him on the cheek. "It should be charged in an hour."

"How're you feeling?" Steve peered at her.

"I'm feeling fine," Kelly said with a smile. "Fat and fine."

"You're going over to the shop, right?" Steve said as he walked out the bedroom door into the hallway leading to the great room.

Kelly followed him, still wearing her long, loose night-gown. "Absolutely. They watch me like hawks over there, waiting for Jack to come. Plus, I'm closer to the hospital there."

"That makes me feel a lot better." Steve gave her a kiss then opened the front door. "Keep me posted. First pains."

Kelly gave a mock salute as he left. "You got it." Then she went to her briefcase bag, which sat on the kitchen table, and pulled out her own phone.

Scrolling through phone messages and texts, she didn't find any from Burt. Curious, Kelly took another big sip of weak caffeine and pressed Burt's phone number. He answered on the third ring.

"Hey, Kelly. I was about to give you a call. How're you feeling?"

"Same story. Feeling fat and fine. I was curious if you had a chance to hear my phone message."

"Sure did. But Mimi and I got back way late last night. Well, late for us." He chuckled. "But I did listen, and I gave Dan a call first thing this morning."

"You think Dan will try to contact that electrician? I got a real buzz when he told me he'd seen Beverly's truck parked on the other side of the shop late in the afternoon. The very day that Giselle Callahan was murdered."

"Oh, I'm sure he will. I know Dan, and he sounded like he was going to contact the guy today."

"Oh good."

Burt chuckled again. "Dan also was amazed that you're still sleuthing around, looking for clues when you're about to give birth any minute."

Kelly had to laugh at that. "Well, I don't have anything else to do. I'm totally caught up with all the accounting for both Housemann and Warner. I've even made some early entries for the first of June, ready to post once June arrives. So, I'm actually bored."

"Oh, Kelly. You should treasure those few totally relaxed days with nothing to do while you can. Pretty soon, you and Steve are about to become busier than you've ever been."

"You're right, I know. But I can't help it. It's like breathing. That's just the way my mind works. We accountants just love to solve problems." She drained the rest of the mug while Burt's laughter came over the phone.

Kelly was about to open Lambspun's heavy wooden entry door when a woman's voice called out behind her.

"Here, let me get that for you," the middle-aged woman said as she quickly walked up to Kelly's side. "You look like you're about to deliver any minute, girl." She heaved open the door and held it wide for Kelly.

"Thank you so much," Kelly said, giving her a grateful

smile as she entered the shop. "I must admit it's been a little awkward opening heavy doors since I got this far along."

"I should say. I remember how I felt years ago when my kids were about to come. I felt like I was carrying a big bag of groceries in front of me all the time." She gave a good-natured laugh as she followed Kelly inside.

"I think I recognize you. Have you been taking some of Lambspun's classes? You look vaguely familiar," Kelly said as she walked into the main knitting room.

"Yes, I have. I took the knitting classes and loved them. Then, I discovered the spinning classes and just fell in love with the wheel." She gave a little shrug. "I've been practicing at home and taking some private lessons from Mimi when she has time." She dropped her large fiber bag on the library table. "I'm Francine, by the way."

Kelly set her bag on the long table. No one else was there. "I'm Kelly. And I simply love to sit and knit with the spinners. I find it calming, soothing almost. Maybe it's the sound of the wheel. I don't know."

Francine cocked her head to the side. "You know, I think that's the same for me. I never thought of it that way. But I do sort of slow down and relax whenever I'm spinning. I kind of get into a zone, so to speak. Have you ever tried it?"

"Ohhhhhh no," Kelly said. "It's calming because I'm sitting there with the spinners. If I tried to do it, there would be yarn all over the place. The roving would twist up into a snake and attack, I'm sure of it."

Francine laughed out loud at that. "I think you're exaggerating."

Just then, Cassie walked into the room, and spying Kelly, she broke into a smile. "Hey, Kelly! How're you doing?"

Kelly settled into one of the chairs around the table. "I'm feeling fat and fine. That's my new motto."

"How come you're not up front in your comfy chair?" Cassie asked.

"Oh, I'll go up front in a minute. I simply wanted to check to see if any emails came in from my clients." She pulled her laptop from her briefcase bag and popped it open.

Cassie walked over and put both hands on Kelly's stomach. "And how's Baby Jack doing this morning?" she asked in a singsong voice. "Kicking any soccer goals?"

"No. In fact he's been pretty quiet this morning so far. We'll see what afternoon brings."

"Hey, Francine," Cassie greeted her. "How's your spinning coming along? That roving you had was a gorgeous shade of blue."

"I'm getting a little more confident every day, Cassie," Francine said as she reached into her bag and withdrew a fluffy bunch of dark turquoise fiber.

"Oh, that is so pretty," Kelly commented.

"It came from Mimi's January hand-dyed class," Cassie said. "Those were some of the most gorgeous-colored fibers Mimi's done. Or rather it was the class doing most of the dyeing."

"One of these days I'm going to learn how to do that," Francine said, fingering the stunning turquoise fibers. "I simply couldn't resist buying it. I can't figure out yet what I want to make with it, but I'm hoping an idea will come to me while I'm drafting the wool."

Cassie pulled out a chair between Kelly and Francine. "Can I draft some, too?" she asked.

"Sure," Francine said with a smile. "There's a lot of wool here, so I can use the help." She handed a bunch of the colorful fiber to Cassie.

Kelly pulled out her travel mug from her fiber bag and unscrewed the top, then poured some of the dark green matcha tea she'd made from the tea leaves Julie had given her from the café. She sipped the strange but tolerable flavor while she watched Cassie and Francine slowly stretch the turquoise fiber in their hands, one section at a time, preparing it to be spun onto the wheel.

Kelly watched for several minutes, then decided she wanted to fondle the fiber herself. Get her hands into it. It had been quite a while since she'd done any drafting. Before long, her hands would be busy caring for Baby Jack. So why not indulge in the totally tactile sensations of drafting wool this morning? It was a lot more pleasurable than checking revenues and expenses.

"Can I join you?" Kelly asked. "It's been a long time since I've drafted any fibers, and I think I need a fiber fix."

"Fiber fix," Cassie repeated. "That's funny."

"I know what you mean, Kelly," Francine said as she passed another bunch of turquoise fiber to Cassie. "Hand this to Kelly, so she can join in."

Kelly put the soft wool fibers in her lap and slowly started to duplicate the motions of Francine and Cassie, gently stretching a small handful of fibers apart, pulling them carefully until they reached their natural resting point and wouldn't give anymore. The soft turquoise fibers caressed her fingers. Soft, soft. This was such an ancient art and was practiced in one form or another by countless civilizations around the world.

"This feels like it's predominately wool," Kelly said. "What did the label say, Francine?"

"You're right on the money, Kelly," she answered. "It's one hundred percent merino wool."

"I remember sheep breeder friends told me about spinning raw wool directly from the sheared sheep," Kelly mused out loud. "It's not washed or carded or anything. They said the fresh wool is still full of natural lanolin from the sheep. So it can be knitted into garments that are naturally waterproof because of the lanolin. That's really useful for hats and mittens and other things worn outdoors."

"I think I remember hearing that at the Wool Market up in Estes Park one summer," Cassie said. "I was looking at bags and bags of sheep and alpaca fiber that were going to be sold in the vendor booths. And I think it was Burt who told me to sink my hands into a bag of cream-colored sheep's wool. And I remember how great it felt. It was kind of oily like. And when I pulled my hands out, there was this smooth residue halfway up my forearms. It really felt good. That's the lanolin, Burt said."

"I remember doing that, too," Kelly said. "It's one of the fun things to do at the Wool Market."

"It will be coming up in a few weeks," Francine said. "I'm looking forward to attending this year. I had to miss it last year because of family travel."

"I don't think I'll make it this year," Kelly said with a smile. "Baby Jack will be less than a month old. And the

Estes Park Wool Market is a full-day trip. And that's longer than I'd be comfortable having Jack out there. So you'll have to take notes on all the new stuff you see when you're there, Cassie."

"Will do," Cassie said, the pile of drafted roving gathering in her lap.

"I'm always amazed at how sensitive my fingers have become over the years," Kelly said, slowly stretching another handful of turquoise fiber. "I've gotten so I can tell if there's something else mixed in with the wool. It feels different."

"Yeah, it does," Cassie said with a nod. Her fingers submerged into the turquoise fibers. "I can tell the difference, too."

"I'm not surprised, Cassie," Francine said as she placed another handful of stretched roving into the large bag next to her. "After all, your fingers are a lot younger than ours, so they're more sensitive."

A peaceful silence fell over the main room then as Francine, Cassie, and Kelly continued to participate in an art as old as time. Ever since humans in various civilizations discovered they could turn the wool on a sheep's back into a fiber that could be made into garments that would keep them warm as frigid winds blew, they have done so.

Kelly continued to draft the wool, enjoying the purely sensuous feel of the wool and indulging herself in the tactile delights of fiber. She lost all sense of time as the separate piles of turquoise roving gathered in her lap as well as the laps of her two companions. None of them spoke for quite a while.

Then Mimi walked into the room and broke into one of her little musical laughs. "Why, goodness me. Look at the three of you. Drafting away peacefully. I simply love it."

"We're helping out Francine," Cassie said. "Do you need my help, Mimi?"

"Just for a few minutes, please. I have to go down into the basement and take inventory of the fleeces we have stored. So I need you to help Rosa with any customers that are up front."

"Sure thing," Cassie said, setting the drafted roving on the library table. "I'll get back to this later, Francine."

Francine made a dismissive wave of her hand. "Don't worry about it, Cassie. You've got work to do, and I'm ready to start spinning now anyway. I don't want to lose that empty wheel in the corner. Burt said it would be vacant today."

"Enjoy, ladies," Mimi said with a smile as she and Cassie headed toward the front of the shop.

"Smart move, Francine," Kelly said, setting the turquoise fibers aside herself. "Those spinning wheels are grabbed quickly, especially by students who haven't bought wheels themselves."

"Don't I know it," Francine agreed as she walked over to the spinning wheel in the corner. "I'm waiting for Mimi to have another of her equipment sales this summer or early fall. That's when I'll be able to buy a wheel myself."

"This is also a reminder that I should check my client accounts. Indulging in the fiber has totally distracted me this morning."

"Yes, but what a delightful distraction it is," Francine said with a smile.

Kelly pulled her laptop from across the knitting table where she'd left it. She logged on to her business email website and checked. No new messages. Several spam-type messages, she noticed. She wondered for the hundredth time how on earth they got through her filters. She scrolled through, then logged out again.

"Nothing important. No business mail, which is surprising. No client accounting entries to make, either."

"That's good," Francine said as she attached an empty spindle onto the wheel. "You've done your duty to your clients."

Suddenly, Cassie poked her head around the corner of the workroom. "Then you can go to the front and relax in your comfy chair, Kelly. Rosa's been looking for you ever since the shop opened. She told me to tell you she was getting worried. Gotta get back up front now," Cassie said, then scurried away.

Kelly slowly rose from the wooden chair, which was already beginning to feel hard and uncomfortable. "Well, I'd better go report in. I don't want Rosa calling out the National Guard to go looking for me." She slid her laptop back into the briefcase bag, slipped the bag over her shoulder, and walked into the central yarn room.

Rosa's face lit up when Kelly stepped down into the front room. "Oh, I'm so glad to see you, Kelly," she exclaimed. "I was beginning to get worried. I didn't want to think of you going into labor as you were driving to the shop."

Kelly had to laugh as she settled into the comfy corner chair. It enveloped her in a welcoming soft embrace. "I'm doing fine, Rosa. As I keep telling people, fat and fine is my new motto. Until Jack comes, that is."

"How's that baby hat coming?" Rosa asked as she walked over to the winding table.

"I've finished it, finally. And just in time." Kelly pulled

out the tiny blue and gray knitted baby hat from her bag. "Here it is."

"Ohhhhh, that's lovely, Kelly," Rosa said, taking the small hat from Kelly's hands. She examined it on both sides. "You did a marvelous job."

"Well, I don't know about marvelous," Kelly said modestly. "I wouldn't say that about any of my knitting projects. Serviceable is more like it."

Rosa shook her head as she returned the hat to Kelly. "Kelly, Kelly, you simply do not give yourself enough credit. You've learned so much these past few years you've been coming to Lambspun. You are not the Beginning knitter you were when you first started. You're Advanced now."

"Oh, heavens no. Intermediate Advanced is much more accurate." She gave a dismissive wave of her hand.

Megan stepped down into the front room then, embroidered knitting bag over her shoulder. "Good morning, you two. I figured I'd find you over here, Kelly. There're so many people in the shop that can keep an eye on you. It's much, much better than your being alone at home."

Kelly smiled at her dear friend. "Everyone says that. Steve even said it this morning before he left for work."

Rosa pointed to a chair at the winding table. "Here, Megan. Have a seat. None of us will be winding any yarn today. We're still spinning that gorgeous turquoise merino wool fiber onto the spindles."

"Thanks, Rosa. That's perfect," Megan said as she dropped her knitting bag on the floor and settled into the chair. "I love this huge window. It makes the whole room so bright."

"I know what you mean," Kelly agreed. "I love the light." She took a sip from her mug.

Megan eyed her slyly. "You're still being good and drinking the weaker coffee?"

"Oh yes. Miserable as it is. But Julie has introduced me to the matcha green tea. That's actually more drinkable, for some reason."

"That's great, too. Tell me, how are you feeling?"

"Fat and fine. That's my new motto," Kelly said with a little laugh.

"Well, you won't be fat much longer." She stared at Kelly's belly. "No Braxton Hicks contractions yet?"

Kelly shook her head. "Nope. Not one. I think Jack has gotten really, really comfortable where he is. He's making no move to leave."

"Did you do your exercises this morning?"

"Yes, Mother Megan," Kelly replied with a sly smile of her own. "I have to do them beside the hassock in the living room so I can get myself off the floor easier. That always makes me laugh."

"I have an idea. It sounds like Jack is getting way too comfortable in the Mommy condo. Let's wake him up. Why don't we take a short little walk outside around the edges of the golf course?" Megan bounced up quickly from her chair.

"Why not?" Kelly said, slowly pulling herself up from the chair's soft cushions. "Rosa, try not to give away the chair while I'm outside."

"Don't worry, Kelly. All the knitters know they have to evacuate the chair whenever you walk into the room."

Megan laughed. "I love it. C'mon. Let's go out the front

entry. It's an absolutely beautiful May morning. Not too hot yet and bright sunshine."

Kelly followed after Megan but at a slower pace. "Don't speed up, or you'll lose me. I can't believe how slowly I walk now. I've always been a speedy walker."

"I know what you mean," Megan said as they both went down the brick steps outside the shop entry. "I felt like I was moving through molasses that last month I was pregnant with Molly. It felt so good to be able to move around fast again after she was born."

Kelly remembered a question she wanted to ask. "Don't forget to make a list of all those post-delivery exercises you used, okay? I'll add those to my exercise routine."

"Sure thing. I bet you've already got them on your list from the obstetrician's office."

Megan walked around the tall cedar trees that bordered some of the golf course, Kelly following. They stepped onto the edge of the well-manicured course. Kelly noticed several golfers gathered around the green that was closest to them.

"Let's walk along the edge of the course," Megan suggested.

Kelly noticed Megan had slowed her pace to match hers. She looked over at the golf foursome of men. Two of the men glanced her way then quickly averted their eyes, she noticed. The other two men followed suit, glancing toward Kelly and Megan then looking away.

"I think I'm scaring the golfers," Kelly said with a little laugh. "All four of them have looked my way then quickly averted their eyes."

Megan grinned. "Typical. So many men stare whenever a woman appears who's clearly in her last month of pregnancy."

Just then, a golf cart scooted around a corner of the greens and slowed to a stop in front of Megan and Kelly. Two middle-aged women sat in the cart. "Hey there," one of the women golfers said with a smile. "If you need a ride, we'll gladly give you the cart. We can use the exercise anyway."

"Thanks," Kelly said. "My friend suggested a short walk, but I think we're scaring the golfers." She nodded in the foursome's direction.

"Yeah. They've been nervously looking over here ever since we came out of the shop," Megan added. "We were knitting in Lambspun." She pointed over her shoulder.

"Oh yes, I've been in that shop," the other woman said. "Lots of pretty things in there."

"For sure. And we'd better get back," Kelly said. "Don't want to scare the guys away entirely."

The first woman gave a wave of her hand. "Don't worry about it. You two keep walking. We'll cruise close by and wave at the guys. You know how easily distracted men are."

Just then, one of the men hurried over. He looked at Kelly anxiously. "Do you need to use a phone to call the doctor or something? I've got my cell here." He held out his cell phone.

"She's fine," Megan reassured him. "She's just started contractions, so we're taking a little walk to speed them along. We'll be heading to the doctor soon."

The man's face turned white as he backed away and pocketed his phone. "O-okay . . . if you're sure." Then he turned and hurried back to the other three men on the green.

Meanwhile, all four women burst into laughter.

Eighteen

"**Hey** there, Kelly. What can I get you?" Julie asked as she walked up to Kelly's table in the shady garden patio later that afternoon.

"Actually, I'm not very hungry right now," Kelly said. "How about another cup of that matcha green tea."

"That's all? It's after twelve. Lunchtime." Julie wiped off another table in a sunnier part of the patio.

"Maybe later. I just don't feel like eating right now."

Julie straightened one of the black wrought iron chairs beside a nearby table. "Why don't I bring a small dish of our raspberry sorbet along with the tea? We're using a new vendor, and the sorbets and ice creams are even more delicious."

Kelly laughed softly. "Okay. I'll try the sorbet along with the tea. Boy, what a combination."

"You got it. Be right back." Julie headed through the

garden patio greenery toward the back door of the café near the kitchen.

Kelly knitted another row of the bright red, green, and blue variegated cotton yarn that Mimi had convinced her to buy this morning. She'd already cast on several rows of stitches, hoping to start a sleeveless top. But the beautiful early summer day kept tempting her to look up at the trees rustling in the breeze instead of watching the needles. Once again she let the yarn drop to her lap. The cottonwood trees above that cast most of the shade for the patio started their musical rippling and rustling. It was such a peaceful sound, Kelly had to listen.

"Just the woman I was hoping to see." Burt's voice came from the parking lot behind her.

Kelly turned to see Burt walking through the garden patio. "Hey there, Burt. I bet you've been out doing errands."

"And you'd bet right," Burt said as he reached her table. He settled into a wrought iron chair across from her.

"You look good, Kelly. How're you feeling?"

"I feel good, too," Kelly said.

"No sign of Baby Jack coming yet?"

"Not yet. I think he's settled into the Mommy condo as Megan calls it."

Burt chuckled. "I love it. Well, just make sure you stay here at the café or inside the shop where we can keep an eye on you."

"Yes, sir," Kelly replied, giving him a mock salute.

"I was hoping I'd find you. Dan called me a little while ago and said he and one of his detectives had a chance to question that electrician this morning."

"Oh good. Did he repeat the story he told us at the shop a few days ago?"

"Sounds like it. Dan says the electrician noticed the vendor truck on the far side of the café after it was closed. He also said that a man showed up later, and the man got in the vendor truck and drove away."

Kelly glanced off into the garden; colorful petunias and impatiens were blooming brightly in three large planters set amidst the greenery. "That still sounds as strange now as it did the first time I heard it. I cannot imagine where Beverly went to. Did the electrician say he went around to the Lambspun shop while he was there?"

"I asked Dan the same thing, and apparently, the electrician said he came and went through the front door of Lambspun because the back doors to the café were locked. And we both know that Pete locks those doors every afternoon before he and Jennifer leave."

"And he didn't see the vendor Beverly again?"

"Dan also asked him that, and the guy says he did not."

"Weird."

"It's a puzzle, for sure. But Dan is good at solving puzzles." Burt gave Kelly a little crooked smile. "You're also good at solving puzzles, Kelly, so if you get any ideas, pass them on."

"Will do," Kelly said as Julie walked up to the table with a small white pot and cup as well as a dish of red sorbet.

"Here you go," Julie said as she set everything in front of Kelly. She then poured a dark greenish stream into a cup and placed a spoon beside the sorbet. "Let me know how you like it, Kelly."

"Sure thing, Julie," Kelly said as she lifted the cup and blew across the top of the hot liquid.

"I don't know how you can drink such hot stuff in the summertime. And it's not even your favorite drink," Burt said with a grin.

"Habit, I guess." Just then, a ringing sounded, which Kelly recognized.

"That's mine," Burt said, removing his cell phone from his pocket. "It's Dan. Let's see if he's learned anything new. Hey there, Dan. How's it going?" Burt said into the phone.

Kelly tasted the cool raspberry sorbet while Burt listened, phone to his ear.

"That's good news. You've got a name and a face of a relative. Now you can track them down and maybe get more answers. I'm sitting here right now with Kelly at the café in back of Lambspun, and I've been telling her what police have learned so far." Burt paused then chuckled. "I'll tell her. Meanwhile, good job and keep us posted." He clicked off.

"Whose relative turned up? Giselle Callahan's?"

Burt shook his head. "Nope. It was Meredith Callahan's sister. Apparently, Meredith had a second smaller life insurance policy, and the beneficiary was her older sister in another state. Dan said the insurance company was going to fax over any records they have for Meredith Callahan. She had a larger policy where the son was her beneficiary, and they already have the details for that one."

Kelly pondered for a few seconds. "Who knows? Most insurance policies are pretty dry reading. But maybe they'll find some more clues to this puzzle."

"Clues can show up anywhere, Kelly," Burt said as he relaxed against his chair. "Dan and the boys have been striking out so far. Let's see if they finally get lucky."

Kelly wrapped the variegated cotton yarn around the knitting needles. There were more than two dozen rows of stitches on her needles, so she was making progress. A light early summer breeze rustled the cottonwood trees above her. Their wide, dark green leaves brushed against one another.

She started another row, then paused. The muscles in the lower part of her abdomen tightened a little then stopped. Kelly continued knitting that row of stitches and another, wondering if the tightening would return. About half an hour later, the tightening returned and lasted a few seconds longer.

Kelly's heartbeat sped up. Labor contractions. At last!

She continued to knit, row after row of red, green, and blue yarn appearing in a pleasing pattern of color on her needles. This would make a pretty knitted top.

The contractions returned. And this time, they felt just a little more intense. The time between contractions was still nearly thirty minutes. Kelly decided she was sure labor had started for real. She reached for her shoulder bag and dug out her phone.

Her excitement building, she couldn't wait to tell Steve. His cell phone rang and rang and rang. And rang some more.

Kelly couldn't believe it. Why wasn't he answering? Kelly knew Steve had his cell phone with him all the time except when it was being charged. Suddenly, she remembered Steve staring at his dead cell phone this morning before he left their house.

Surely his phone would be charged up by now, she thought, incredulous. What's the matter? Is his crew making so much noise hammering and nailing that he can't hear the phone ring?

"Hey there. Can I get you anything?" Jennifer asked as she walked up to Kelly's table.

Kelly debated saying anything at first. "I'm fine. Just sitting here, waiting for Baby Jack to check out of the Mommy condo."

Jennifer laughed lightly. "Sounds like he will when he's good and ready."

Kelly paused then decided, what the heck. She smiled at Jennifer and said, "Actually, I think he's started to pack his bags now. Some low-level contractions started about an hour ago. About half an hour apart and not lasting long. But I noticed the last one was a little stronger."

Jennifer's brown eyes popped wide. "Really! Ohmygosh! We have to get you to the hospital!"

"Not until they come more frequently. Or they get stronger."

Jennifer's expression changed to worry. "Are you sure, Kelly? What if they speed up real fast? You don't want to deliver out here in the garden, do you?"

Kelly smiled. "I think we'll be okay. It's only five or ten minutes down Lemay Avenue to the hospital."

A familiar car pulled into the shop driveway then, and Lisa stepped out. "Hey, you two!" she called as she walked through the garden toward them.

"Thank goodness, there's Lisa!" Jennifer said anxiously. "Maybe she can convince you to go now."

To Kelly's relief, Jennifer waited until Lisa approached their table before saying anything.

"Lisa! Maybe you can talk some sense into Kelly. I can't."

Lisa pulled out a chair across from Kelly. "Jennifer, this is Kelly. You know that's not going to happen."

"She's going into labor and she's still sitting here, knitting!"

Lisa's expression changed quickly. "How far apart are the contractions, Kelly?"

"About half an hour. But the last one just now was stronger and lasted a little longer."

Now Lisa's eyes grew wide. "Kelly, I agree with Jennifer. You need to head for the hospital."

"You need to call Steve now," Jennifer said. "He'll want to take you to the hospital."

"Can you believe he's not answering his phone?" Kelly said. "I've tried several times."

"Good grief," Jennifer exclaimed, then waved at the balcony above. "Cassie! Can you come down right now, please?"

"Sure, Jen," Cassie answered, then headed for the back steps.

"I'd drive you but I have to get to the PT office in a few minutes," Lisa said.

"Cassie can drive her. She's got her learner's permit and she's really careful. Kelly will be the licensed driver in the front seat. Pete and I can pick her up later."

"Okay, okay." Kelly gave in with a smile. "I don't want you two hovering and staring at me anymore. Let me call my OB first." She searched her directory for her obstetrician's office phone number. That phone rang two times before it was answered.

"I'm an OB patient of Dr. Jefferson," she said to the office receptionist. "My contractions have started. And they're getting a little stronger. Low-level now, but I'm full-term, so I figure labor has started." Then she rattled off her name and birth date.

"How far apart are your contractions?" the woman asked.

"About twenty-five minutes, but I notice they're getting a little stronger each time."

"It sounds like you're going into labor, for sure," the woman's cheerful voice said. "Let me check with Dr. Jefferson's nurse, but I'm sure they'll want you to head over to the hospital now."

"Okay, I'll hold."

"Oh Lord!" Jennifer rolled her eyes.

Just then Kelly felt the beginning of another contraction. The tightening slowly, slowly built up more then released and eased away into nothing again.

A couple of minutes later, the office receptionist returned to the line. "Yes, the doctor wants you to head over to Poudre Valley Hospital now. We'll alert the OB staff that you're coming in."

"Thanks so much," Kelly said. "I'll head over there now." She clicked off her phone, then paused. "Let me try Steve again," she said as she shoved the knitted top into her bag.

"Kelly, I can call Steve, and I'll keep calling until he answers," Lisa said, pulling her cell phone from her knitting bag. "You go to the hospital."

"Yeah, I think I'd better. This contraction just now was definitely stronger."

"And they're coming faster!" Jennifer glanced over at Cassie. "Cassie, please take Kelly down the street to the hospital. Her contractions have started!"

Now Cassie's eyes popped wide. "*Really!* Oh wow! Let me get my stuff and the car keys." Cassie turned then raced out of the garden and back up the café steps.

"I'm dialing Steve's number now," Lisa said.

"Jen, your order is up," Eduardo called from the café back door.

"I'll keep checking on you, Kelly," Jennifer said as she sped toward the café's back steps. Cassie was already coming down the steps, a small backpack over her shoulder.

"It's ringing busy, but I'll keep calling Steve, Kelly," Lisa said. "Don't worry. You just take care of yourself and the baby now. I'm going back to the PT office, and Jennifer will keep me posted. And she'll tell everyone else." Lisa rose quickly, punched in Steve's number again, then hurried from the garden patio, cell phone to her ear.

Kelly rose from the chair just as Cassie walked up to the table. "Okay, Cassie. You know where Poudre Valley Hospital is," she said with a little smile.

"Right down the street," Cassie said, taking Kelly's arm as she started to guide Kelly out of the garden patio.

Kelly was glad the lunch crowd was lighter today and the café patio was empty. She glanced above at the huge, tall cottonwood trees rustling their leaves high above and wondered how many childbirths those old cottonwoods had witnessed while they sheltered generations of Native Americans then American settlers more than two hundred years ago.

Cassie angled the older sedan into the entrance to the hospital emergency room and pulled up at the curb. "Wait, Kelly, I'll help you get out," Cassie said, putting the car into park. She jumped out of the car and raced around to the other side, then opened Kelly's door wide. "Here, let me help you out," she said, offering Kelly both hands.

"Thanks," Kelly said, taking both Cassie's hands to help her stand up. Over Cassie's shoulder, she noticed a blue-garbed man rushing through the wide glass doors, pushing a wheelchair.

"Don't worry, Kelly," Cassie said, as the hospital aide approached with the wheelchair. "I'll call Eric now. He's at the building site, and he can tell Steve."

"Thanks so much, Cassie," Kelly said as the aide pushed the wheelchair up to the curb.

"Here you go, ma'am," the hospital aide said as he took Kelly's arms and helped her into the chair. "Have contractions started?"

"Yes, indeed," Kelly answered. "Coming faster."

"I'll take you right up to delivery."

"Take care, Kelly," Cassie called out as the hospital aide quickly pushed Kelly toward the hospital's ever-opening glass doors.

Cassie quickly jumped back into the sedan and drove around the corner to the extra large hospital parking lot in the rear of the hospital. She pulled into one of the parking spaces then retrieved her cell phone from the small backpack on the floor between the seats. Scrolling through the smartphone's directory, she pressed Eric's number. She waited through five rings before he picked up.

"Cassie? What's up?" Eric answered.

"I just took Kelly to Poudre Valley Hospital. Her contractions started."

"Whoa! I figured it was something important for you to call me here at the work site."

"Yeah, and you've gotta go tell Steve now! Kelly's been calling him over and over but his phone doesn't answer."

"You're kidding! I'll go get him now. We had a work truck break down here at the site this morning, so he's been really busy. I bet that's why he didn't hear his phone."

"Hey, I'm over here in the hospital parking lot now. Gotta park because there's no longer a licensed driver in the passenger seat. So I'm gonna go inside to the ER waiting room. Come find me when you bring Steve over, and we can make calls. Everybody will want to know."

"Sounds good. I'll see you over there."

Eric pocketed his smartphone and swiftly scanned the building site. The new house in the Wellesley neighborhood was all framed in. Walls, both exterior and interior, and support beams. The smell of freshly sawed wood hung in the air. Eric had grown to really like that smell.

He glimpsed Steve's bright blue hard hat through one of the window openings of the framed house. Eric took off running, his work boots stomping through the packed dirt. "Hey, Steve!" he yelled.

Steve didn't turn around, obviously not hearing his name called.

Eric rounded one of the framed house corners and yelled again, now that Steve was closer. "Hey, Steve!"

Steve jerked his head around. "What's up, Eric?"

Eric scooted to a halt in front of Steve. "I got a call from Cassie right now. She just took Kelly to the hospital. The contractions started."

Steve's eyes popped wide. "Really? Why didn't she call me?"

"Kelly told Cassie she tried but your phone kept ringing and didn't answer."

Steve reached into his pocket and drew out his smartphone. The screen was black. "Damn!" he swore, scowling at the phone. "I charged it this morning, but it's dead!"

"You can use mine if you want," Eric offered.

"Naw, I gotta get over to the hospital now!" Steve said in an anxious voice.

"Listen, why don't you let me drive you?" Eric suggested. "We don't want you running a red light because you're hurrying. Cops would be writing you a ticket while Kelly's delivering Baby Jack." He grinned at Steve. "You can be the licensed driver in the passenger seat for me."

Steve gave in quickly. "Okay, okay. Let's play it safe. Here are the keys." He dug his keys from his pocket and dropped them into Eric's hand. "Let's go. Hey, Dutch! Take over! Kelly's at the hospital! I gotta go!" And he rushed off.

The older man looked up in consternation. "Oh Lord!"

was all he said as he stared after Steve and Eric, who were walking away swiftly.

"That's what Dutch says to everything," Eric joked as they hurried across the building site.

Eric carefully drove Steve's truck up to the hospital emergency room entrance then pulled to the curb. Steve was already opening the passenger door. "Make sure you and Cassie call everybody, okay?" he said before he jumped down from the truck, slammed the door, then hurried toward the hospital entry doors.

"Will do!" Eric called after him. Watching Steve disappear through the glass doors, Eric drove around the corner to the emergency room parking lot and pulled into a space. Closing all the windows and locking the doors, he hurried over to the waiting room area inside the hospital. Scanning the entire room, he spotted Cassie seated on one of the black cushioned chairs, her head bent over her phone.

"Hey, Cassie. I just dropped off Steve. Did you see him come in now?"

"Yeah, I saw him for a second," she said, looking up. "But he was talking to the nurses at the front, then one of them took him around the corner. And I haven't seen him since. So I bet he's upstairs with Kelly."

"Probably," Eric said as he sank into the chair next to hers. "His phone was dead. That's why Kelly couldn't reach him. Man, was he steamed."

"I bet. Listen. I've reached Lisa over at her PT clinic and

Jen and Pete at the café and told them that Kelly's here at the hospital now, and you were bringing Steve because his phone's dead. And I left a message for Megan. Jen will tell Mimi, and Mimi will tell Burt. I thought I'd call Jayleen next."

"Okay, I'll call Marty and Greg. Just in case Lisa hasn't told them yet. Then I'll call Grandpa Curt. Spreading the word."

"Those ancient Aztecs we studied spread the word with those drums. Sure would be faster," Cassie joked as she pressed another number in her smartphone's directory.

"Ohhhhh yeah," Eric agreed with a smile.

Nineteen

Steve grasped Kelly's hand and stared intently at her face. "They must be getting stronger from the look on your face." He held her hand and leaned forward next to Kelly as she half sat, half reclined in the hospital bed. A nurse stood on the other side of the bed, holding Kelly's wrist as she stared at her watch.

Kelly nodded, not wanting to distract herself from the breathing techniques she had practiced in the labor and delivery classes.

"They're also coming faster," the nurse said. "We'll be taking you into delivery pretty soon now."

"Good," Kelly whispered.

Steve didn't want to distract her. He simply kissed her hand as he leaned forward and whispered, "You're doing great, Kelly."

Kelly focused on her breathing as the contractions grew stronger and stronger and stronger. She kept concentrating as they wheeled her into the delivery room. The urge to push was immense. Finally, she heard her obstetrician's voice beside her. "Okay, Kelly, you can push now."

And she did. As strong as she could. Three big pushes. Then she heard a nurse call out, "It's a boy!"

"A good-sized one, too!"

The next sound Kelly heard was a baby's cry.

"He's kicking, too!" a nurse said.

Kelly turned her head and saw Steve's eyes glisten just as she felt hers do the same. "Thank God," she breathed. Her next thought was of her dad as she pictured him smiling at her in his special way. Smiling at her and Steve and Baby Jack. Smiling and happy.

Kelly leaned back into the bed pillows and looked down at her baby's little scrunched face, eyes tightly squeezed shut. "He's beautiful," she whispered. "Even all red and wrinkly."

Steve moved his head closer to hers as they both hovered over their newborn son. "He's perfect."

"Hello, Jack," Kelly whispered. "You're beautiful. You know that?"

Steve leaned over and kissed Jack on the top of his head. "Hey, Slugger. Welcome to the family."

"I guess we're a real family now," Kelly said, touching Jack's baby-soft cheek.

"Yeah, we are." Steve held his finger close to Jack's tightly clasped hand. The little baby hand opened then curled up beside Steve's finger.

"Good thing the nurses make us slather on all that antiseptic hand wash," Steve said.

Kelly thought for a moment. "You know, I keep getting these memories of my dad smiling at me. Maybe that means he's looking over me . . . or something."

"I'm sure he is. He's looking out over both of us. And Jack."

Kelly liked that idea. Then she remembered something. "You know, we have to call everybody. Cassie and Eric have told all of them by now. Tell them Jack is here all safe and sound."

"Good idea," Steve said, digging Kelly's cell phone from his pocket. "I'll start with Pete and Jen. They've probably got Cassie and Eric with them. They can help spread the word." He scrolled through the phone directory and pressed a number.

"They're all probably gathered together at someone's house," Kelly said. "Waiting to hear."

"I bet you're right," Steve said, phone to his ear. "Pete? We wanted you to spread the word. Jack Flynn Townsend is here. All eight pounds of him."

Kelly watched Steve's face spread with a grin. "Kelly and I figured you'd all be gathered together. He's perfect. All his fingers and toes. And beautiful, even all red and wrinkly."

Kelly motioned to Steve. "Hold the phone next to my ear."

"Pete, Kelly's on the line, too," he said, then held the cell phone between them both, close to their ears.

"Pete, tell Cassie and Eric we appreciate those careful rides to the hospital. Both of us. Steve said Eric wouldn't let him drive. And I couldn't."

"Ha! Good for him! Cassie said you were counting minutes between contractions," Pete said.

"Oh yeah. Jack was getting ready to move out," she said with a laugh.

"Let me give everyone the details," Pete said, then his voice moved away. "Hey, guys, Jack Flynn Townsend is here safe and sound. Eight pounds, and all his fingers and toes."

Kelly heard a background cheer come over the phone. "They're cheering," she said to Steve. "Hey, Pete, put us on speakerphone. So everyone can talk."

"Okay, but it's gonna be a circus," he said with a laugh.

"He's putting us on speaker," Kelly said to Steve, handing the phone to Steve to hold.

Jennifer's voice spoke first. "Kelly, how're you doing?"

"Doing fine, Jen. Tired, but happy."

"Okay, rest. Here's Lisa."

Lisa's anxious voice came over the phone. "Kelly? How was it? It sounds like you went kind of fast."

"Once the contractions began, things started moving faster for sure," Kelly said. "Actually, I was surprised how fast everything moved toward the end."

"Hey, Kelly," Greg's voice sounded. "Tell Baby Jack to get a move on and grow up. We can always use another big bat."

Kelly heard her friends' laughter bubble up in the background. Then, Megan came on the line. "Hey, good job, Kelly!" Megan cheered. "You knocked it out of the park, girl!"

Kelly laughed softly while Steve laughed louder. "Sounds like you, Megan," Steve teased.

"Oh, she's in rare form," Marty said next. "We just told Molly, and she's super excited. She can't wait to see Baby Jack. She insisted Megan take her shopping for a Baby Jack toy."

"Oh, that is so sweet. Give Molly a kiss for me, will you?" Kelly said. "And tell her 'thank you' for Baby Jack. He'll love it."

"We'll have a get-together over at our house with everyone once we get home," Steve said. "Assuming nobody has a cold. If you do, you'll have to sit outside on the patio," he said with a chuckle.

Greg's voice sounded in the background. "I think we should make Marty sit outside for safety's sake. If Baby Jack takes a good look at him, he'll break out in tears, for sure."

The sound of laughter and teasing echoed in the background. Pete's voice sounded then. "As you can see, Kelly, it's business as usual around here. We'll look forward to seeing you and Baby Jack."

"You guys are great. You know that?" Steve said.

"All except the skinny redhead," Greg yelled in the back.

Kelly listened as the sound of laughter and love spilled out and over the phone. She felt blessed. Truly blessed.

Twenty

"**You** hungry?" Steve asked his newborn son as he lifted him from the baby bassinet. "Don't worry. Your mommy is right here," he said as Jack started making little sounds.

In the couple of days since Jack's delivery, Kelly had learned to recognize those unique cries. More like squawks than cries. Hunger squawks had a distinctive anxious tone.

"Hey there, Jack," Kelly soothed as she took the baby in her arms. "Don't worry. It's right here." She guided Baby Jack to her left breast, and watched him eagerly latch on and start to suck. Breast milk had already escaped at the sound of Jack's crying. Reflex responses as old as time.

She watched Jack gulp several swallows of milk then relaxed back into her favorite armchair in their living room. Jayleen had made a gift of the cushioned and comfy armchair to Kelly and Steve as her present to Baby Jack. She'd already given Kelly a wonderful maple rocking chair as soon as she and Curt learned Kelly was expecting.

Kelly recalled Jayleen's words. "Every expectant mother needs a comfy armchair for feeding the baby and a rocking chair to soothe the baby when he's crying." Good advice.

"Did you buy a lot of snacks for the Gang? Since we're not going out, you know Greg and Marty will want to make a meal out of chips, dips, and sweets."

"Oh yeah. And I will, too," he joked. "Don't worry. I've got more than enough, even by Greg and Marty's standards."

Kelly looked down at her son, blissfully nursing, then back into Steve's eyes. "I think we're beginning to settle in, don't you?"

"Oh yeah." Steve smiled back at her. "At last," he said, then laughed softly.

"At last," Kelly agreed with a little laugh of her own.

"Whatsa matter, Jack?" Marty asked as he walked around the room, baby in his arms. "Are you pooping in your pants?"

Kelly had to laugh as she sat in the comfy armchair. All her friends were spread out across Kelly and Steve's living room.

"If he's scrunching up his face, it's because he caught a glimpse of Marty's," Greg teased.

"He scrunches up like that when he's hungry," Steve observed from his relaxed slouch in the other living room armchair.

"Here, let me hold him," Pete said, springing out of the love seat where he sat beside Jennifer.

"Hey, some of us have bigger appetites than others, right, Jack?" Marty asked as he walked over to Pete and carefully transferred newborn Jack into his arms. "Here's your uncle Pete. You'll love him. He's around food all day."

Kelly watched Pete gently swaying in place as he held Jack. "Hey there, Jack. When you're big enough, Uncle Pete will make you one of his special pecan pies. With ice cream on top."

Jennifer stood up beside Pete and made little cooing sounds as Pete rocked the baby.

"Boy, you two make great babysitters. You've got that baby rocking down pat," Steve said.

"We've had a lot of practice with Molly," Jennifer said with a grin.

"Ohhhh yeah," Pete agreed with a laugh. "Miss Molly loves to be rocked and talked to. And sung to. If you know how to sing."

"Don't we know it," Megan said with a weary sigh.

"Oh yeah," Marty agreed. "Sometimes we'd sing nursery rhymes to Molly. She seemed to really like the rhyming sounds."

"I swear, I went through my entire childhood copy of those wonderful nursery rhymes for babies and young children," Megan said.

"Don't tell Jack that," Kelly broke in with a laugh. "I can only remember one nursery rhyme, and it's short. Not enough to rock a baby to sleep."

"Now I'm curious. Which one is it, Kelly?" Lisa asked from her spot in another cushioned chair beside the sofa.

"Okay, it's silly, but cute," Kelly said. "Jack Sprat could

eat no fat. His wife could eat no lean. And so between them both, you see, they licked the platter clean."

Everyone chuckled at the nursery rhyme. "Ohhhhh, now I'm starting to remember one, too," Marty spoke up from his perch on the arm of Megan's chair.

"I can't wait to hear what it is," Jennifer tempted with a grin.

"Oh Lord, Jennifer, don't encourage him," Megan warned.

Marty bounded up from his perch and began to recite in perfect schoolboy tone, "As I was going to Saint Ives, I met a man with seven wives. Each wife had seven sacks. Each sack had seven cats. Each cat had seven kits. Kits, cats, sacks, wives, how many were there going to Saint Ives?"

"Damn, I don't have my calculator with me," Greg said with a frown.

"Mine's in my briefcase if you want to dig it out," Kelly offered.

Steve rose from his spot next to Kelly. "I'll get it if anyone actually wants to calculate."

"Sit down, Steve." Pete waved his friend back down in his chair. "I already have the answer. And so does Marty, I bet." He grinned at Marty. "The answer is one."

"One?" Greg said, eyebrows raised. "Okay, that's got to be a trick answer."

"Kind of," Marty explained. "You see, the person who is asking the question said he was going to Saint Ives. Then, he says he met a man with seven wives and so on. That means all of them were coming from Saint Ives. You see?" A broad grin spread across his face.

Kelly joined her friends in a loud collective groan. "Oh, tricky. Tricky!"

"Of course!"

"Love it, love it."

"I can't believe I fell for that," Greg admitted with a groan. "It must be lack of sleep."

"Excuses, excuses."

"Why aren't you sleeping?" Jennifer asked.

"Ohhhh, I've just been thinking about stuff. Lots of stuff on my mind. Making future plans. Things like that." He sprang from his chair. "Here, Baby Jack has quieted down, so let me take a stroll with him."

Pete carefully transferred Jack into Greg's outstretched arms. "Here you go, Jack. Take a stroll with your uncle Greg."

"Hey there, Jack," Greg said, looking down at Jack's sleeping face. "We're all waiting for you to grow up big and strong so you can bring in some runs for the team."

"You and Lisa do have some big changes coming up," Steve said. "The baby is due when, again?"

"The doctor said the best guess is mid-November. Maybe earlier. It depends," Lisa answered.

"You're healthy and fit," Megan said. "Why would the doctor expect the baby to come early?"

Greg glanced over at Lisa. "Should we tell them?"

Lisa simply smiled in reply.

"Tell us what?" Marty inquired, in his attorney voice.

"The obstetrician did an ultrasound, and it looks like we will be having two babies. Twins," Lisa said with a smile.

Kelly felt her mouth drop open. All her friends had the

same response. A chorus of "What!!" bounced around the room.

"Twins!"

"I don't believe it!"

"Oh my gosh!"

"Two? Two!"

"I gotta sit down," Pete said as he sank to the sofa beside Jennifer again.

"How . . . how are you guys gonna handle it?" Steve asked. "Handling one newborn is more involved than Kelly and I imagined. Handling two?"

"To start out, we may have to hire a student nurse from the nursing school at the university in Greeley," Lisa answered. "I've been asking around, and I've heard very good things about them. Everyone who used one of those nursing students was pleased. In fact, they hated to see them leave."

Kelly stared at her friend. "Lisa, I have no doubt you can handle it. But Greg . . ." She gestured to Greg half walking, half bouncing around with Baby Jack in his arms. "With twins, yet."

She tried to picture crazy Greg, prankster Greg, food-hound Greg as the father of twins. Suddenly, a vision came into focus in her mind. Greg, a crying baby under each arm, bounce-walking around his living room . . . and she started to laugh. And laugh. And laugh some more. All she could think of to do was point to Greg and say, "Greg?" And then another spasm of laughter took over. Maybe it was just part of the complete relaxation and release she felt after Jack's delivery. Whatever its cause, the laughter felt good.

By then, all of Kelly's friends started laughing as well.

Loud guffaws, soft chuckles, snorts, whatever. Even Lisa was laughing.

Greg, for his part, was laughing as well as he bounce-walked Baby Jack around the room. Then the musical sound of the doorbell ringing cut through the laughter, and Steve opened the front door. Burt, Mimi, Curt, and Jayleen stood on their doorstep, Cassie and Eric beside them.

"We heard there was a new resident in Fort Connor meeting friends and family this evening," Burt announced with a big grin.

"You heard right," Steve said with a laugh.

"These two young'uns couldn't wait any longer, so we decided to take a look ourselves," Curt said, his arms around Eric and Cassie as they stepped over the threshold.

Both Eric and Cassie craned their necks. Cassie spotted Baby Jack first. Greg was returning him to Steve's arms.

"There he is!" Cassie squealed.

"Go on in, kids," Curt said, giving them both a little push. Cassie and Eric raced over to Steve and hovered on either side of him, peering at the small bundle in Steve's arms.

"Jeeeeeez! He's way bigger than my little sister was!"

"Ohhhhhh, he's *so* cute!" Cassie exclaimed. "Look at his little face!"

"He was eight pounds at birth," Steve told them. "That's why he looks bigger than your sister."

Eric nodded. "Yeah, she was six pounds, I think."

Curt and Jayleen appeared beside the teenagers. "What a cutie pie!" Jayleen declared with her trademark big smile.

"All healthy and sound, looks like to me," Curt decreed

with a tone of authority. "Good job, Kelly-girl." He gave her a wink.

Kelly smiled and gave Curt a nod as she rose from the armchair and walked over to greet her friends. "Glad you folks approve. You're both fine judges of sound stock."

Curt chuckled as he and Jayleen stepped aside so Mimi and Burt could come closer. Mimi had both hands clasped over her chest in what Kelly recognized as her "worry mode."

"He's healthy and sound," Kelly said, reassuring her dear friend.

Mimi gazed at Baby Jack and her eyes glistened. "Ohhhhhh, he's beautiful!" she cooed.

"He sure is," Burt agreed, leaning over. "I can't wait to watch you grow up, Jack. We're having a great time with Miss Molly. So you'll just add to the fun!"

"Yes, you will, you pretty thing," Mimi cooed some more.

"Enough with this pretty and beautiful stuff!" Greg decreed. "Call him handsome. Girls are pretty and beautiful."

"Well, then, I think he's handsome like his daddy." Burt revised his statement with a grin.

"Now that's going too far," Marty joined in, scooping up fiesta dip with a large tortilla chip.

"You folks are a hoot and a half," Jayleen said as she settled into a vacant armchair. "It doesn't matter a lick if Jack is handsome or looks like the back end of a horse. As long as he's smart like his mama and daddy, he'll be all right."

Kelly stopped mid-sip of iced tea. She tried to gulp it down but wound up sputtering over the sink as she laughed. The entire room filled with laughter once again.

"Ohhh no . . ." she tried when she caught a breath. "Not the back end of a horse. Please, no!"

Burt walked over and handed her a new bottle of iced tea. "Take a deep breath before you take a drink," he advised as he guided her to a chair. "I've had to learn new skills with this group."

Kelly settled into the cushions. "Thanks, Burt. I was laughing so hard I thought I'd fall down," she said with a smile. "It's so wonderful to have all of us together like this." She glanced around.

"Yes, it is, Kelly. And I thought I'd grab a quiet moment to catch you up on the findings of Dan's investigation." Burt had lowered his voice, even though everyone else in the room was laughing once more as Marty made a joke.

"Oh yes, I'd love to hear it," Kelly said, sitting up straight. "What did Dan learn when he questioned Beverly, the snack vendor?"

"Quite a lot, actually. Before he even brought Beverly in for questioning, Dan and the department had received those records I told you about earlier. Names of the insured's next of kin or something. There was one name that turned out to be quite interesting. One medium-sized policy did not have Meredith Callahan's son listed as the beneficiary. Her sister from Ohio was listed instead. One Elizabeth Beverly Sorenson. A resident of Ohio."

Not recognizing the name, Kelly asked, "Have they gone to Ohio to question her?"

Burt gave a half smile. "They didn't have to. She was right here in Fort Connor."

"Really?"

"Yes. Elizabeth Beverly Sorenson is Beverly, our friendly snack vendor. She was going by the name of Beverly Jones once she came to Fort Connor. She moved here shortly after her sister's death."

"Wow . . ." Kelly pictured the smiling face of the snack vendor. "She came after her sister's suicide. Did any of the Callahan family recognize her?"

Burt shook his head. "Apparently, she did not attempt to contact them. She focused her revenge strictly on Giselle Callahan. It seems she was intent on avenging her younger sister's death. She blamed Giselle Callahan for her sister's desperate suicide. She told Dan she waited until one afternoon when Giselle was alone on the golf course. Then Beverly changed her clothes in the van and combed back her short hair. Trying to look like a man. Beverly is a good-sized woman anyway. Then she parked behind the café near the steps and walked into the garden, then headed toward the golf course. She told Dan she had the razor-blade knife in her hand, ready to use. She announced to Giselle Callahan that she was with grounds maintenance and walked behind her. Then she grabbed Giselle and slit her throat. Then walked away. Left Giselle lying there to bleed out and die. She told Dan she threw the bloody razor blades in the Dumpster trash in a shopping center as well as the clothes she was wearing."

"Good Lord . . ." Kelly whispered. "What a sad, gruesome story."

"Indeed, it is."

"Did she appear remorseful at all?" Kelly mused out loud.

"No. Not a bit. Dan said Beverly looked him straight in

the eye and admitted she killed Giselle Callahan and said she would do it again if necessary. In her opinion, Giselle Callahan was a wicked woman. That's what she called her, Dan said. 'A wicked woman.' She willingly confessed and said she doesn't care if she spends the rest of her life in prison."

"Good Lord," Kelly said again. "Well, I guess she'll get her wish, won't she?"

"Indeed she will, Kelly."

Marty's voice cut through the loud conversations as he waved his smartphone. "Hey, you guys! We need a photo! Of all of us! Let's gather up."

Kelly and Burt both rose to join the others. "Who's going to take the photo? One of us would be left out."

Everyone started talking at once, then Eric's voice rose above as he shouted, "Hey, guys! I'll take one photo, then Cassie can take another. That way we can get everyone."

"That'll work," Steve said as he gestured for Kelly to join him.

"Kelly, you and Steve and Baby Jack settle on the sofa," Burt said, gesturing to them. "Then everyone can cluster around in our usual unruly mob."

"Hey, I like that," Pete said as he and Jennifer joined Kelly and Steve, filling the sofa. "The Unruly Mob. That should be our new nickname."

"Why not?" Burt said with a chuckle. "It's pretty darn accurate."

Kelly snuggled up beside Steve and looked down into the face of their sleeping son. "We are so lucky," she whispered.

"Ohhhhh yeah. And blessed. That's what Jennifer said to

me earlier. 'Blessed.' I like the sound of that, don't you?" Steve smiled into Kelly's eyes.

"Oh yes," she said in a quiet voice. "We're truly blessed. Our son is healthy and strong."

"And so are we," Steve added with a smile. "And according to Dutch and the boys, we're going to need to be."

Kelly laughed softly. "Blessings and challenges on the road ahead, everyone says."

"We're ready, don't you think?" he said with a grin.

"Oh yes. Absolutely," she agreed with a little laugh.

Kelly gazed at her sleeping son's face again and sent a sincere, heartfelt thank-you out into the Universe. She was happier than she had ever been in her entire life. And she was grateful. Truly grateful.

Fuzzy Hat

The Sweetheart Baby Hat in the back of the Knitting Mystery *Close Knit Killer* is the best baby hat pattern the Lambspun staff has found. But if you are an experienced knitter, you could also make this pattern in a smaller baby-sized version by using smaller No. 6 or No. 8 needles.

FINISHED MEASUREMENTS IN INCHES:

Head Circumference (inches): 16, (18, 20, 22)

MATERIALS:

2 balls Alpaca Bouclé (~130 yds)
1.5 ounces Lambspun yarn (~130 yds)

NEEDLES:

U.S. Size 11—16-inch circular needle
U.S. Size 11—double pointed needles

GAUGE:

3 sts = 1 inch

INSTRUCTIONS:

Using one strand of each yarn, held together, CO 48 (54, 60, 66) sts. Join in a circle, being careful not to twist the sts, and mark the beginning of the rnd.

Rnds 1-9: Knit.

Rnd 10: *Purl 1 rnd, knit 1 rnd. Repeat these 2 rnds three times. Knit 6 rnds.* Repeat from * to * 2 times. If hat needs to be longer, repeat from * to * again.

Decrease for Crown:

Rnd 1: *K4, k2tog* Repeat from * to * around. (40 (45, 50, 55) sts remain).

Rnd 2: *K3, k2tog* Repeat from * to * around. (32 (36, 40, 44) sts remain).

Rnd 3: *K2, k2tog* Repeat from * to * around. (24 (27, 30, 33) sts remain).

Rnd 4: *K1, k2tog* Repeat from * to * around. (16 (18, 20, 22) sts remain).

Rnd 5: *K2tog* Repeat from * to * around. (8 (9, 10, 11) sts remain).

Finishing:

Cut yarn, leaving a strand long enough to thread through the sts and pass through center to inside of hat. Pull sts together. Weave in all ends.

Pattern courtesy of Lambspun of Colorado, Fort Collins, Colorado. Pattern designed for Lambspun by Lynn Davies.

This is a tasty as well as easy casserole that can be put together quickly. A perfect main dish that Kelly and the Gang would serve whenever they got together.

Easy Hamburger Casserole

2 medium potatoes, sliced
1 onion, sliced
1 package (10 ounces) frozen lima beans
1 teaspoon salt
1½ pounds ground chuck beef
1 cup soft bread crumbs
1 can (8 ounces) tomato sauce
2 tablespoons water
1 teaspoon prepared mustard
1½ teaspoons seasoned salt
1 tablespoon instant minced onion
¼ teaspoon black pepper

Put vegetables in 2-quart casserole and sprinkle with salt. Mix remaining ingredients and spread on vegetables. Bake, uncovered, in preheated moderate oven (350 degrees) for about 1 hour. Makes 4 to 6 servings.

If you missed out the first time around,
keep reading for an excerpt of
the second book in Maggie Sefton's
New York Times bestselling Knitting Mysteries . . .

Needled to Death

One

Kelly Flynn grabbed her empty coffee mug as she opened the glass patio door leading to her cottage's small backyard. "Go for it, Carl. Another sunny day. Squirrels are waiting." She gave her Rottweiler a parting pat as he raced outside, clearly eager to face the furry tormentors that kept him running.

Spying the deep rose circlet of yarn that rested on the dining room table, Kelly snatched her knitting bag with her latest project. The silk-and-cotton, raspberry sherbet yarn had tempted her for months in the knitting shop across from her home.

Kelly paused near her desk, nestled in a sunny corner of the cozy white stucco and red-tile roof cottage. It was her cottage now. When Aunt Helen was killed, Kelly inherited everything, and her life turned upside down.

Glancing at her corporate client's folder beside the computer keyboard, she checked the clock. The analysis of the client's financial statements was going smoother than she'd anticipated. Some accounting issues were easier to solve than others. There was ample time for a knitting break.

The caffeine lobe deep in her brain sent out another insistent signal—coffee, now. Kelly headed for the front door. She could almost taste Eduardo's potent brew. The knitting shop had an attached café with the best regular coffee Kelly had ever tasted. Eduardo, the genial cook, always laughed when she asked about his secret for the coffee that kept her coming back for more.

July's intense heat radiated in the Colorado air even though it was only mid-morning. Afternoon would be brutal and in the high nineties, Kelly decided as she glanced at the shimmer coming off the adjacent golfing greens. That reminder caused her to turn and check on her dog's whereabouts.

Carl had developed an unfortunate habit these last three months she'd stayed in Fort Connor. Golf balls. They were an irresistible temptation to which Carl frequently succumbed. Kelly had tried several tactics to discourage him from climbing the fence and racing onto the greens to steal balls. Memories of angry golfer encounters were still fresh in Kelly's mind.

She spotted Carl standing, paws up on the chain-link fence. "Don't even think about it, Carl," she warned in her best attempt-to-control-dog voice. Carl looked over his shoulder in pleading mode. "Nope. You've gotten us in enough trouble already. Go play with your legal stash over there." Kelly pointed to a cluster of golf balls near several decorative pots filled with colorful shade plants.

Carl rolled his soft brown eyes in an obvious last effort to convince, then lay down in the grass and stared longingly at the greens.

"I know it's more fun to chase down stray balls, but you just can't. I don't want to have to bail you out of doggie jail," Kelly warned as she headed across the driveway toward Aunt Helen's former farmhouse, now turned knitting shop.

Passing by the oaken front door with its carved sign that read HOUSE OF LAMBSPUN, Kelly followed the flower-bordered pathway around the sprawling stucco and red-tile roof building to the café entrance. The enticing aroma of coffee greeted her as soon as she opened the door. She glanced around at the tables filled with customers lingering over late breakfast and brunch until she spotted a familiar face. One of her knitting friends, Jennifer, worked mornings at the café and afternoons as a real estate agent.

Kelly aimed straight for her. "Cof-fee, cof-fee," she demanded in a deep, raspy voice, mug in outstretched hand.

"Look, it's the return of the Coffee Zombie," Jennifer joked to the café owner. "Hide, Pete. She hasn't had her caffeine yet."

Pete's round face spread with a wide grin as he poured orange juice into a glass pitcher. "It'll only be a minute, Kelly. Eduardo's got some brewing. We had a business breakfast group in here this morning, and they drained the last drop."

Kelly's heart almost stopped. "Pete, don't even joke about something like that," she warned.

"It'll only be a moment. You can make it," Jennifer teased. "C'mon, have a doughnut." She gestured to the tempting pastries displayed in a nearby glass case.

Kelly tried to ignore them, but one lemon-glazed creation

called her name. "Okay, but sugar's not gonna do it. I need coffee. I can only last so long on that supermarket brand I have at home. I've already spent most of the morning combing through one corporate account, and I've got several more waiting."

"Boy, you're surlier than usual this morning," Jennifer observed, handing her the napkin-covered doughnut. "Numbers not adding up? Clients getting unruly? I can help with that." She winked.

"Actually, everything's going smoothly. I just want to work ahead so I can take the whole day off tomorrow," Kelly said before she sank her teeth into the sugar.

"You guys have a game tomorrow?"

"Games all day. It's the Fantastic Fourth at the Fort tournament. Teams are coming from all over the state."

"I'd better tell Eduardo to put some more shoelaces in the coffee, then. You'll need it," Jennifer said with a laugh as she took Kelly's mug and headed for the kitchen.

Kelly brushed sugar flakes from her T-shirt and checked the barrette holding back her chin-length, dark brown hair. One of the best things about telecommuting to her office in Washington, DC, was she could dress the way she liked. And in Colorado in the summertime, that meant a T-shirt and shorts.

Tomorrow would bring back a ton of memories, she was certain. She remembered playing in that same softball tournament years ago when she grew up here in Fort Connor. Lots of memories. In fact, that's all she had left from the past. The people were all gone—her dad, her aunt Helen, everyone.

"You're saved," Jennifer announced, coming toward her,

mug in hand. "Coffee's ready, and you're all set. Go forth and knit." She handed the mug to Kelly. "I'll be over on break."

"Thanks," Kelly said and headed for the doorway that led into the knitting shop.

As always, her senses went on overload the moment she entered the shop. Room after room of the renovated farmhouse was filled with yarns of every hue and texture—frothy mohairs in ice cream colors, nubbly wools and luscious alpacas, seductively soft silk spun with cotton or wool or all alone. Kelly couldn't get through a room without stroking a fat skein or squeezing some enticing fiber. She'd become a "fiber fondler," as the shop's knitting regulars called themselves.

Rounding the corner into what was once the farmhouse living room, Kelly went straight to the long library table that now dominated the room. "Hey there," she greeted two of her friends who sat around the table knitting.

"How's the sweater going?" Lisa asked, glancing up from the lacy ribbon vest she was creating.

"Well, okay, I guess. I'm still doing the ribbing along the edge," Kelly replied as she settled into a chair.

"Getting used to the circular needles?" Megan asked, pausing over the vivid purple froth that lay piled in her lap. Was that one of the new boa eyelash yarns that were so enticing?

"Yeah, gradually. It still looks strange, but I hope to finish the ribbing soon so I can start knitting the sweater. I mean, it doesn't feel like a sweater yet, just this circle of yarn." She held up the circle of rosy red yarn. The two slender wooden needles were connected end to end by a ribbon of thin plastic. Kelly scrutinized the rows of ribbing that covered the entire circumference and frowned. "You sure this is gonna work?"

Lisa grinned and brushed a lock of blond hair from her forehead. "Ohhh, it'll work all right. Trust us."

"Wait'll you see those rows of stockinette stitch appear, then you'll be convinced," Megan added with her usual bright smile. With her fair, fair skin and almost black hair, Megan always looked delicate to Kelly—except, of course, when she was on the softball field. Underneath the porcelain, Megan was tough as nails.

"Okaaaay," Kelly said, still skeptical. "If you say so. I still don't understand how I'll get stockinette if all I do is the knit stitch. I mean, when I did my first easy sweater with the chunky yarn, I had to do it the regular way—one row of knitting, one row of purling. How do you get stockinette without doing that?"

"It just happens," Megan reassured.

Kelly pondered that and drank deeply from her mug, savoring the coffee's familiar harsh assault on her taste buds. "That's no answer. There has to be a reason why it works."

"Trust in the process," Lisa said with her enigmatic smile.

"That's what Jennifer always says, but that's hard for me," Kelly admitted, picking up the circular needles. "I mean, I spend most of my days examining the process with all my accounts. It's hard to switch off."

Mimi, the owner of the shop, leaned around the doorway. "It's magic," she said with a smile. "I couldn't help overhearing you, Kelly. Don't worry. It'll be fine."

"What'll be fine?" Jennifer queried as she approached the table, knitting bag over her arm.

"Oh, Kelly's worrying about knitting in the round," Mimi

explained and went back to straightening the surrounding shelves of books and magazines.

"That's Kelly's standard operating procedure," Jennifer said, pulling a luscious, multicolored, fringed yarn from her bag. "Whenever she starts a new project, she always worries that it won't turn out."

"Hey, not always," Kelly protested, compelled to defend herself even though she knew her friends were right.

"Yeah, you do."

"Always."

"I rest my case." Jennifer grinned. "You'll be fine. Just trust—"

"In the process, I know, I know." Kelly drank from her mug as she reached out one hand to fondle the glistening and vibrantly colored fibers that Jennifer was knitting into one of those new trendy scarves. Yummy soft. "I'm going to have to make one of those scarves. They are simply irresistible."

"Get a little further along on your sweater first, before you leave it," Megan advised. "I know what it's like to be tempted away from a bigger project."

Kelly nodded and went back to creating the ribbing that would be the bottom of her new sweater. At first, it seemed strange to knit two stitches, then purl two stitches, but after a few rows, she actually saw the ribbed effect appear. Another few rows and she'd have created the inch required to form the sweater's edge.

Lisa broached another subject, one that had been niggling in the back of Kelly's mind. "How long do you think your boss will let you work away from the office? Did he give any clue when you went back to DC last month?"

"I don't know. He was doing his cool, aloof routine when I spoke with him. He does that whenever he wants to keep someone off balance." She frowned at the memory of sitting in her corporate CPA firm's offices, pleading her request for an extension of family leave.

With the death of both her aunt and her long-lost cousin, Martha, Kelly was suddenly the heir and beneficiary of a good deal of property. It would take several months to sort through both estates, even with trusted family lawyer Lawrence Chambers overseeing the process. Kelly didn't have a clue when she'd be able to return to Washington—or if she even wanted to.

"Well, you know how we all feel," Megan spoke up. "We want you to stay here with us."

Kelly felt her heart give a little squeeze. Deep inside, that's what she wanted, too.

"Any chance of that happening?" Jennifer probed. "You're managing those huge mortgage payments on the cottage, right? And you've got a renter for your town house back in Virginia. How's that working?"

"Oh, Chuck is great. He absolutely loves the place," Kelly replied. *All the more reason to let him have it*, the little voice inside whispered. *If it were only that simple*, Kelly thought. "But it's a delicate balance. The only way I can manage the cottage mortgage payments is with my CPA salary." She shook her head. "I can't quit my job."

"Well, we'll simply have to find a way for you to earn money here," Jennifer declared.

"Boy, that's not as easy as it sounds," Kelly said. "Consulting on my own simply wouldn't cut it. I've done some checking, with Megan's help."

"Something will come up. I can feel it," Jennifer said.

The front door's jingling bell sounded. More customers. Over the past three months that she'd been a regular, Kelly had noticed the ebb and flow of customers. Mid-morning to lunchtime was often hectic, with classes and customer questions. Then a brief pause often occurred before the afternoon press of customers and more classes began. Of course, weekends had no pause at all. It was nonstop shopping and classes the entire day. Kelly marveled at how Mimi managed to handle the constant flow of questions and instruction and helping customers find "just the right yarn" while staying so warm and reassuring. It must be her passion. It flowed over into everything she did and all she'd created. Kelly glanced to the billowy mohairs that draped against the walls and the stacked bins that bulged with summer-bright yarns. Mimi had truly created a wonderland here. No wonder knitters flocked to the shop.

"Well, hello, everybody," a woman's voice spoke from the doorway. "Looks like half the Tuesday group is here."

Kelly turned in her chair and recognized Vickie Claymore, another of the Tuesday group regulars. "Hey, Vickie. What brings you out of that beautiful canyon and into town?"

"Nothing much. Errands, that's all," Vickie said as she joined them at the table.

"When are you bringing some of your weavings?" Lisa asked. "I've got a friend who's been dying to buy one ever since she saw mine."

"That's great! Thanks, Lisa," Vickie said, her suntanned face breaking into a grin. "I hope to have some more ready by next week." She brushed her dark brown hair off her shoulder.

Vickie was one of the few fifty-plus women Kelly knew who could still wear her long hair hanging behind her back in a ponytail. Even mixed with gray, it still looked good on her. Kelly admired Vickie not only for her lively personality, but also for her artistic creativity and her shrewd business sense. Vickie was a successful alpaca breeder and rancher as well as a talented spinner and weaver. Instead of knitting on Tuesdays, Vickie would spin, sometimes on the drop spindle. Other times, she'd borrow a wheel from Mimi.

"Boy, if I lived in that gorgeous canyon, I wouldn't want to leave," Megan said.

"You would if you wanted to buy groceries and eat," Vickie said with a laugh. "Plus, it's good to get a break from the ranch. Makes me appreciate it more." She poured herself a cup of tea from the always-present teapot at the center of the table.

"Are all your baby alpacas born? Any more deliveries?" Kelly asked, remembering Vickie's concern for her herd.

"Yep," she replied, brushing dust from her jeans. Ninety degrees or not, boots and jeans were necessary around the ranch. "All the cria are safely delivered—thank goodness and natural alpaca mother instinct."

Lisa looked up from the ribbon vest. "Cria?"

Vickie nodded. "That's the name for baby alpacas. We've got twenty new ones."

"Wow. Is that a lot to care for?" Megan asked.

"Actually, the mothers do most of that. I just have to make sure the moms are well fed and cared for." She grinned, and her eyes lit up. "Just like with humans, moms do most of the work."

"Doesn't your cousin, Jayleen, help out?" Mimi asked as she rearranged a bin of eyelash yarns. "You have nearly forty animals."

"Thirty-eight with the babies, and, yes, Jayleen comes every day."

"Oops, I almost forgot! I need to ask you a favor, Vickie," Mimi said, abruptly turning from the bins. "There's a group of out-of-town knitters from the Midwest who're visiting Fort Connor. They're a touring group. Apparently they take yearly trips to different areas of the country."

"Wow, touring knitters. Now that's something new," Jennifer observed.

"Actually, there're several knitting groups that tour, I've heard," Mimi added. "This group is coming to see the shop after July fourth, and they asked if I knew of any alpaca ranches they could visit. I know this is short notice, Vickie, but would they be able to tour your ranch Friday afternoon?"

Vickie leaned back in the chair and sipped her tea. "Friday. Yes, I think that would be all right. What time would they come?"

"They're planning to have lunch at Pete's, so we can drive them into the canyon afterward. Probably about two o'clock. Does that work?"

"That'll work," Vickie agreed, smiling. "I take it they've never seen an alpaca before, right?"

"Probably not."

"Okay, I'll give them the grand tour." Vickie drained her teacup before she stood up.

"Vickie, you're a doll," Mimi said, her face losing its worried expression. "Thank you so much. Now all I need are some volunteers to take them to the ranch." She surveyed the table. "Any of you girls want to take a drive into the canyon Friday? We'll need shepherds for this flock."

Kelly started to speak up, but Jennifer beat her to it. "I'll be glad to escort them, Mimi," she said. "I've been wanting to drive past some property in the canyon anyway."

Picturing herself driving through the shady, deep green canyon northwest of Fort Connor, Kelly chimed in, "Count me in, too, Mimi. I could use an afternoon in Bellvue Canyon."

Mimi beamed. "Thank you so much, girls. I'll take care of all the arrangements."

"I'll see you two on Friday, then," Vickie said as she headed toward the doorway. "If your flock behaves, I'll show them my looms. I'm weaving a new piece now with some of my herd fleeces. It's really striking, if I do say so myself."

"I'll bet it is," Kelly said. "I remember that beautiful rug you showed us last month. The patterns were gorgeous."

"You can see it when you come. It's on my floor now. Take care, folks." Vickie gave a wave as she left.

"Boy, Kelly, I didn't think you'd be up for supervising knitters after the last time," Megan teased.

Kelly remembered helping Megan last spring when they escorted a group of senior knitters to the regional Colorado wool festival. "Ohhhh yeah." She grinned, recalling one mischievous knitter's antics. "Well, let's hope we don't have any 'Lizzies' in this flock."

Mimi threw up her hands in remembered horror as she scurried back to her office while Kelly and her friends laughed out loud.

Kelly sat down on one of her teammates' blankets that dotted the ridge above the city reservoir. She'd forgotten to bring a blanket of her own. Heck, it was all she could do to get to the field this morning.

After a long night spent poring over her client accounts, Kelly had overslept, awaking to the sound of an angry golfer's shout outside. "Damn dog! I knew he stole my ball," the man yelled.

Bolted awake, Kelly was about to go to Carl's rescue when she saw the time. It was past eight o'clock, and her softball team's first game was at nine. She vaulted out of the bed and into the shower, setting a new speed record even for her. She raced through the kitchen, poured a double ration into Carl's doggie dish, and shoved it under his nose. The golf ball scolding would have to wait. Carl, clearly ecstatic at the unexpected bowl of plenty, dug in.

Grabbing her first baseman's glove and her dad's USS *Kitty Hawk* baseball cap, Kelly raced out the door and into her car, hoping she had all her clothes on. There was no way she'd let her teammates down by not showing up on time. Thanks to uncommon good fortune with traffic lights and an unexpected parking spot, Kelly raced onto the field where her team gathered. Two minutes to spare.

"Boy, girl, you like to live on the edge, don't you?" Lisa joked.

"No, she just likes to give us all heart attacks," Megan said over her shoulder as they took the field. "I'm backup first base, and I'm lousy at it. So don't do that again."

Kelly swore alarm-clock vigilance and took her base, grateful for green lights.

Relaxing now under the blue velvet night sky, Kelly let out a sigh. So many stars. She was always surprised when she returned to Colorado and noticed the night sky. Not only was she a mile closer to the heavens, but there were more stars to see. Big-city light pollution kept her from stargazing back in the DC metro area. Occasionally, she'd driven out into the Virginia countryside to find a beautiful Blue Ridge mountain knoll just so she could see the heavens more clearly.

But it wasn't the same. The sky looked different here. And this ridge was right on the edge of town. She gazed up and tried to spot her favorite constellations, the ones her dad had taught her to see back in her childhood. She visually outlined the Big Dipper, then found the North Star and was looking for the Little Dipper when a familiar low voice sounded beside her.

"Want one? It's your favorite," Steve Townsend said as he sank to the blanket beside her.

"Thanks," Kelly said, accepting the bottle. "You read my mind."

Steve seemed to be doing a lot of that lately, Kelly noticed. Whether it was running interference for Carl with the angry golfers or taking time from his busy construction business to appear at her door with coffee when she needed a break from corporate accounts, Steve showed up. He was a nice guy. A really nice guy who had turned into a good friend—even if he was the star player for a rival team.

Kelly tipped the bottle with the colorful label and drank. Her hometown had developed into a center for special microbrewed boutique beers. The amber ale's cold, crisp tang fit perfectly with the summer night. The intense heat of the day had subsided now, and the air was gradually cooling, especially up on the ridge—one of the many benefits of mountain living.

"How's your knee?" Steve asked as he leaned back on his arm, stretching out his long legs, which were even longer than Kelly's.

Kelly checked her newly scraped right knee. The sting of injury had lessened so much that Kelly had forgotten about it.

Her knees were always skinned when she was growing up. Softball, basketball, soccer—all took a toll. She was used to bandages. But living in the corporate world these last several years had taken her far away from simple pleasures like sliding into base, knees be damned. Suits and stress were the uniforms and routine of the day with no time allowed for standing outside in the sunshine. The clock inside Kelly's head ruled her schedule in six-minute intervals—billable hours. These last three months had given Kelly a taste of a different kind of life, delicious and tempting like a forbidden dessert. If only she could find a way to stay here and not starve.

"Oh, it's fine. I completely forgot about it. Actually, it feels kind of good to have skinned knees again."

Steve grinned. "How's that?"

Kelly let out a sigh and leaned back on her hands, staring out over the brightly lit city spread out in a carpet below. The fireworks display in City Park would be starting soon. "It reminds me of when I was growing up here and all the other places my dad and I lived. I was always playing ball and getting hurt. It's amazing I have any knees left." She laughed softly in the gathering darkness. The blue velvet sky had turned to black. "I didn't know how much I missed it until I came back and met Lisa and Megan and started playing again."

"Wasn't there a team in DC where you could play?"

"Oh, sure. Lots. But it was always a question of time. Never enough time. I worked late a lot at the office. Until my dad got cancer, that is. Then I made sure I visited him every night." Kelly felt an old familiar tug of remembrance as she pictured her father.

"That must have been tough."

"It was."

The aroma of hot dogs and hamburgers drifted by. "Last chance for hot dogs and burgers," Lisa called to the scattered players relaxing along the ridge. She wound a path through the blankets and chairs, a platter in each hand piled with cookout leftovers.

"Hey, I'll take another burger," a guy said as he slipped up behind Lisa and made off with his prize. "Who's got the beer?"

"Beside the grill, over there," someone else called out.

"I've got some chardonnay, if anyone wants it," Wendy, the team's catcher, said, waving from a nearby blanket.

"Boy, hot dogs and chardonnay," Steve joked. "That just doesn't work."

"Hey, I can't help it," Wendy explained with a laugh as she grabbed a glass from the guy beside her. "I don't like beer."

"And you call yourself a catcher."

Kelly let the sound of relaxed laughter float over her like the evening breezes that came over the mountains. It felt good here. Really good. Deep inside, she felt the warmth that always came whenever she considered staying in Colorado.

"Well, for what it's worth, you sure look a lot more relaxed and happy than when you first came into town back in April," Steve said.

"Yeah," Kelly admitted with a sigh. "That's because I am."

"Relaxed or happy?"

"Both."

Steve didn't reply. After a few minutes of comfortable silence, which Kelly spent tracing star patterns, he spoke up. "Well, maybe that means you should stay."

"If it were only that easy."

"You know, Kelly, there's a huge amount of business going on in this town. There're all sorts of ways to consult—"

A collective "Ahhhh!" spread along the ridge as the fireworks display blazed into the sky.

"Whoa," Kelly said. "I'd forgotten how pretty it is from up high. Even prettier than being right beneath. That's where I usually was back in DC. My dad and I would go find a spot near the Washington Monument."

"Sounds like fun."

"Yeah, it was. If you don't mind being crammed in with several thousand people. We could barely move."

"More than at City Park?" Steve teased.

Kelly sent him a look. "Ohhhh yeah. Way more." She watched a spectacular flare of reds, blues, purples, and greens shoot through the black mountain sky. "It's nicer here," she said softly. "It's good to be back."

"Well, for the record, I'd be glad if you could stay, too." He gestured to Kelly's teammates, oohing and aahing at the colorful displays. "Even if you guys did beat us this afternoon."

Kelly grinned. "I'll take that as a compliment."

"Do that."

Two

Kelly eased the huge SUV around the curving canyon road more slowly than usual. These monster vehicles had a different feel to them, not at all like her sporty, super-responsive road car. She glanced into the rearview mirror. Jennifer was right behind her in Mimi's blue minivan, loaded like the SUV with touring knitters.

"How much farther is it? I thought you said it was 'just up the road,'" the knitter in the front seat asked for the third time in twenty minutes.

Kelly took a breath and searched for patience. This woman was something else. She'd done nothing but complain ever since she'd gotten into the automobile. It was too hot. The air-conditioning was too cold. She was tired. She was thirsty. Weren't there some alpacas they could visit in town? She didn't like curving roads.

Noticing the other women's rapt attention to the beautiful scenery outside the windows, Kelly tried to distract the woman, or at least her impatience. "This canyon is much greener and more deeply wooded than some of our others. That's because it's a north-facing canyon, and it holds the snow longer. That means there's more water available."

Fussy Knitter piped up, pushing her glasses to the ridge of her nose. "Yes, and more snow to shovel, too, I'll bet."

"Absolutely," Kelly said with a laugh. "In fact, some of the upper roads don't get plowed by the county. The home owners have to pay to have it done."

"Now, I wouldn't like that at all," Fussy declared, setting her mouth. Kelly noticed hard lines already etched in her face. Too much frowning, she figured.

"Well, the people who don't like it usually move back into the city after a couple of years, I'm told," Kelly observed. "You have to love being in the mountains to live comfortably here."

"Ohhhh, I'd love it," a woman's voice spoke up from the middle seat.

"Me, too," agreed another.

"Is that the place, over there?" Fussy asked, pointing to a farmhouse nestled between trees. Cows grazed in the pastures.

"No, but we're getting close," Kelly answered. "Just around this curve." She spotted Vickie's sprawling farmhouse in the distance and slowed as they approached the driveway.

"Well, finally!" Fussy declared.

Kelly kept her smile to herself as they bumped along the rutted driveway, listening to the stream of complaints coming from the next seat. The other women were laughing and chattering excitedly as they approached the farmhouse.

"Oh, look! Alpacas!" a woman proclaimed, pointing to the corral and pastures adjacent to the weather-beaten red barn.

"How do you know they're alpacas?" Fussy asked. "They look the same as llamas."

"Well, you're right. They are very much alike. But I've been to Vickie's ranch before. Otherwise, it's hard for most people to tell."

"What's the difference?" a woman asked.

"About a hundred pounds. Alpacas are smaller than llamas," Kelly replied as she pulled the SUV into a graveled area near the barn and parked beside Vickie's beat-up gray pickup truck. Exiting the auto, she motioned to a parking spot for Jennifer, who was coming up the driveway behind them.

"Okay, ladies," Kelly addressed the women who were unfolding themselves from the vehicle. "Let's get everybody together, then we can start our tour. Meanwhile, smell that mountain air." She took a deep breath. Out of the close confines of the car at last.

Jennifer parked the van, then hopped out and helped her charges alight, laughing and talking the whole time. Kelly wished she could be as entertaining as Jennifer, but she seemed to be missing that gene. Maybe she could foist Fussy off on her for the ride back into town.

"Wow, this is one beautiful place," Jennifer observed as she approached Kelly. "I haven't been here before, have you?"

"Yes. One time I came with Mimi when she was doing some weaving with Vickie. They were developing a workshop together." She glanced toward the farmhouse across the drive, wondering why Vickie hadn't come out to greet them. It certainly wasn't for lack of noise.

The gaggle of knitters had gathered around the fence, pointing and exclaiming at the alpacas scattered about the pastures. For their part, the alpacas simply gazed back with huge brown eyes and continued to graze peacefully. Kelly noticed one or two headed toward the fence, clearly as curious about the visitors as the visitors were about them.

Of course, their approach delighted the knitters to no end, and cameras appeared from purses. Digital and film, the cameras snapped away as the women leaned over the fence. Thank goodness it was sunny, Kelly figured, or the flashes would have spooked the gentle beasts for sure. It did halt their approach, however, much to the ladies' disappointment.

"Will they let you pat them?" one woman asked.

"Some will. But we'll let Vickie be in charge of that," Kelly replied, wondering again why Vickie hadn't come out to greet them.

Checking her watch, she saw it was after two o'clock, so they were right on time. Maybe Vickie was in her sunny workroom in the back of the house, absorbed in her latest weaving project.

"She may have forgotten that we're coming," Jennifer offered, stretching, arms overhead. "Does she have a workroom or something?"

"Yeah, in the back. She may be working and waiting for us to ring the doorbell. I'll go check. You keep track of them," Kelly suggested and started across the gravel driveway.

She headed toward the front porch with its rough-cut pine beam posts and overhang that created an inviting, shady spot for the rocking chairs that were angled to enjoy the mountain view. A wide wooden deck also extended around the corner of the log home and along the side, creating a large, sunny patio.

As Kelly's foot touched the front step, she heard an altogether too familiar voice right behind her.

"Why isn't she out here to greet us?" Fussy demanded, catching up with Kelly. "Isn't that her truck in the driveway?"

"She's probably in her workroom in the back and couldn't hear us. Why don't you wait with the others while I go get her, okay?" Kelly suggested as she crossed the porch, hoping Fussy would take the hint.

She didn't. "I've already seen the animals. I want to see those weavings the shop owner was talking about."

Kelly reached for the doorbell, then stopped when she noticed the door was ajar. She rang the bell anyway and waited. And waited. Fussy wasn't good at waiting, she noticed, so Kelly rang again and waited some more while Fussy fidgeted.

"Well, where is she?" Fussy demanded. "Don't tell me we came all the way out here for nothing."

"Oh, she probably didn't hear it, that's all," Kelly reassured. She pushed open the heavy door, and they stepped into the entryway. "I'll go check her workroom. Why don't you stay here and admire the décor, okay?" This time Kelly let her voice assume a formal tone, and she gave Fussy an I-mean-business look for good measure. Fussy stayed put.

"Vickie? Hello?" Kelly called. "Jennifer and I are here with the tour group. Where are you?"

No answer. Kelly stood for another moment, letting her gaze sweep over the spacious log home. One whole side of the living room was floor-to-ceiling windows, affording a gorgeous view of the canyon and the mountain ranges in the distance. Vaulted ceilings and skylights allowed light to flood the room, highlighting the furnishings, some rustic, some modern.

Vickie had eclectic tastes as well as an excellent eye for art. Patterns and fabric and color were everywhere. A still life in the style of the old masters was separated from a colorful abstract by one of Vickie's striking weavings. Everywhere Kelly looked she saw art—painted, sculpted, woven, or carved. It was a visual feast.

Wishing she could simply stand and drink it in for several minutes like she did on her last visit, Kelly headed through the living room toward the back of the house. Once the touring group was enthralled in Vickie's demonstrations, she and Jennifer could enjoy their surroundings. Glancing over her shoulder, she noticed Fussy was edging out of the entryway.

"Wait right there," Kelly said, gesturing to the woman. "I'll be back in a minute."

When she skirted around the rust-colored leather sofa, however, Kelly came to an abrupt halt. Vickie lay on the floor, her dark hair spread out on the handwoven rug in stark contrast to her pale face. A pool of blood, blackish red, swirled across the intricate pattern woven into the gray and white wool.

Kelly's breath caught in her throat. What had happened? Why all this blood? Was Vickie still alive? Suddenly, she spotted an ugly red gash across Vickie's neck. Kelly swallowed down her revulsion. Vickie's throat had been cut.

She knelt beside her friend and gingerly placed her fingers on Vickie's wrist, hoping to feel a pulse. There was none.

Vickie was dead. She'd bled to death. And hours ago, too, from the look of the blood. It was dried already in places where it had soaked into the fabric. The icy lump in Kelly's throat sank to her stomach. Was this a suicide? Or was it murder? Who would kill Vickie?

"Oh my God!" cried Fussy, right behind Kelly's shoulder. "Would you look at that! There's blood everywhere!"

That did it. Kelly snapped into command mode. She jumped up and wheeled on Fussy, pointing straight at her. "*You!* Out! This minute. Go get Jennifer and tell her to bring her cell phone right away!"

"Well, I never—" Fussy huffed.

Kelly dropped her voice two octaves into the I'm-warning-you-Carl range. "Do it. *Now.* This is a crime scene, and the police need to be called. Go!"

Mention of the police clearly got Fussy's attention, because all color drained from her pinched face. She turned and ran from the house. Kelly took a deep breath and forced herself to look at her dead friend once more. How was this possible? Vickie was always so full of life and energy. Who would kill her? It had to be murder. Vickie had so many plans for the future. Kelly remembered her friend excitedly describing how her baby alpacas were already sold to other breeders. As soon as they were weaned from their mothers, she'd be "playing stork," as Vickie laughingly referred to her delivery trips. No. Vickie hadn't killed herself. Kelly was convinced.

She slowly walked around the great room, trying to absorb every detail she could in case she was asked later. She disturbed nothing but noted everything. There was no sign of a knife anywhere. Did the killer sneak up on Vickie? There was no way Vickie would stand still and let a crazed person slit her throat. *So, what happened?* Kelly wondered.

As she circled behind the sofa, Kelly spied a bronze bust lying on the floor beneath an end table. She remembered that piece because Vickie nearly knocked it over when she was hauling a huge weaving into the room to show them on their last visit. The Mozart bust. Kelly glanced to the cherrywood bookcase where she'd remembered it last. The space was empty.

Jennifer burst through the front door and raced into the room. "Kelly! Is it true? Did someone kill—?" She skidded to a stop when she saw Vickie. "Oh my God," she breathed, hand to her throat. She went almost as white as Vickie.

"Jen! Jennifer, give me your cell," Kelly ordered in a sharp voice to snap her out of it.

Color started to rise in Jennifer's cheeks, and she shook her head as if to clear it. "Here." She offered the phone. "I'm not sure we'll have a signal, though. I lose it a lot in the mountains."

Kelly snapped open the cover, and, sure enough, there was no signal. One of the downsides of mountain living. "Damn," she said. "I didn't want to use the landline."

"Why?" Jennifer asked, turning away from the gruesome sight.

"There may be fingerprints. I don't want to smudge any before the police get here." She searched her pockets. "Do you have a tissue or something I can use?"

"Yeah, here." Jennifer dug in her back pocket and handed one over.

Kelly approached the kitchen, searching for a phone. Spying one on the wall, she carefully draped the tissue over the receiver and used her T-shirt to cover her dialing finger while she punched 9-1-1. She sincerely hoped she hadn't accidentally wiped off any other fingerprints in the process.

When the police operator came on the line, she calmly reported what she had found, where they were, and identified herself. The operator informed her that an investigative unit would be on the scene right away. Kelly gave the woman the description of Vickie's farmhouse as well as how far up the canyon it was located before she hung up.

Turning back to Jennifer, she saw her hovering at the edge of the sofa casting furtive peeks at Vickie. Death held an undeniable fascination for most people. Kelly remembered how her father looked when he died, but he was barely recognizable having wasted away with lung cancer. It wasn't the same. Vickie had been in the prime of her mature life, full of anticipation for the future and joyful, loving her work and her art. Kelly glanced at her dead friend. It wasn't the same. It wasn't the same at all.

"Do you really think someone killed her?" Jennifer asked softly, as if someone was listening.

"It has to be murder," Kelly declared, even more emphatically now. "Vickie wouldn't kill herself. But even if she planned to, she would have done it another way. If she'd wanted to bleed to death, she'd have done it in the bathroom or in the tub or something. Not on top of her gorgeous rug." Kelly shook her head.

Jennifer shuddered. "What a gruesome thought. I mean, I've been down sometimes, but never enough to do that." She grimaced again. "Who in the world would kill Vickie?"

"I don't know. I can't imagine—"

Suddenly, voices. Voices everywhere as the flock of touring knitters swarmed into the house and scattered about the great room, tittering and squealing and shivering in turns as they pointed and peeked.

Kelly and Jennifer stood rooted in the kitchen, both clearly appalled at the sight. Vickie had been their friend, Kelly fumed within. Her death was not a stop on the tour schedule.

Fussy fluttered to the head of the flock and pointed to the victim. "There she is!" she proudly proclaimed. "I found her just like that!"

"That does it!" Kelly exploded as she strode over to the women. They were just like a bunch of magpies. She purposely stood between the flock and her fallen friend, then pointed to the door.

"Get out now!" she ordered. "Vickie was our friend and you have no right to invade her privacy like this. *Out!*"

"That's right, ladies," Jennifer spoke up. "This is a crime scene. You could get in trouble with the police for disturbing it. Now leave." She shooed them away.

Jennifer's stretching of the truth worked. The flock squawked and scattered out the door. Fussy, however, held her ground. She puffed out her chest in full huff. "What about you two? You have no right to be here, then."

Kelly was beyond the point of politeness. Manners be damned. She pointed right between Fussy's eyes. "You. Not another word. I mean it, or you'll walk back to Fort Connor." If Kelly's voice sank any lower, it would be in the river at the bottom of the canyon.

Fussy blanched, then turned and stalked out of the house, feathers dropping in her wake.

"Whoa, you go, girl," Jennifer teased. "I'd hate to see you really mad."

Kelly released a huge breath. "It's not a pretty sight, trust me."

Just then, the sound of a wailing siren pierced the air, farther away, then coming closer. The police. *Thank God.* Kelly sighed in relief.

"C'mon, let's get out of here." Jennifer prodded and motioned to Kelly.

Kelly took one last look at her murdered friend and followed Jennifer out the door.